where there's a

Will

KAREN KELLEY

sourcebooks
casablanca

Published by Sourcebooks Casablanca, an imprint of Sourcebooks, Inc.
P.O. Box 4410, Naperville, Illinois 60567-4410
(630) 961-3900
FAX: (630) 961-2168
www.sourcebooks.com

Library of Congress Cataloging-in-Publication Data
Kelley, Karen.
  Where there's a will / Karen Kelley.
     p. cm.
  (trade paper : alk. paper)
  I. Title.
  PS3611.E443W44 2012
  813'.6–dc23

                            2012019830

        Printed and bound in the United States of America.
              VP 10 9 8 7 6 5 4 3 2 1

To Paula, Brenda, Arturo, Becky, Jill, Esther, and Trey.
Thanks for all the support and the wonderful friendship
you have given me. Laughter is the best medicine!

Chapter 1

"Please, Lord, you have to send me a miracle. A man, in case you want specifics."

Haley Tillman really needed to get laid before she incinerated. If a man looked cross-eyed at her, the only thing left would be a pile of smoking ashes.

Just one little bitty miracle. Was that too much to ask?

She was thoughtful for a moment, then decided she'd better revise her prayer. Once, she'd asked for a stuffed bunny rabbit. The next day her dad took her to the taxidermist to pick up Fifi, the family dog that had died two weeks before, or as Haley preferred to call the beast when no one was around, The Tasmanian Terror. The mongrel was more her mother's pet. Her father had had the miniscule creature stuffed.

There was also a sale on stuffed rabbits. She hated the glass-eyed zombie rabbit and hid the nasty looking creature in the back of her closet. There was no escape from Fifi, though. Her mother placed the silent menace in the living room where everyone could see the dog.

So maybe a prayer revision might be in order. "Not just any man. I want a really hot, drool-worthy, sexy man." That still wasn't good enough. "No, he has to be more than a normal man. He has to stand above mere mortals. No more dweebs, losers, or rejects." She figured it wouldn't hurt to ask for the best.

And no more crying jags like the one last night just because she'd been stood up. She threw the cover back and grabbed her black-rimmed glasses off the nightstand before heading toward the bathroom.

A miracle would be nice. She snorted. As if a miracle was ever going to happen. She was pretty sure hot and sexy would never make it to her front door. Her *almost* date hadn't been drool-worthy. She supposed Ben wasn't bad looking, in a *GQ*, polished sort of way.

Haley sighed. Being stood up was nothing new. Anyone with a little bit of sense would be used to it by now, but not her. Okay, so maybe she sort of expected it because she'd cornered him. She did not wear desperation well.

"Ben could've said no," she mumbled as she walked inside the bathroom and flipped on the light. Her coworker from the bank owed her. Haley had worked all week crunching numbers for him.

She casually glanced toward the mirror and saw an apparition.

Her heart pounded inside her chest. She stumbled back, bumping into the bathtub. Before she toppled inside, she slapped a hand on the toilet seat and regained her balance.

As her pulse slowed to a more normal rate, she cautiously scanned the tiny room. She was the only one there. Her imagination was getting the best of her. That's all it could be. Over-tired, stressed, of course she was seeing things. She came to her feet, nerves stretched taut. Her stomach rumbled.

Please don't be the ghost of Nanny.

She loved Nanny, but her grandmother was gone, and though Haley had lots of fond memories, she wanted her to stay gone.

She was still trembling when her gaze landed on the mirror. She jumped, heart pounding again until she realized it was only her reflection that stared back. Fantastic, she'd scared herself. This had to be an all-time low.

She closed her eyes and took a deep breath, then opened them again. Mornings were not good. She should drape black silk over her mirrors until she at least had her first pot of coffee. Not that she was monstrously hideous, but she was no beauty queen, either.

She had her father's looks. Her father was tall. Haley was five feet seven inches. She also had her father's dull, dishwater blonde hair. Her hair had turned bright orange when she attempted to color it in the eighth grade. She decided dull blonde was better. Her boobs were too big, too, but they matched her hips.

All the magazines she read said you had to like at least one thing about yourself. Her legs were nice and long. When she wasn't tripping over her feet, she was fairly satisfied with them. Except her life was never going to change. And miracles? She stopped believing in miracles a long time ago.

She brushed her teeth, then dragged a comb through her tangled hair so it didn't look quite so much like a rat's nest. There was a half gallon of ice cream in the kitchen freezer. It wouldn't be too difficult to eat herself into sugar oblivion. She could bring new meaning to the phrase *death by chocolate*. What would her sister say? Rachael never, absolutely never, let sugar cross her lips, and she always said Haley was killing herself. Right now, she didn't really care.

The buzz from her doorbell blasted through the tiny two-bedroom house that she'd inherited from Nanny, effectively drawing her away from her dreary thoughts. Bummer. She'd already started planning her funeral. She sighed. It was way too early for doorbells.

She grabbed her faded pink terry-cloth robe off the hook on the door and pulled it on over her green froggy flannel pajamas and left the bathroom. The doorbell buzzed again.

"Okay, okay," she mumbled.

Once she stood at the front door, she peered through the peephole her father had installed for safety, as if anyone would ever break into her house. What would they steal? Her hand-me-down furniture?

She blinked. No one there. Were they hiding?

Hmm, serial killer lurking outside her door? Would that count as a date? Nope, they didn't have murders in Hattersville. Nothing, absolutely nothing, ever happened in the small town. She shook her head and opened the door a crack, making sure the chain was secure.

"Hello?"

A man stepped into her line of vision. Haley's mouth dropped open. *Good Lord!* This had to be the guy who invented tall, dark, and sexy! Her thighs quivered.

At least six feet one inch of pure testosterone stood on her porch. He had the dark good looks of a male stripper, only with clothes on. The stranger removed his black Stetson, slowly dragging his fingers through thick, coal-black hair. His deep blue eyes held her gaze before sliding down her body as if he could see more than the sliver revealed from the slightly open door.

Warm tingles spread over her like a Texas wildfire in the middle of summer. She could barely draw in a breath as her gaze moved past broad shoulders and a black Western shirt that hugged his scrumptious muscles. Then her eyes slipped right down to the low-slung jeans riding his hips, past muscled thighs, all the way to his scuffed black boots.

Oh, Lord, her every fantasy stood on her front porch!

She forced herself to meet his gaze.

I want him! She felt like a kid in a candy store with lots of money to spend. *Mommy, Mommy, can I have the hot sexy cowboy? Pleeeeeeeeease!*

If only it was that easy. No way would she ever have the opportunity to have sex with someone who looked like him. What was he doing at her door, anyway? Lost?

"Haley, right?" he asked with a slow drawl that made her body tremble with need.

How did he know her name? She grasped the door a little harder. He smiled as though he knew exactly what she was thinking. Her world began to tilt. She remembered that breathing might not be a bad thing so she drew in a deep breath. "What?" the word warbled out. She cleared her throat and tried again. "Do you need directions or something?"

"You're Haley."

She nodded.

He smiled wider, showing perfectly straight white teeth. "Mind if I come in?"

Her fantasy of this cowboy's naked body pressed against *her* naked body shattered like rocks hitting a mirror. Oh, this guy was good, real good, but she wasn't born yesterday. He'd obviously seen her name on the mailbox out front. She raised her chin. "I don't need a vacuum. I have all the pots and pans I will ever use—including waterless cookware. There's a complete set of encyclopedias on my e-reader *and* I have a double-barrel shotgun for protection. Now, do you want to tell me why you're ringing my doorbell at this time of morning?"

"You prayed for a miracle. I'm the answer to your prayer." He rested his hand on her grandmother's white rocking chair. Her rocker had always sat in that same spot on the porch for as long as Haley could remember. The cowboy lightly set the chair in motion. Back and forth, back and forth, his thumb lightly caressing the weathered wood.

Wow, her prayer had really been answered? The man upstairs had given her more than she'd asked for. She reached up to smooth her hair about the same time reality set in. Had she lost her mind?

"Go away!" She slammed the door shut. Her pulse raced so fast Haley thought her heart would jump out of her chest. At this rate she was going to have a heart attack before she turned twenty-seven! Who was he? Definitely the wrong house. Shoot, the wrong town. No one who looked like him lived in Hattersville. Definitely a salesman. As if she needed another vacuum cleaner. Three were quite enough. Another magazine subscription might have been nice. One could never have enough magazines.

But wouldn't it have been nice if he was sent in answer to a prayer? How had he known she'd prayed for a miracle? Not that it mattered since she'd slammed the door in his face.

Oh, hell!

What was she thinking? Haley smoothed her hands down the sides of her robe, took a deep breath, and started to open the door. She remembered at the last minute to remove her glasses and stick them in her pocket. Rachael had said they made her appear to be more professional. Haley thought the glasses made her look like Buddy Holly. She wore them out of habit rather than a need to see. She pasted a smile on her face and opened the door as much as the chain would allow.

The cowboy wasn't there.

Had she only imagined him, too? She closed the door enough so that she could slide off the chain. Her smile was still firmly in place when she opened the door again. Nothing. Only old Mrs. Monroe watering her lawn across the street. She looked up and waved as her crotchety husband came around the corner of the house, getting a face full of water. Mrs. Monroe quickly dropped the hose.

"Damn, thought we'd finally got some rain," he sputtered.

"Oh, I'm sorry." She rushed toward him, raising her flowered apron as she went.

"That's okay, sweetie. You can cool me off anytime."

Haley smiled, then glanced down the street. Her smile dropped. Not a soul, darn it. Her fantasy lover, possibly an answer to her prayer, showed up on her porch and what did she do? Slammed the stupid door in his face.

Maybe she only imagined the guy. Really, who could actually look that good? She took a cautious step past the doorway. Maybe Mrs. Monroe saw the cowboy. But her neighbor had already turned off the water and they were going inside.

Haley stepped off the wide, covered front porch, her eyes narrowing as she looked up and down the street. Still nothing.

Chelsea, the former cheerleader, high school football sweetheart, beauty-queen-turned-slutty-bank-teller stepped out of her house next door, then gave a surprised jump when she caught sight of Haley. Chelsea's gaze swept over her.

"You really should take a little more pride in your appearance." She shrugged. "But then I suppose nothing would help, so why try?"

Haley's lip curled. Why had her coworker bought the house next door? To taunt her? Her ploy was working.

Chelsea closed her front door, but immediately returned her attention to Haley. Oh, no, Chelsea wore her fake pouty look. Haley braced herself.

"I'm sorry about last night. Ben and I happened to be working late at the bank, and afterward we decided to have a drink. He totally forgot about his date with you until it was too late. I hope you weren't *too* disappointed."

Haley took a step back as Chelsea hurried down the front steps to her sporty little red Mustang. Chelsea had to know about the date. Then it hit her. Of course Chelsea knew. That was exactly why she'd coerced Ben into taking her for a drink. Chelsea loved hurting people. It was a game to her—one she played very well.

Haley tried to think of something smart to say. "You… you…" Darn! Why couldn't she think of a good comeback? She probably would later when she wouldn't need it. "I hope you get a flat tire," she finally sputtered. Oh, that was a real winning line. Sheesh!

Chelsea was right, though. Haley's looks left a lot to be desired. But Ben was her date. Of course Ben would rather be with Chelsea. Chelsea looked hot with flaming red hair and she was cute.

Haley marched back inside and closed her door a little harder than necessary. Out of habit, she jerked the chain through the slot and turned the lock. Not that it mattered. An intruder would take one look at her and run screaming in the other direction. Was that what happened to the sexy cowboy? He'd barely gotten a glimpse. What would he have done if he saw the whole picture?

No, she didn't want to think about his reaction. Her day was already depressing enough. She aimed toward the kitchen and turned the coffee pot on, then grabbed a diet soda out of the fridge. "Caffeine," she sighed and took a drink. She would get dressed, then figure out what she would do for the rest of her boring day.

She trudged into the bedroom and came to a dead stop. She could feel the color drain from her face. The cowboy casually reclined on her bed with his back braced against her headboard, his booted feet crossed at the ankles.

And he was reading her diary. Her very naughty diary. Oh, Lord! All her fantasies were in that diary. She'd even made up a few she thought might be interesting. Pages and pages of—*sex!* Good girls didn't write about sex. Except Haley *did* write about sex. All her dreams were kept hidden between her mattress and box springs. No one was supposed to ever know just how naughty she could be!

"That's my diary," she choked out.

He glanced up. "And very explicit. Do you actually fantasize about stripping in a club?" His words were lazy, with just a slight Texas drawl that washed over her like hot fudge dribbled on vanilla ice cream. When his heated gaze trailed down her body, she melted.

Haley's body temperature jumped from hot to cold to burning up. He was reading about her private desires. Every fantasy she'd ever heard about, read about, or even imagined, was on those pages. She wanted to die!

Wait a minute. What was she thinking? A strange man was inside her home and she was worried he was reading her stupid diary? She threw the can of soda at him and whirled around. She only had to make it out of the house.

But when she slid into the living room, he was leaning against the front door, still reading her diary. How'd he get there first?

He glanced up, looking quite unconcerned that she was about to have a heart attack. "This might be interesting. I've never made love in a closet while there's a party going on in the other room."

For a split second, she could see herself locked in his embrace, crammed between a soft fur coat and a leather jacket, naked bodies straining, naughty words whispered as country music blared on the other side.

Oh, God, she had to be mentally unhinged to even imagine having sex with an intruder. She rushed forward and snatched her diary out of his hands, then put distance between them. "Who are you? I don't have any money."

He smiled. "I don't want your money."

Her frown deepened. "Did you confuse houses? Chelsea lives next door."

He shook his head.

"Then who the hell are you and what are you doing in my home?" she demanded, not feeling as brave as she tried to pretend.

He looked at her as though she should know. "I'm an answer to a prayer. *Your prayer.* You asked for a miracle, so here I am. You can call me Ryder. I'm an angel—sort of."

"Your name is Ryder and you're an angel."

"Sort of."

She eased closer to the end table and the heavy, brown ceramic lamp sitting on it. "Believe me, I've never met a cowboy who was anything close to being an angel."

"Have you met other angels?" He crossed his arms as if he felt quite comfortable breaking into someone's home.

"No."

"Then how would you know what we look like?"

It didn't matter. She was close enough to her weapon. She dropped her diary and grabbed the lamp. She wasn't quite so vulnerable holding the heavy lamp! She started to shake it at him, hoping to put the fear of God into him, but was held up by the cord. This was not the fierce image she wanted to portray.

She jerked the cord out of the socket then quickly faced him again. "The soda can might not have done much damage, but I guarantee this lamp will."

"You're the one who prayed for a miracle," he pointed out.

Her eyes narrowed. "Lucky guess, but I'm not buying that you're an angel."

"Sort of," he reminded her.

"What the hell is 'sort of' supposed to mean?"

"I'm a nephilim." He took a step toward her.

She raised the lamp, which was getting a little heavy. "Don't come any closer."

He stopped, but darn it, he didn't look a bit put out that she had a weapon. He'd changed his angel story, too. "What's a nephilim?" And why the hell was she engaging in conversation with someone who had obviously escaped from the state hospital?

"My father was an angel, and my mother was a mortal. They mated and created me, a nephilim. An immortal."

"Yeah, right." Oh, Lord, he was crazier than she thought. "A cowboy, who's half angel. Nope, I've never seen that, either." There were plenty of cowboys in Hattersville and they only loved three things: their horses, their trucks, and drinking. Sexy, yes. Angelic, no.

"I'm here because you asked for a miracle."

"If you'll just leave my house, I promise not to call the police."

He took a step toward her.

She took a step back.

"I'm not going to hurt you."

"Stay where you are," she warned.

But he didn't stop moving toward her. She hated violence, especially when it involved her. Well, he couldn't say she didn't warn him. With all the strength she could muster, and the surge of adrenaline created by her mounting fear, she threw the heavy lamp at the cowboy.

The lamp went flying right at him. He jerked his hand into the air, palm up. The lamp stopped midair. The cord dangled, swinging back and forth.

"How did you do that?" Haley whispered.

"I told you, I'm a nephilim." He snapped his fingers and the lamp was back on the side table; even the cord was plugged in.

The room began to spin around. Haley reached for something to steady herself, but only connected with air. She never fainted.

Strong arms suddenly were around her. He picked her up and carried her to the sofa, setting her down gently as darkness closed in around her. This was it. The best looking man to ever knock on her door was an angel. She *was* dead and didn't even know it, and here he was about to take her to—*Heaven?*

Pfft. And why not, she'd never sinned. Not one blasted time. Well, unless she counted all her sexual fantasies, and apparently they didn't count. Nope, her strict moral upbringing guaranteed her a place in Heaven.

"Are you still with me?" he asked.

Something cool and wet pressed against her face. Her eyes fluttered open. A washcloth. He was still there. This wasn't one of her dreams. She whimpered. He pulled her closer to his chest. She breathed in a heady scent that reminded her of leather and a clean country breeze. Except she didn't feel comforted because she knew exactly what was happening. "I don't want to be dead," she sobbed. What had she died from? Brain tumor? Car accident—well, probably not a car accident since she was inside her home.

He began to lightly stroke her back. "You're not dead."

Not dead? That was a relief. His touch was soothing. She could feel herself begin to relax, until she remembered she still didn't have answers. "Then why are you here?"

"I told you. I heard you praying for a miracle."

She frowned, only remembering she'd prayed for sex. Or maybe she was thinking about sex and prayed for a miracle. It made sense because she thought about sex a lot. She leaned back and looked into his eyes. He had nice eyes. They were a startling shade of blue. So intense. Her gaze moved over his face. Delicious. Was he really an answer to her prayer? There was one way to find out. "Okay, if you're my miracle, then kiss me."

Without hesitation, his lips lowered to hers, the warmth of his breath whispering against her cheek right before his tongue scraped across her lips. She opened her mouth and his tongue slipped inside. A deep, shuddering sigh swept over her as he explored her mouth, caressing her tongue with his. She was starting to grow damp when he pulled back.

"Wow, please don't wake me up," she finally said.

"You're not asleep." He grinned, and once again she was mesmerized by his smile.

This was the best dream she'd ever had! She squeezed his arm. Her heart skipped a beat.

If it was a dream, then why did he feel so real?

Chapter 2

"HALEY?" THE STRANGER'S VOICE vaguely filtered into her muddled brain.

"Hmm?" She never dreamed this real. Sometimes her dreams seemed real, but when morning came the lover she held close was always stuffed with cotton and covered with a pillowcase.

"Are you still with me?"

Her attention was drawn back to—Ryder? She distinctly remembered he'd told her that his name was Ryder. Angels weren't cowboys and they didn't have names like Ryder. Serial killer moved back to the top of her list.

She pushed out of his arms and scooted to the far side of the sofa, but immediately regretted the loss of his warmth. Had he cast some kind of spell on her? No, the guy was a nut or this was a practical joke, but he definitely wasn't an angel.

"You're a good magician. Now, who put you up to this? Was it Alexa?" Maybe her friend had bought her a male hooker so Haley could fulfill her fantasies. No, a guy who looked like this one would cost way too much money.

When he shook his head, a lock of hair fell forward. He casually reached up and brushed it back in place. It was all she could do to stay focused.

"I haven't lied," he told her.

He made himself comfortable on the floor, leaning one arm on her sofa cushion, then stared at her until she began to fidget.

"What?" she finally asked.

"You're so beautiful," he told her.

Her coworkers could have taken up a donation for her. They were always giving to one charity or another to impress the boss. Someone might have started a fund for her. Something like: take-pity-on-the-dateless-frump campaign. She pushed her glasses higher on her nose. Except she was pretty sure they didn't think twice about her away from work, even though she'd been with the bank four years and had lived in Hattersville her entire life.

Her sister could've given him a key, and then when Haley had gone into the kitchen, he might have slipped inside her home. But Rachael was a stick-in-the-mud and had such very high convictions about the difference between right and wrong that Haley couldn't see her sister doing anything like that, even for her frumpy, sex-starved sister.

It didn't explain how Ryder removed the chain from the front door or stopped the lamp in midair. Okay, deep breath and figure this out. Her eyes narrowed. "So, what are you supposed to do? Grant me three wishes?"

He chuckled. "That would be a genie."

"You're telling me that genies exist?" She cocked an eyebrow.

"Not that I know of."

"But you just said they did."

"No, you asked if I could grant you three wishes. I told you genies do that, at least in children's books."

"So, what can you do for me?"

"I can help you believe in yourself."

"Well, great, it worked." She jumped to her feet and stepped back, hugging her arms around her middle. "I believe in myself. Now get out of my home and I won't call the police."

He shook his head, looking dejected that she still doubted his story. For a second, she almost felt sorry for him, but she quickly reined in her emotions.

"No one ever believes in me or miracles. What has the world come to?"

"Really?" She planted her hands on her hips. "I mean, really? You dress like a cowboy, your name is Ryder, and you expect people to believe you're an angel?"

"Nephilim," he corrected.

"Whatever."

"I only came because you were so upset last night. I thought you might do something foolish."

The loud drumming inside her head made it almost impossible for her to think. "What do you know about last night?"

He shrugged. "I know you were stood up again. Ben went to a bar with Chelsea rather than take you out. He's an ass. I don't know why you were so distraught that you would cry yourself to sleep. He wasn't worth your tears."

How could he know all that?

"And Chelsea wants your job."

He was right again. Chelsea was a teller at the bank who wanted desperately to be a loan officer. There was only one problem: no opening. Well, unless someone left or got fired. Chelsea had attempted to put Haley's head on the chopping block more than once. Except Haley was pretty good at her job. And why wouldn't she be? It wasn't as though she had anything better to do on her weekends.

Ryder cleared his throat, returning her thoughts to the present.

She really needed to pay attention. Ryder was much too close for comfort. She quickly moved to the other side of the sofa. "How did you know I was stood up last night?" Before he could answer, she held up her hand. "And no more lies about being an angel."

He came to his feet. She was ready to make a run for the front door if he came any closer.

"I won't hurt you," he said.

"I won't give you the chance." That sounded brave, except she wasn't a brave person. She rarely stood up for anything, especially herself.

"Everyone always wants proof," he mumbled, shaking his head. He closed his eyes and crossed his arms in front of him.

Now what was he up to?

A golden light suddenly surrounded him. It was the most beautiful light Haley had ever seen. The soft glow bathed her in a flood of warm air that made her skin tingle. Something popped, then pure white wings appeared, stretching out on either side of him. The wingspan was impressive. It couldn't be real, she thought, shaking her head. Tentatively she touched one of the feathers and it began to sparkle, right before it disappeared.

"You *are* an angel," she whispered. A cowboy with wings!

"Nephilim," he corrected.

The room began to spin, and her legs refused to hold her up.

Ryder cursed, folding up the wings, but he couldn't reach Haley before she landed on the floor with a clunk. He grimaced.

Laughter sounded behind him. He frowned and looked over his shoulder. Chance stood behind him with a big grin.

"Do you think the wings might have been a bit much?" Chance asked as he moved closer and stared down at Haley's motionless body.

With a snap of Ryder's fingers, the wings were gone. "I couldn't convince her without them." Mortals had images firmly planted in their minds about angels having wings. Not that he was a true angel, only half. The wings were something he used when he needed to convince someone he was part angel. It always worked.

He scooped Haley into his arms, marveling at how comfortably she fit. He carried her back to the sofa where he gently laid her down, putting a pillow beneath her head.

"Not your usual type," Chance commented as he studied Haley.

Ryder straightened her lopsided glasses before he stood. "She needed a miracle."

"From the looks of her, she might need more than a miracle."

"Not funny."

"It wasn't meant to be." Chance shook his head. "You're walking a fine line by even showing yourself to her as an immortal."

"As if you've ever followed the rules."

Chance's expression turned serious. "True, but I've always kept my identity a secret, most of the time. You know as well as I do the longer you stay, the deeper the imprint that angels actually exist, that *you* exist."

Chance was right. Showing himself as an immortal could get him into a lot of trouble. "If it makes you feel better, I don't plan to stay long. I only want her to feel a little more confident in herself. She's a beautiful, sexy woman, but she doesn't see it."

Chance raised his eyebrows.

Ryder sighed. "Trust me on this."

"Okay, but you've got to trust me, too. And don't forget the rules."

"Never."

"Word of honor?"

For as long as Ryder could remember, there was a special bond between him and Chance. Their word meant something. His gaze strayed to Haley. There was so much he wanted to show her. Would he have time?

"Ryder?" Chance prodded for an answer.

"Yes, I promise," Ryder finally told him, knowing Chance wouldn't leave until he did.

"Good." Chance closed his eyes and disappeared.

Ryder couldn't blame Chance for being overprotective. Hell, he was just as bad when Chance faced a demon while trying to save Destiny. They were nephilim, immortals up to a point. It didn't mean they couldn't be killed.

There were other nephilim, but only four in their group—Chance, Dillon, Hunter, and himself. Their fathers were angels, exactly as he'd told Haley. Centuries before, some of the male angels had come to earth and mated with beautiful mortal women. When the women bore children, a new race was created. Immortals with powers, demigods. The nephilim.

But their offspring didn't follow the same rules as mortals, or the rules angels lived by. The nephilim broke more rules than they kept. Still, there was a fine line they weren't allowed to cross. If they kept their noses clean, the Powers That Be looked the other way.

Ryder sat on the floor next to the sofa near Haley. He watched the even rise and fall of her chest. There was something about mortals that made him want to get closer. Mortals reached out and grabbed life, even though the challenges they met could knock them to their knees. They kept getting right back up, even Haley. Although a few more years like the ones she'd been having and she might give up. Her tears had been the breaking point for him. Ryder had to help.

Haley's eyes fluttered open. She blinked twice. "Oh God, you're still here."

"Most people are glad to see me."

She pushed up on the sofa and scooted to the far end. If she didn't stop moving away, he was going to get a complex.

"Tell me again why you're here?" She eyed him with more than a little trepidation.

"You prayed for a miracle. I want to help."

"What? Are you going to wave your arm and make me beautiful?"

"You already are."

A short burst of laughter escaped from between her lips. "I guess that's why I have men lining up at my front door." Her words broke on a sob that she quickly swallowed. "I need more than a miracle."

He came to his feet and held out his hand. "Will you trust me to show you just how beautiful you are?"

She shook her head. "No, I don't want to trust you at all. You're... you're a cowboy. You're not even wearing white."

He waved his arm in front of him and suddenly he wore a white Stetson, white shirt, white jeans, and white boots. The change was disarming, to say the least. Her eyebrows drew together. "You looked better in black."

Ryder waved his arm again and the clothes changed back.

Her stomach rumbled and she thought she might be sick. This couldn't be happening. But what if it was, and he could make her beautiful?

"I can leave and your life will be exactly as before. Would you rather that happen?" He waited patiently, knowing she hated her life, but it had to be her decision.

She nibbled her bottom lip. He could see the warring emotions crossing her face. She didn't want to go back to the way things were, but stepping out on blind faith meant taking a risk. Safe might not look so bad to her right now. He hoped she would make the right choice.

"Okay, fine, but I still don't trust you." She came to her feet, ignoring his hand, but he continued to hold it out to her. Something close to a grumble slipped past her lips right before she slapped her hand inside his.

He liked this side of her. It reminded him a little of the woman in her diary. The woman she secretly yearned to be. He started toward her bedroom, but she tugged on his hand.

"Where exactly are we going?" she asked. The distrust was on her face again.

"Your bedroom."

Her cheeks turned a rosy shade of pink. Damn, she was such a mixture of contradictions. Innocent yet passionate, even though she hid her desires behind heavy glasses and bulky clothes. She'd never truly had the chance to express her sensuous side. He knew a little about Haley. She'd only been with six men, each one more sexually disappointing than the last. Not one of them had been able to appease her appetite, so she tamped it down, pouring her secret fantasies onto the pages of her diary.

"You have to trust me."

She finally exhaled a defeated breath and nodded.

"Don't worry, Haley. I'll never hurt you." He didn't stop walking until they stood in front of the full-length mirror in her bedroom.

"This really isn't making me feel more confident." She grimaced at her reflection.

He only smiled as he stood behind her. "Let me show you." He reached around her and untied her robe.

She pushed his hands away and stepped back. "What are you doing?" she gasped.

"You have to trust me."

"Why should I?" she countered. Her hands gripped her robe so tightly that her knuckles turned white.

"Because I can give you everything you've ever desired." Ryder watched as she struggled to accept what he promised. "Or I can leave now. It's up to you."

She nibbled her bottom lip before meeting his gaze in the mirror. Her face reflected her fear, her indecision. How badly did she want her life to change?

"You really are an angel?"

"Half angel, half mortal."

"A nephilim," she finished.

"Yes."

"This isn't a practical joke?"

"No."

He knew the moment she gave up the fight. Her shoulders slumped in defeat and her hands dropped listlessly to her sides. He silently breathed a sigh of relief. He wanted to make her life better and end her suffering, but she had to say the words.

"Help me," she finally whispered.

"Good decision," he told her and positioned her so she stood directly in front of the mirror again. Her body trembled. Ryder swore to himself he would make everything better.

"Maybe you can help, maybe not. I still look the same." Her eyes met his. It was as though she dared him to prove his words.

He smiled, enjoying the fact that she still held on to a little stubbornness. She'd need even more in the future. He removed her robe, then pushed the first button on her pajama top through the hole, then the next button, and the next.

Her face turned from a rosy hue to draining of all color. Uneasiness and embarrassment flowed from her body. Was he pushing too quickly? But no, it was the only way. He didn't have time to take it slow. He never did.

Their eyes met in the mirror. Haley looked away. He caught her chin and turned her face until she met his gaze once more. "I'll never hurt you," he said. "But if we're to continue, you must trust and obey me."

"What exactly does that mean?" Some of her spark returned.

"Whatever I ask you to do, you must do without question."

She stared at her shirt, every button undone. One slight movement and the two sides would part, showing more than the tempting sliver of pale skin. "I can't." She shook her head, then grabbed the sides of her shirt, pulling them together.

Maybe he wouldn't be able to help her. Disappointment filled him. "If you don't trust me, I'll have to leave. I won't be able to change your life." Ryder had hoped for more. Her desires were pressed tightly inside the pages of her diary and that was where they would stay. He took a step back.

"No, don't go. I'll do"—she swallowed hard—"whatever you ask. I want my life to be different."

He nodded and stepped nearer. Her shoulders shook as she let her hands drop to her sides. "You're so very beautiful," he said as he slowly pulled open her shirt, exposing her breasts.

"I'm not," she whimpered, her words shaky.

"Why do you say that?"

"Because it's the truth." Her shoulders drooped in defeat.

"Who told you this?"

"My mother. My sister. Everyone. Maybe not in so many words, but I knew what they meant."

"And you believed them?"

"They love me. Why would they lie? Why would strangers lie?"

Her words were barely audible. Ryder knew her shame ran deep. He wasn't sure he could change her visual image of herself. If someone is told often enough how ugly they are, then changing their mind might prove difficult.

"They lied," he said simply. "Maybe their intentions were good, but their words held no truth. When people let doubt creep into their world, fear takes hold. But you can conquer your fear." She didn't move. Hell, she barely breathed. He wasn't sure if she heard his words or not. At least she was still here. That was something.

Ryder brushed his hands over her shoulders. The cotton material slid down her arms, drifting to the floor. Her trembles increased, but she didn't stop him. He knew she desperately wanted to shield herself from his view, but he wasn't about to let her. He loved looking at her too much. She had the most perfect breasts he'd ever seen, and he couldn't resist touching them.

He slipped his hands around her until he held the weight of her breasts in his hands. She sucked in a deep breath, reached up, but then at the last minute, let her arms drop back down.

"I love the way your breasts fit into my hands," he told her.

"They're too big." Her expression dared him to say she lied.

"You're wrong. Women would envy your full breasts. Men would get hard just looking at them."

She turned her face from the mirror. "It's a sin to look at naked flesh."

The lies mortals told, all in the name of what they thought was right or wrong. It always amazed him. "The body is a beautiful thing to look at, to touch." He brushed his fingers across her nipples. She jumped like a nervous filly taking her first steps. But Haley's nipples betrayed her desire when they turned to hard nubs. "See how easily you respond to my touch." To prove his point, he tugged on her nipples, rolling them between his thumbs and forefingers.

She moaned, her eyes closing.

"Open your eyes. Watch as I touch you."

She dragged her eyelids open, leaning back against him. Her breathing came in short gasps. "Please," she begged.

"Not yet, but soon." He stepped back, moving his hands to her shoulders until he knew she wouldn't stumble backward. "This is the end of lesson one." If he didn't stop, he would go too far, and there was so much more that he wanted to show her.

She nodded, used to disappointment, and reached for her shirt.

"Did I tell you to put your shirt back on?"

"But I thought—"

"No, I don't want you to think about anything except the way it felt when I touched your breasts. Today, you're not to wear a top. Not for any reason. Agreed?"

Her forehead wrinkled. "But—"

"Complete obedience."

She opened her mouth, then snapped it closed. "Okay, okay."

"Good." He closed his eyes and was gone in an instant.

Haley blinked, then turned. Ryder had disappeared. Had she only imagined him?

Of course she had. A miracle? Yeah, right. Her fantasies were getting more bizarre. She reached for her top, but when she would've pulled it back on, she caught the scent of leather and a clean country breeze. Her hand tightened on the material.

What if it was real?

She finally threw her shirt on the bed and stomped out of the room. She was losing her mind. Maybe she needed to make an appointment with a psychiatrist and have her head examined. Had she written a sexual fantasy in her diary where an angel gets her sexually aroused, promises to make her life better, then pops out of her life, leaving her half-naked? Maybe she was trying to bring her fantasy to life? She shook her head. Nope, she'd never had that fantasy before. She would definitely have remembered it.

She stopped in front of the refrigerator and opened the freezer door. The cold air immediately caused her nipples to tighten. For a moment, she closed her eyes and remembered how Ryder's hands felt holding her breasts, how his fingers squeezed her nipples.

"It wasn't real," she said as she opened her eyes and brought out the double chocolate brownie ice cream. She shut the freezer door, grabbed a spoon and strode into the living room. This was real, she told herself as she sat on the sofa.

Her diary was still on the floor where she'd dropped it. She stared at the black cover with the word *Diary* written in bold gold letters. The book practically screamed that everything had really happened.

She shook her head, set the carton of ice cream on the end table, and picked up the diary. Nothing had happened. A vivid dream, that's all it had been. And, of course, she was losing her mind.

After she safely tucked her diary between her mattress and box springs, she returned to the living room and grabbed the carton of ice cream. How much time would pass before her parents and sister realized she'd lost her mind? Did insanity run in her family?

Tears formed in her eyes as she dropped to the sofa. Would they institutionalize her? How the hell was she going to get laid if she was in the state hospital? She sniffed as she scooped up a spoonful of ice cream.

Her phone began to play "Wild Thing."

She jumped.

The glob of frozen ice cream landed on her bare chest. She sucked in a breath and reached for the ice cream as it ran down one breast. She caught the ice cream at her nipple, and stilled.

Her phone abruptly stopped playing "Wild Thing."

She glanced at her phone, then down at her chest as guilt filled her. The cold against her skin felt incredibly erotic. This was wrong, she told herself, but she couldn't stop from moving the ice cream back and forth across her nipples. Excited tingles rippled over her. She once wrote in her diary how she would love to have a man slide an ice cube over her naked skin. Ice cream was just as good, better, in fact. Without really thinking about what she was doing, she scooped out more. It was cold in her hand, but she didn't care. She smeared the chocolate over her chest, across her nipples, then tweaked them, gasping with pleasure.

Her phone began to play again. Two notes, then stopped. She glanced down at her chest. She was covered in chocolate ice cream and chunks of brownie. Correction, melting chocolate ice cream and chunks of brownie. Sticky melting chocolate ice cream and falling-off-her-chest-to-the-floor chunks of brownie.

"You really know how to kill a good time," she grumbled as she glared at her phone. When she stood, she looked at the caller ID. *Ryder* flashed across the screen. She swallowed past the lump in her throat as the blood drained from her face.

"You aren't real. Only a fantasy."

Or maybe she *had* lost her mind.

Chapter 3

"I'm very real."

She whirled around; the carton of ice cream fell to the beige carpet. The cowboy nephilim was back! Oh, hell, he'd seen her feeling herself up. "You were watching?" she gasped.

"Your emotions flowed through me."

"I want to die," she groaned.

"Watching you was a hell of a turn-on."

"Why would you do that?"

"I couldn't resist." He shrugged. "I'm half human. I have needs that are difficult to control at times."

"What? Not enough happening at your home on the... the cloud? You have to spy on me?"

With one finger, he tilted the black Stetson higher on his forehead. She was mesmerized by that one move.

"I don't live on a cloud."

"Next you'll be telling me you own a ranch."

He smiled a slow, disarming smile.

One eyebrow rose in sarcastic disbelief. "Seriously? You own a ranch? What do your neighbors think of having a nephilim living nearby?"

Something close to sadness shone in his eyes before it abruptly disappeared. "No one knows my true identity. I don't interact with mortals very often."

"No, you just spy on us." When his gaze lowered, Haley wished she could call back her words. There was a moment of awkward silence. She wondered if he would disappear again, but then he raised his gaze.

"You're sexy covered in chocolate," he said, changing the subject.

Sexy? Her? She studied Ryder's face. Was he feeding her a line of bull? No one had ever said she was sexy.

His gaze roamed over her, touching her breasts, sliding over her hips, caressing between her legs. It started an ache deep inside her. She could almost believe she was sexy.

He tossed his hat. The Stetson landed on the sofa. She couldn't take her eyes off it.

"Haley, what are you doing to me?"

"Nothing," she said, dragging her gaze back to him.

He stepped closer and removed her glasses, putting them on the end table. Her eyesight wasn't that bad. Sometimes she wondered why she even wore them. Rachael had talked her into buying the heavy black frames. She said they would give her an edge in the banking business. Not that she needed an edge as a loan officer.

Her thoughts were rambling. And why not? A hot guy had told her that he thought she was sexy and he was looking at her as though he wanted to make love—with *her*! Her thighs clenched and she had to fight the urge to throw herself at him. She wasn't that kind of girl. Except she was half-naked and covered in ice cream.

He rested his hands on her hips. She almost jumped out of her skin.

"I think you know exactly what effect you have on me," he drawled.

But she didn't. How could she when nothing like that ever happened. And oh damn, she didn't want it to stop. From the look in his eyes, she didn't think it would. At least, not right away. She was transfixed as she watched Ryder lean down. Her thighs trembled. He licked the ice cream off one nipple, then sucked the sensitive nub into his mouth.

Haley gasped and grabbed his head as flames nipped her skin. His mouth sucking on her breast felt so incredibly good. Just as quickly, he moved away.

"You make me forget what I'm doing," he said. "But not yet. It's too soon."

"No, it's not too soon." She ached for more. Yes, she was begging! She didn't care.

He hesitated, as though he struggled with his decision. "Maybe you're right."

"I am," she whispered. She waited breathlessly to see what Ryder would do next. His gaze lingered on her breasts. Again, she was caught between desire and the lessons that were drilled into her since she was a child. He must have sensed her dilemma because he raked a hand through his hair and mumbled something about her making it more difficult.

"Okay, we'll move to lesson two," he said. "But that will be all for today."

"Yes, lesson two." She thrust her chest forward and moved closer, but he only took her hand and pulled her toward the bedroom. He was right. Having sex would be much more comfortable if they were on the bed, except he stopped in front of the stupid mirror again.

"Lesson two," he said as he slipped his fingers in the waistband of her pajama bottoms and slowly pushed the material downward.

Haley grabbed the waistband before he could lower her pajama bottoms more than a couple of inches. "Can we turn out the light?" No man had ever seen her completely naked.

"I want to see you."

Oh, God, she was going to throw up. The passion she'd felt only moments before evaporated as quickly as dew on the grass at sunrise. She closed her eyes tight. "I can't."

"Haley?"

"What?" Her voice cracked.

He let go of her pajama bottoms and ran his hands over her hips. Up and down. The tension inside her began to ease. With her eyes closed she almost felt as though it was dark inside her bedroom. His touch was nice, making her believe she could have everything she'd dreamed about when it came to a man.

Ryder's hands moved to her ass.

She tightened. The relaxed state he'd brought her to quickly disappeared. What was she doing? He said he was some kind of half angel-half mortal, and she believed him? Was she a moron? Her eyes flew open. She stared in panic at the stranger who knelt in front of her.

"Shh, I won't hurt you," he whispered.

Something in his eyes said he spoke the truth. She trusted him. She couldn't really say why, but she did. Maybe because he'd already changed her life to some degree. At least it wasn't boring.

He began to massage her butt cheeks. Haley let herself be swept away by the sensations he created inside her. He squeezed, then released. His hands set off a chain reaction that sent tingles to other parts of her body.

Was it so wrong that no matter what he asked her to do, she would probably do it? His fingers were magical. If his touching her was a sin, then why did it feel so good?

She drew in a sharp breath when he pressed his hand against her... sex. Sheesh, she couldn't even say the word. The most she'd ever uttered was damn or hell, and she'd always been careful not to let anyone hear. She was a good girl. She really was. She'd always...

Ryder pressed his palm harder against her flesh, then began to move it in a circular motion. Oh yes, right there! She wiggled against his hand as thoughts of being good flew out the window.

"Do you like when I touch you?"

She nodded.

"I'll have to stop if I can't undress you all the way."

Stop? Her heart skipped a beat. No, she didn't want him to stop.

He moved his hand away. Frustration filled her. Her hips moved forward, silently begging for more, but Ryder only looked at her. He didn't touch.

"Okay, okay," she muttered.

"Say it."

The man could be so aggravating. "Yes, you can remove my"— she swallowed, then almost choked on her next words—"pajama bottoms." She couldn't believe she'd told Ryder he could strip her. But it wouldn't be too bad with her eyes shut. She squeezed them closed. That was better.

She waited.

Nothing happened. She heard a car go down the street. The next door neighbors' black lab barked.

Ryder didn't attempt to lower her pajama bottoms. She gave him permission. Now what was he waiting for?

"Open your eyes." His words were soft, like a caress, but he might as well have set off a bomb the way they jarred Haley.

Really! Really? It wasn't enough that she'd actually told him he could strip her? He wanted more?

The alternative was unacceptable. Who in their right mind would want a super sexy cowboy nephilim to disappear from their life? So what if he wanted her to open her eyes.

"Haley, you're stalling."

Maybe she was. Deep breath. She inhaled then exhaled.

Her lids would not lift. She stretched her facial muscles, but nothing happened. How hard could it be to open her eyes? She strained, finally admitting defeat. "I can't," she told him.

"Yes, you can."

He ran his hand over the front of the cotton material. She gasped as he bumped against her nerve endings. Up and down, up and down. Then he stopped.

Nooo… She bit her bottom lip.

Drat! Okay, fine.

She opened her eyes and glared at him. "There, are you satisfied?"

"Not quite." He didn't wait for her to change her mind as he jerked the bottoms downward, revealing her hips, her mound, her curls. The pajama bottoms puddled around her ankles when he let go of them. "Now I am."

She stood naked before him, absolutely mortified. Never once had she been naked in front of a man with the light on. Her first instinct was to cover herself, but he'd said he would leave if she didn't obey him. Haley had a feeling it would be like before, and she wasn't supposed to hide anything from him. Fantasy or reality, she didn't want it to end. Not yet. She was such a slut! Shame filled her. Good girls didn't act like that. She was a good girl, except for maybe the sex fantasies she jotted down in her diary. But other than that, she rarely sinned. Haley was pretty sure what Ryder was doing had to be sinful.

"Nice," he said.

She raised her chin. Shame on him for lying. She wasn't nice to look at, and he teased her. Haley knew the truth and she would let him know it didn't matter to her. "I'm… fat, but I don't care." She raised her chin.

He shook his head. "Curvy, not fat. Never fat. Sexy curvy. Jane Russell curvy. Marilyn Monroe curvy."

Curvy? Rachael had always said Haley was a little too heavy. Her sister was never wrong. Rachael did whatever she set out to do. She'd worked nights and went to school in the daytime, but now she was a lawyer in a prestigious law firm. She was always right.

Right?

Haley looked at her reflection with more than a little skepticism. She looked ridiculous wearing nothing but streaked chocolate ice cream and a couple of clumps of brownie. Curvy? No, she didn't think so. She hated what she saw. How could any man ever want her?

Ryder moved in front of her. For a moment he only looked into her eyes, then he took her face in his hands and lowered his mouth to hers. As soon as his lips touched hers, a shudder of need swept over her. His tongue caressed, sucked, stroked, until she couldn't remember what she was thinking. The kiss ended all too soon, and left her wanting a lot more.

"Lesson two," he said, then knelt in front of her. His face was only a few inches from her... Oh good Lord! Her... sex.

Haley was pretty sure she was going to die of humiliation. The only one who saw her like this was Dr. Parker during Haley's yearly exam, and the doctor was a female. Haley's sexual encounters never included getting naked with the light on, and very little foreplay.

Ryder's warm breath drifted across her curls, drawing her attention back to him. Tingles of pleasure rushed over her. Oh, my, that felt very nice. *Did it really matter that she was naked?* She didn't think so. Not when he made her feel so good.

But he stopped touching her. She wiggled her hips. She needed more. She wanted him to touch her... there.

Except he didn't. No, his hands skimmed over her hips, down her legs. That felt nice too, but not as nice as the other. He began to massage the backs of her knees. A deep, throbbing ache swirled inside her, and all the time her gaze stayed focused on the mirror, watching what he did as if she viewed someone else. The woman looking back at her wasn't Haley. No, that woman was a stranger. She was sexy and curvy, not fat at all.

"I love how your body responds to my touch," he said, drawing her attention back to him. His hands moved to the insides of her knees. "Are you damp with need?"

She moaned, unable to talk. She only wanted the sensations he created to go on forever. It was what she dreamed about. It was what she wrote about in her diary, her secret fantasy world.

"Open for me, little flower," he told her.

This wasn't happening. It couldn't be real. She would awaken any moment and he would be gone. She glanced down. He watched her, waiting for her to obey. Haley looked at the woman in the mirror, waiting to see what she would do. The woman staring back trembled, but she parted her legs just a fraction.

Ryder's hands traveled farther up, massaging. It was all Haley could do to drag a breath into her starved lungs. He ran one hand between her legs, inching closer, but not quite touching that secret spot. "Beautiful," he breathed on a sigh. He moved a little to his right, just until she could see all of the woman in the mirror.

Haley's doubts came rushing back. The image of the seductress shattered as tears filled her eyes. She saw herself for what she was and shook her head.

"You're beautiful and sexy."

She nibbled her bottom lip.

"Say it." His words were gentle.

"I can't."

He ran the backs of his fingers through her curls. She gasped, her body jerking. He opened her, exposing all of her to his view, then licked his finger before running it down the fleshy part of her sex. "I want to kiss and suck on you, right here. But you have to say it." He drew his finger down her slit once again.

Her mouth was so dry, she couldn't swallow. He plucked at her sex, teasing her. She looked in the mirror. She wasn't sexy. She wasn't beautiful. But, damn, she wanted what he could give her. "I'm beautiful and sexy." Her words were tight, forced between dry lips.

"I don't think you meant it." He licked once up her leg, coming close but not quite touching that special place with his mouth.

"I meant it," she moaned.

He licked her thigh, then slipped a finger inside her. Her body clenched as spasms rippled over her. Just as quickly, he slipped his finger out.

"I was right, you are damp. And you want what I can give you. You want me to suck your pussy."

Oh, damn! He'd said the *p* word! She wanted to die right on the spot.

"Would you like that?" he asked.

She opened her mouth, but no words came out. Her throat was parched. She could barely breathe, but before she could gather enough outrage over his suggestion, she imagined his mouth on her… sex. That was exactly what she wanted him to do.

She nodded.

Rather than giving in to her need, he moved back a fraction and looked up at her. Haley knew what he wanted. Her eyes moved back to the mirror and suddenly she saw herself in a different light. Had he cast a magical spell on the mirror? She stood naked, with a sexy man at her knees, his fingers lightly dragging back and forth through her curls. Her legs were parted, as though she was a warrior queen and Ryder her slave, begging for her favors. "I am beautiful and sexy," she stated firmly. She looked down at him.

His mouth covered her. She gasped as his tongue darted out, massaging her clit, sucking her inside his mouth. She cried out, pulling his head closer still. "Yes, oh yes." Her hips began to rock, moving against his mouth. She had dreams about a man taking her inside his mouth, but this was the first time it had happened, and it was better than any dream.

"You taste sweet and musky," he said as he moved back. His hand continued massaging where his mouth had been. "Each woman has a different taste."

He licked her. Her thighs quivered.

"Your taste is unique, more potent than aged brandy. Even now, I want to suck you back inside my mouth."

Her legs wobbled. He came to his feet, picked her up in one swift movement, and lowered her onto the bed. He stood back and removed his shirt and she finally got to see his tanned muscles, his defined abdomen. The hard ridges. She wanted to run her hands over each sinewy muscle, feel the firmness of his chest pressing against hers.

"I want you," she said.

"Open for me," he told her.

It wasn't real, she told herself. It was only a very good wet dream and she never wanted the fantasy to end. She spread her legs.

He stopped in the process of unzipping his jeans. "I can hardly wait to bury myself inside you." He dragged his zipper down, his gaze never leaving her body.

It didn't matter what the truth was. Right then, she felt sexy and she felt beautiful. "Hurry."

He shoved his jeans and briefs down at the same time. She stared. He was hard and thick and big. She opened her legs wider. He kicked out of his clothes, then knelt between her legs. He licked her, drawing her into his mouth. He sucked. Her hips rocked. His fingers massaged the insides of her thighs. She moved her head from side to side as sensations she'd never experienced engulfed her.

Her body burned with the heat he created. "I can't," she gasped. "I need… I need…"

He sucked harder, his tongue pressing against her clit. He slipped his hands beneath her bottom, pulling her in, closer to his mouth. She gasped. Her body tightened. Wave after wave of pure ecstasy swept over her when she came. Haley thought she might have cried out, but she didn't know. She shuddered as she was taken to the edge and pushed over.

Oh, yes! The world around her splintered into a thousand tiny pieces. Her body shuddered with release. He pressed the palm of his hand tight against her until she slowly returned.

This was what she'd dreamed about all her life. She knew orgasms could be earth-shattering, but she never expected to have one. For the first time in her life, she felt complete, and sexy, and so very satisfied.

She stretched, smiling.

He moved up in the bed and laid beside her as the bedroom came back into focus. "You're so beautiful." He stroked his hand over one breast, tweaking the nipple.

"Am I really?" She searched his face to see if Ryder meant what he said. He looked sincere.

"Yes. And damn sexy when you come." He smiled as he moved off the bed, tugging on her hand.

Haley hesitated before taking it. What else could happen? She was naked in front of a stranger. But one who had given her the wildest orgasm she ever had in her life. She would follow him just about anywhere.

Ryder only led her to the bathroom where he turned the water on. Once the temperature was to his satisfaction, he flipped the lever. Her gaze traveled over his tanned skin, the bulging arm muscles, his sexy ass. He stepped under the spray, ducking his head so his hair got wet. She swallowed as her eyes moved to the front of his body. The man was hung very well. Her thighs clenched as she imagined how it would feel to have him buried deep inside her.

Why hadn't she prayed for a miracle a long time ago?

"Haley?"

She forced herself to meet his eyes, then felt the heat rise up her face when she realized he'd caught her staring.

"It's okay to look," he said.

She opened her mouth, but nothing came out. What could she say? Great, then turn around and give me a full frontal view?

Ryder turned and did exactly what she imagined. Could he read her mind? She certainly hoped not

Her gaze drifted down. "Wow," she breathed.

"Does my cock excite you?"

Heat flooded her face.

"Haley, you can be truthful."

She nodded.

"Then say it."

"Out loud?"

"Out loud," he confirmed. When she didn't say anything, he started to turn away.

"Cock," she blurted.

Haley cringed, cautiously looking up. Not one lightning bolt struck her. Did she really expect to be struck dead just because she'd said a dirty word out loud? It was just a word.

Her gaze moved down. But oh, what a word.

He circled his hand around the flesh and slid his foreskin down. Water from the showerhead moistened the tip. His cock practically invited her to come nearer and examine its magnificence. So she did. Ryder took her hand and moved it so that she held him. Her heart began to race. His erection felt even more wonderful than it looked.

She ran her thumb over the velvety smooth head of his penis. He grew hard as she fondled him.

"You... excite me very much."

He quivered.

Pleasure swirled inside her. Growing bolder, she slid the foreskin down. He gasped and she was afraid she might have damaged him, but when she glanced up, she saw pleasure on his face. Her gaze moved downward again. She'd never held one that she could actually examine so closely. The few times she'd had sex were always in the dark, and magazines just didn't do the male anatomy justice. Nothing compared to the real thing.

"Join me." He held his hand toward her.

Did she have to let go? She didn't want to let go of the new toy.

When he didn't move, she assumed he wasn't giving her a choice. Well, fine, then. She clasped his hand, but she didn't like letting go of his cock.

There was only a smidgeon of room left and that was right in front of him. She squeezed in, the spray hitting her right smack in the face. Drowning was not an option, so she ducked. His erection sandwiched against her ass.

He groaned.

She froze.

Awkward!

"Uh, sorry." She quickly stepped closer to the showerhead, banging her head against the metal. Water sprayed her face again. If she didn't drown, she'd probably die from embarrassment.

Ryder grabbed her shoulders and turned her until she faced him. Before she could say another word, his lips brushed hers, and then he was kissing her. Her brain stopped functioning when her nipples pressed against his chest and his cock nudged her belly.

Please don't let this be a dream.

She wanted his kiss to last forever, to feel her body pressed intimately against his. She raised her arms, wrapping them around his neck, her body molding closer, water tickling her backside. For the first time in her life, she felt sexy, and wanton, and hot.

When he ended the kiss, they were both breathing hard. Knowing she had that effect on him was a heady experience. Power surged through her. Ryder made her feel as if she'd climbed to the top of the mountain, as if she could conquer anything. She never wanted this moment to end, never wanted the outside world to intrude, never wanted...

Someone banged on the bathroom door and her new world came crashing down around her.

"Haley, are you okay?" The door slammed open and her sister's shadowy figure appeared on the other side of the beige shower curtain.

Ryder suddenly vanished. One second he was holding her close, his sexy body pressed against her, and in the next second, poof, he disappeared and she was left grabbing tile to stay upright. Had he really left? Haley's gaze frantically scanned the inside of the shower.

What? Did she think he might be hiding behind the soap? He was gone. Period.

What if her sister had scared him off for good?

"Haley?"

"I'm fine!"

"Well, you don't have to get testy."

Haley poked her head from behind the curtain and frowned at her sister. "I was taking a shower and would have liked a little privacy. How did you get in?" She distinctly remembered locking the front door.

"Back door. It was unlocked. You really should be more careful."

Drat, she'd forgotten to lock it. "In Hattersville?"

Rachael raised a disdainful eyebrow. "Crime happens everywhere. Even in Hattersville. Believe me, I know. I see it every time I'm in the courtroom."

Please don't let her talk about her current case! Her sister could go on for hours and hours and hours... It might be different in the city where Rachael worked, but the only crime in Hattersville was boredom and there was plenty of that to go around.

"I asked you to call before you dropped by," she said, quickly changing the subject.

Rachael shrugged her delicate shoulders. "I'm your sister. Besides, you're never doing anything important."

"You never know." She raised her chin. "What if I had been having really dirty sex with a hot cowboy?"

"Haley Tillman! You better use the soap to wash your mouth out!"

"Really? I mean, really? Are you going to stand there and try to convince me you're still a virgin?"

Her sister's cheeks turned a rosy hue. "I'll meet you in the living room." She turned on her heel and left quickly, closing the door behind her.

Guilt flooded Haley as she shut off the water and stepped out of the shower. Her sister really tried to set a good example. Rachael meant well, even though she often went about things the wrong way. She probably didn't realize how insulting her words could be or how much they hurt. Haley *did* have a life!

Until she'd been rudely interrupted, Haley had been doing something very important. Like having sex in the shower. And just this morning she'd had her first real orgasm. She bit her bottom lip. It had been such a fantastic orgasm. She pressed her legs together.

And then Ryder had disappeared again.

"How could today start off so well, then turn to… shit." Again, nothing happened. She wasn't turned into a pile of ashes for cursing. Imagine that, two bad words and she was still among the living. She grabbed a towel out of the cabinet and dried off.

They were just words. Haley didn't know what all the fuss was about. She grimaced, still remembering the taste of Ivory soap. She was thirteen when she mumbled the word *crap*. Her mother had heard. Cursing was not permitted in the Tillman household. Her father had said *crap* earlier that morning, but Haley never told her mother where she heard the word. She was a little afraid her mother would wash her dad's mouth out with soap. Her dad was pretty cool. Not as uptight as her mom.

And her sister wouldn't wait in the other room forever.

Haley snorted. She'd be lucky if she could get dressed before Rachael came to check on her. After tossing the towel over the shower curtain rod, she hurried to her bedroom and grabbed her terrycloth robe off the floor. She slipped her arms into the sleeves and tightened the belt as she left the room. She might as well get Rachael's impromptu visit over and done. As soon as the thought entered her mind, another wave of guilt washed over her. Rachael really meant well.

Her feet came to a dead stop when she entered the living room. Rachael was on all fours cleaning the floor where the ice cream had melted into a chocolate blob on the carpet. Oh, drat, she'd forgotten about the ice cream.

"What happened in here?" Rachael looked at her, waiting for an answer.

This was not good. Haley had never been able to lie well. She could barely tell the truth! "I was eating ice cream and dropped some on my… uh… new sweater. That pretty pink one you picked out." She didn't add that it was the one that reminded her of the pink stuff in her mom's medicine cabinet. She'd always hated the taste.

"You were eating out of the carton?" Rachael dropped the wad of chocolate-soaked paper towels on the carpet and sat back on her heels.

She flinched. "Saves on dishes?"

Rachael frowned. "It serves you right that you ruined your favorite sweater." Her gaze was critical as she stared at Haley.

Haley didn't look away. Ryder had made her feel sexy and Rachael wouldn't steal her newfound confidence. Nothing she could say or do would make Haley feel bad. She wouldn't crumble. Not this time.

Why did Rachael keep staring as though she had a huge wart on her nose?

"Stop giving me that look!"

One of Rachael's eyebrows rose. "And what look would that be?"

"You know exactly what look I'm talking about. The one you always give me."

"Did someone wake up on the wrong side of the bed?"

If only she could tell her sister the truth. Then she wouldn't be so full of herself! Not that Rachael would believe her. Any arguments inside her suddenly died. She wasn't so sure her imagination hadn't run away with her. Sexy cowboys did not appear on her porch and make wild passionate love to her, claiming they could answer her prayers.

Maybe she'd hit her head or something. She could be in a coma and not know it. If that was the case, her sister needed to leave. It was bad enough Rachael always interfered in Haley's life; being in her subconscious was even worse.

Rachael scooped up the paper towels and carried them toward the trash in the kitchen, but spoke as she went, "You know, if you would stop eating junk food, losing twenty pounds wouldn't be that difficult."

Haley opened her mouth, but just as quickly closed it. Why try? She never won. Her sister was right. The need to refute her words was strong, though. "I only need to lose fifteen pounds."

Rachael returned to the living room. "Fifteen or twenty, what's the difference?"

"Five pounds." She smugly smiled.

"It's still fat."

Why did Haley always feel the need to argue when she knew she wouldn't win? "Curvy," she stubbornly insisted.

Rachael narrowed her eyes, studying Haley with a critical eye. "We need to go shopping."

Oh, good Lord! Not shopping. Rachael had no more sense of style than Haley when it came to picking out Haley's wardrobe. In some instances, her style was worse. Rachael was petite and cute. Her hair was pale blonde and her skin was porcelain perfect. Haley remembered when they were growing up how boys fell all over themselves to be the first one to open a door for her big sister. She was the little princess. Haley, on the other hand, was the ugly duckling.

Rachael's looks were the reason she won a lot of court cases. No one took her sister seriously. A lawyer? Really? Men didn't think she had a brain in that pretty little head. They always underestimated her, and she let them, even pouring on the soft southern charm, right before she cut their throats in the courtroom. They never knew what hit them until it was too late. Haley had to admit, she was secretly proud of her sister. She'd always wished for just a smidgeon of her bravado.

But shopping with her older sister would be a huge mistake. Rachael always talked her into buying clothes that looked even worse hanging in her closet. Like the dainty pink sweater. Haley didn't do dainty or pink well. Not that she had any better luck with *her* choices. Nothing ever looked as good as it did on the store mannequins.

"I hate shopping," Haley told her.

"If you'd lose the extra weight, you wouldn't."

"Yes, I would."

"How did your date go last night?"

That was Rachael. Change the subject and throw your opponent off guard.

Haley drew in a deep breath. She might as well tell the truth. "Ben had to work late. He called to apologize." She braced herself for another blow to her ego.

Rachael's lips thinned to a grim line. "Why you like him is beyond me. There's something wrong with a man who uses more hair products than a woman. "You're too good for him."

Haley was starting to lean more and more toward the idea that she'd hit her head and was in a coma.

"What?" Rachael asked when Haley didn't say anything.

Haley shrugged. "I guess I thought you would say something about my being stood up again."

"By Ben? I don't think so. You always choose the wrong men. Ben is a user." Her mouth turned down. "I might be a little critical of you, but I'm your big sister and I only want you to be happy." She stepped closer, then in a rare move she put her arms around Haley and hugged her.

Shock, and something pretty close to sisterly love, filled Haley. Rachael moved before Haley could reciprocate.

"Whose black cowboy hat?"

"Huh?" There she went, changing the subject again. "What are you talking about?"

Rachael nodded toward the sofa. Haley turned. Her heart skipped a beat when she saw Ryder's Stetson. How would she explain a man's cowboy hat in the house? Casually mention she'd been visited by a nephilim? That she'd almost had real sex? Her sister would have her committed and Rachael knew enough judges who would sign the order. *Think!* Deep breath. She could do this.

"The Old Settler's Reunion is next weekend. I bought the hat to wear." Rather than meet Rachael's gaze, she spotted her glasses on the end table where Ryder had set them. She put them on before she faced her sister.

Rachael shook her head. "I'm not sure you're the cowboy hat type. Do you even own a pair of jeans?"

"No." She shrugged. "I thought about buying a pair, though. It's almost sacrilege to be a Texan and not own a pair."

"Sometimes I wonder about you." She sighed. "I've got to go to the office this morning, but I wanted to stop by and remind you we're having dinner with mom and dad tonight. Why don't you pick up ingredients for a salad? You can buy some healthy groceries while you're at it. Get rid of the chips in the pantry. Especially if you plan to squeeze into a pair of jeans." She was out the door before Haley could say anything.

"Why does she always stab me right where it hurts?" Haley mumbled.

Ryder suddenly appeared in front of her. She jumped, slapping a hand to her chest. "You need to stop popping in like that! I could have a heart attack!"

His grin was slow and sexy. "Want me to leave?"

Chapter 4

RYDER WAS ASKING HER if she wanted him to leave? Her gaze met his. Passion burned in his eyes. He looked at her as though he wanted to throw her on the floor and make love to her all day. Leave?

She shook her head. "No, I don't want you to leave. Just make some kind of noise before you pop in. You scared me."

"I could blow a trumpet, if you'd like. Maybe borrow Gabriel's horn."

Was he serious? His eyes twinkled.

"Not funny." She didn't want to think about anything remotely angelic when he was around.

He moved closer, tugging on the cloth belt of her robe. "No clothes."

She sucked in a deep breath as he pulled the belt from the loops. "I couldn't very well parade around the house naked with my sister here."

"Why not? The naked body is a beautiful thing. It's to be admired."

"And I'd never hear the end of it. My sister is very prim and proper."

He shook his head and laughed.

"What?" She frowned.

"Your ideas about other people are funny."

Her frown only deepened. "Believe me, I know my sister. Men might drool all over themselves when she's around, but she has high standards."

"You were right when you said she wasn't a virgin."

"Do you always eavesdrop on other people's conversations?"

"I only listen in on the important ones." He pushed her robe off her shoulders. It fell to the floor with barely a whisper.

Haley's first instinct was to cover herself, but he anticipated her move and took her hands in his. She swallowed hard when his gaze slowly roamed over her body.

Think about something else! Anything else! "I know Rachael isn't *that* prim and proper, but she doesn't fall into bed with every man who dates her, either."

"Everyone has their sensuous side. Don't let people fool you."

"Is that the next lesson?" She pulled her hands free and crossed her arms in front of her. That was a smart move! She only made her chest stick out farther.

He shook his head. His gaze was definitely focused on her breasts. She let her hands fall to her sides, then casually moved her hands so that her lower half was shielded from his view. Only then did she breathe easier.

"No lesson right now. I only want to make love to you."

Heat crept up her face. He smiled. His hand moved to her breast, pulling on the nipple. She exhaled on a sigh as ripples of pleasure erupted inside her.

He continued to lightly massage her breasts, teasing her nipples. His hand ran over her ribs, tickling, before moving to her abdomen. "Do you like that?"

"Yes, it feels good." His hands were warm on her cool skin. She didn't want the sensations he created inside her to ever stop.

"Did you like when I sucked on your pussy?"

Oh, jeez! Her thighs clenched as her eyes drifted closed. She visualized his head between her legs, his tongue scraping across her sex. "You know I did." Her words were scratchy and dry. A need deep inside her rose to the surface.

"But I want to hear you say it."

Her eyes flew open. "I... I can't." She'd already said *cock*, but she was under extreme duress. What would her mother say if she knew her youngest daughter had even said *cock*? Haley bet she'd get more than a taste of soap even though she was twenty-six years old!

How many times had she *talked dirty* since Ryder showed up? And without stuttering. Fantastic, one day with an angel, okay, half angel, and she wallowed in the gutter. Hmm, that didn't say much about him.

"Are you sure you're part angel?" she asked, pushing her glasses higher on the bridge of her nose.

"Positive. Why, do you doubt me?" His fingers played up and down her arms.

A shiver ran down her spine. She had a feeling he was only halfway paying attention to her. He seemed much more interested in her body. "I never thought angels would act like you do."

"But the other half is human and I have all the desires of any mortal man." He inched his fingers past hers and ran them through the curls at the juncture of her legs.

Oh, damn! His touch was heavenly.

Duh!

He leaned close to her ear. "Say it. Tell me how much you loved that I tasted you."

She should be mortified that he would want her to talk about how he'd made her feel. How he made her feel right now. Except her body betrayed her, pushing closer to his fingers, responding to his touch. A moan escaped her lips when he pressed his hand against her slit and began to slide it up and down. She gasped, moving her hips. She never wanted him to stop touching her.

"What did you love?" he asked, then slipped his tongue inside her ear and swirled it around.

She groaned as she lost herself in his touch, heat spreading over her body.

He tugged lightly on her earlobe while his fingers continued their assault on the lower part of her body, then suddenly moved his hand away.

She whimpered, rocking her hips, silently pleading for more.

"Just tell me what you want."

Her mouth was so dry that she wasn't sure she could say anything, but her body ached with need. She didn't really care if Ryder was angel, demon, or just a very vivid dream. "I loved when your mouth was on me."

"What do you want me to do?" His warm breath whispered against her face.

There was more? Of course there was more. There was always more.

"Tell me exactly what you want me to do, and I'll do it." His tongue moved over her jaw line, tracing the edge.

She whimpered, her body arching, silently begging for more. Her eighth grade English teacher was probably turning over in her grave. Miss Crane had painted pictures with words and made Haley want to increase her vocabulary, but Haley didn't think her teacher would approve of the very vivid images Ryder painted. But oh, how she wanted him. He made her feel alive and sexy and wanton. "I want you. I want all of you."

"That wasn't so hard, was it?" Ryder scraped his fingers across her one more time then unbuttoned his shirt. This was her fantasy. He was the dream lover she imagined, except he was real.

Wasn't he? She touched his chest. He felt real. His shoulders were wide, his biceps tight. She ran her hand over his chest, down to his six-pack abs. He sucked in a deep breath. She met his gaze and saw the passion on his face. Had she done that? Had she made him want her touch?

Incredible.

Ryder pulled his arms out of the sleeves of his shirt and let it drop to the floor. His eyes never left her body as he quickly toed off his black boots, then removed his socks. He seemed almost eager. Having a man want her this much was a new experience and she liked how it made her feel.

His hands moved to his jeans. Haley hugged her middle, waiting in anticipation for his pants to follow the rest of his clothes. She wasn't disappointed when he tugged the top button through the hole then jerked the zipper down. She held her breath when he pushed his jeans over his hips, down his muscled thighs, then kicked out of them. She didn't let out her breath until he slipped his fingers into the waistband of his briefs and released his very erect cock.

His very large cock. She wanted to drop to her knees and suck him inside her mouth. Let her tongue roll over the head, her teeth scrape across him. But when he stepped closer and trailed his fingers through her curls, she lost herself in the quivers of excitement that trembled over her. She swayed toward him. In one swift movement, he picked her up and carried her toward the bedroom.

Ryder made her feel as light as a feather and as delicate as a rose petal when he laid her on the bed. But when he looked at her, when she could almost hear his thoughts blending with hers, asking her to spread her legs, that's when she broke the rules drilled into her since childhood because she did exactly what he silently asked.

He dragged his gaze from between her legs and met her eyes. "I'll do anything you want."

"Kiss me," she said. Her words sounded husky, sexy. As though someone else spoke them. It didn't sound like her voice at all. No, a seductress suddenly took possession of her body. That wasn't who she was, not really. Good girls were more reserved.

Ryder moved her arms so they were stretched above her head. He lightly grazed his knuckles down the side of one breast, over her ribs, past her hip, down her leg, only stopping when he reached her ankle.

Haley didn't care about her mother's morals as a rush of fire nipped down her body. She grew bolder. "I loved it when you tasted me." Her body throbbed with renewed need as he moved between her legs.

"Nice," he said, looking down at her. His hand encircled his cock. She couldn't look away as he slid his foreskin down. A drop of moisture formed. She sat up, unable to resist temptation, and reached out, running her finger over the tip of his penis. He groaned. Power surged through her. If she had completely lost her mind and lived in a fantasy world, then she could do whatever she wanted. She licked her lips.

He drew in a sharp breath. "Not this time. I want to love you."

Ryder might be a dream, but that didn't mean she didn't get embarrassed. Before she had time to think about her bold actions, he lowered his head and stroked her with his tongue. She squirmed beneath him as tremors of delight spread over her. "Yes! Oh please, don't stop." He licked then sucked her inside his mouth, nibbling on her sensitive flesh. She couldn't draw in a deep breath. Her lungs felt as though they would burst. Her hips rose, grinding against his eager mouth. She needed more, she wanted more, she demanded more!

He slipped his hands under her bottom, bringing her closer to his mouth. He sucked, then released, only to suck her inside his mouth again. His tongue swirled around her flesh, licking, as lights flashed inside her head.

"Touch your breasts," he told her. "Pleasure yourself."

She whimpered.

"Please." He licked her slit, teeth tugged on her flesh.

She squeezed her nipples, gasping when they tightened, not realizing her body would be so sensitive. She watched him through half-closed eyes. He drew her inside his mouth, his tongue hard against her flesh. She massaged her breasts, fire burning inside her. Yes, this was what she imagined sex could be like. Oh, yes!

She tensed as spasms gripped her. Before she could recover from her orgasm, Ryder straightened, lowering her hips to the bed. She whimpered. He took one of her hands and moved it between her legs, moving her fingers so that she touched herself. She moaned as he stoked the fires inside her once more.

He entered her, just a little at first. She drew in a sharp breath, her fingers stilled.

He was big, maybe too big. She wasn't that experienced. She hadn't been with enough men. Fear penetrated the fog of passion, wiping it away. What if—

"I won't hurt you. Let your body adjust to my size."

His eyes told the truth. Ryder would never hurt her. She relaxed as his words soothed. He moved his fingers over her, teasing.

Ryder was too big. She wouldn't be able to take all of him. "I can't."

"Shh…" He didn't move, letting her become accustomed to his cock inside her. Her breathing slowed. She relaxed, knowing he wouldn't force her to go farther than she was willing to go. Then something happened. Another heat began to build. She wiggled, trying to get closer to the warmth he created. He pushed deeper. She gasped as he filled her, afraid he would rip her in half.

"Remember me drawing you inside my mouth, sucking on you. God, you tasted hot. I thought I would come before I ever got the chance to fuck you. I loved licking you, hearing you cry out when you came."

Her nipples tightened. She wiggled beneath him as erotic images formed inside her head. Her fingers moved over her flesh, her body straining for more.

"I want to do everything you wrote about in your diary. Promise that you'll let me."

Flashes of her diary whipped through her mind. Everything?

He moved out, then in, filling her body, stroking her.

"Promise that I can do everything you wrote about." He leaned forward and ran his tongue over her lips.

She tried to capture his tongue, but he moved, licking up the side of her neck. A shudder of longing rolled over her. Her body adjusted to his size, and she found herself wanting more. She wrapped her legs around his waist, drawing him in deeper.

He gasped. His eyes closed then opened, as if he tried to stay focused.

"I want to do everything in your diary," he repeated.

Ryder wasn't moving. She needed him to make love to her. Why wasn't he moving?

"I want to experience each of your fantasies with you," he said.

Now? Wasn't she doing that already?

She wiggled against him, but he moved back before she received any kind of satisfaction. What had she put in the silly diary, anyway? Nothing specific came to mind as he dipped back inside. She wrapped her arms around his neck. He stopped moving again. Most of the pages had been filled with fantastic orgasms, so what did it matter?

"More," she pleaded.

He tugged on her earlobe with his teeth, then let go. "Say it."

"Yes. Okay." She would agree to anything right now. Just as long as he didn't stop what he was doing.

He drew out, then plunged inside her again. She gasped. Her hips rose.

She watched his face, saw his need, saw the pleasure she gave him. She met his thrust. He drove harder. She rocked her hips against his.

"You're so freakin' tight," he said between gritted teeth.

"Yes, right there," she cried out.

He plunged inside her. Harder. Faster. She clenched her inner muscles. He groaned.

Faster, harder.

Her body came alive beneath him.

"You're so damn hot," he gasped.

Yes! She wanted him to talk dirty!

His cock slid deep inside her. He pulled almost all the way out, then drove inside her again. Stroking her. Inflaming her as exquisite sensations of pleasure rushed over her. Each nerve felt exposed. Each breath she took scorched her starving lungs. She cried out, raising her hips to meet each hard thrust.

His body stiffened. He growled with pleasure.

Flames licked her body. The heat was almost too much. The friction too intense. Release came fast and hard, spreading quickly over her, leaving trembles in its wake, then turning warm as her body relaxed.

He slowly lowered himself until his length covered her. When he rolled to his side, he took her with him. Their ragged breathing echoed through her bedroom. She held him tight, not wanting the feeling to end, a little afraid he might disappear again.

It was much later when he broke the connection between them. How long did they lie there? She felt so satisfied, and so incredibly tired. In her drowsy state, Ryder pulled the cover over her. Then he whispered close to her ear. "Lesson two, you're not to wear any clothes for the rest of the day. You will not use anything to cover yourself. If someone rings your doorbell or knocks, answer the door, but do not put on any clothes. Understood?"

She snuggled the pillow closer to her.

He laughed. "Haley, do you understand? No clothes, no sheet, no towel."

"Umm, whatever you say." She only needed to rest for a moment.

Chapter 5

HALEY PULLED THE PILLOW closer to her and yawned. That had to be the best dream she'd ever had. She'd never felt so relaxed. At this rate, if she ever had sex again with a real man, he probably wouldn't live up to her fantasy lover.

She glanced at the clock. Eleven. Wow, she'd almost slept the morning away. She tossed the pillow to the side and sat up.

"Ow." Man, she didn't know a dream could make a person sore.

She probably slept wrong or moved too fast and pulled a muscle. Where were her glasses? Not on the night stand. She rested her hand on the mattress and discovered what had become of them. She put them on before she hobbled to the bathroom. There was a towel hanging from the shower rod. She touched it. Still damp.

She reached up and touched her hair. It was damp, too. Her heart began to pound.

No, it wasn't real. In her dream, she vaguely remembered dropping ice cream on her chest, which had turned quite erotic. Then her angel guy—correction, nephilim—had appeared again and they had hot sex.

Her eyes narrowed. What if—

She shook her head. It hadn't happened. The ice cream, maybe, but nothing else. She vaguely remembered she planned to eat herself into a sugar stupor. The emotional trauma of being stood up the night before, then indulging in too much ice cream had been too much. She must've fallen asleep or something after that and dreamed the whole thing.

But the sex fantasy was great.

And in her dream, Rachael dropped by to remind her about dinner with their parents. Her forehead wrinkled. Which *was* tonight, now that she thought about it.

That still didn't make it real, so she might as well stop dwelling on it. She turned on her heel and marched to the kitchen, then slowed when she neared the trash can.

"So what if I emptied a carton of ice cream," she mumbled. Rachael was right when she warned Haley to stay away from sweets. Maybe she was a diabetic and she'd had some sort of hallucination.

She suddenly found the humor in her situation.

Oh yes, and her dream lover told her not to wear clothes for the rest of the day. She laughed. Her imagination was getting better and better. She had to remember to write that one down in her diary.

A cold chill rippled down her spine. If it wasn't real, why was she standing in the middle of her kitchen completely naked when she always wore pajamas to bed? Goose bumps popped up on her arms.

Nope, she wasn't going there. She needed to forget all about her dream. She returned to the bathroom and turned on the water in the shower. Before she took off her glasses and stepped under the spray, she noticed a hickey near her right breast. She turned so she could get a better look at it. Oh, Lord, it sort of looked like wings.

She was only twenty-six. Too young to be losing her mind. She stepped into the shower, sticking her head under the spray. Maybe it was only temporary insanity.

When she finished washing, she turned the water off and got out, feeling like her old self. The steam from the shower had cleared her head enough that she could think straight again. She grabbed a towel to dry off. Of course she'd dreamed the whole thing.

"Wild Thing" began playing in the other room. She quickly knotted the towel between her breasts and put her glasses on before she hurried into the living room. Her phone had stopped ringing by the time she picked it up.

"One new voice mail." She didn't recognize the number. Probably a salesman. She decided to listen to it anyway.

"*I told you no clothes,*" a familiar voice told her.

The blood rushed to her head. She dropped the phone. It landed with a soft thud on the carpet. "No way. It was only a dream." She looked around the room, but she was the only one there. When she reached for her phone, there was a white feather next to it. She jerked her hand back.

This wasn't happening. There were no such things as angels—nephilim—whatever the hell he called himself. Ryder wasn't real! She had a very vivid imagination, that was all!

Her head began to pound. Cautiously, she reached for the feather, picking it up as she straightened. It lay on her open palm, taunting her. When she touched it, the feather sparkled, then vanished right before her eyes.

Her phone began to ring again. She was definitely changing the ringtone. No way was she picking it up, either. It continued to play "Wild Thing." Over and over the cell phone blasted out the damn song. The tune was going to drive her crazy. She scooped the phone off the floor just as it stopped. Another voice mail. She pushed play and brought the phone to her ear.

"*I want to touch you again. I want to taste you.*"

She trembled as his words wove an erotic image in her mind.

"*But you're not following the rules.*" His voice took on a sterner note. "*No clothes today, remember? If someone rings your doorbell or knocks, you're to answer it naked. If you don't obey me, I can't help you.*"

She closed the phone and carefully set it on the end table. It was real. And the sex had been awesome. Or maybe she was dreaming again. Who the hell cared? It was still the best sex she'd had in a year. She frowned. The only sex, actually.

Ryder wanted her naked, so be it. She loosened the knot and let the towel fall to the floor. "Please don't let anyone ring my doorbell today," she prayed. Or worse, what if her mother came by? She swallowed past the lump of fear that formed in her throat. "Mom would have a heart attack." She immediately pushed her paranoia away. Her mom wouldn't come over, not when Haley was going to her parents' home for dinner tonight.

Alexa wouldn't be dropping by, either. Her friend had been forced to endure a shopping trip with her mother and sister for her sister's upcoming wedding. Haley breathed a sigh of relief. She was safe. No one else ever came to see her. Her mouth turned down. That was actually kind of sad when she thought about it.

A sudden cold chill washed over her. The house was too cool for running around naked. *Naked!* Not a stitch of clothes on. She glanced down. Her nipples were hard little nubs. Had she totally lost her freaking mind?

No one could make her do anything. Why not get dressed? She scooped up the towel and headed for the bedroom, but when she stepped inside her room, she was met with a familiar scent—leather and country breezes. Visions of what Ryder had done to her filled her head. He brought her body to life and, for a little while, he made her feel beautiful.

She stepped closer to the mirror, and with a critical eye studied her reflection. Her hair was dull, dishwater blonde. She'd tried dying it once and only managed to turn it orange. Her gaze traveled downward. Her boobs were way too big, but at least they didn't sag. Her hips were still too wide, but her legs were long. Long enough to wrap around Ryder's waist and pull him in deeper.

And he wanted her.

Who was she kidding? He only felt sorry for her. Hadn't he told her that he was answering her stupid prayer? She pushed her glasses higher on her nose. She was a charity case, nothing more, and nothing had changed. Her life was still the same as it was the day before.

Except for the sex.

The sex was incredible. She supposed as long as she obeyed him, he would hang around, at least for a while. If it meant walking around naked all day, that was okay by her. It wasn't as though she was expecting company or anything.

"You want me naked," she spoke aloud. "Then here I am." He said lesson two. She wondered what exactly she was supposed to learn.

Apparently, she would be stuck inside all day. What to do? She went to the other room and sat on the sofa, grabbing the remote. A quick search gave her a choice of infomercials, cartoons, or sports. She turned off the TV and tossed the remote. Boring! Sex would be nice. She shifted her bottom to a more comfortable position. The friction was kind of nice. Did she have batteries for her vibrator? It had been forever since she'd used it. The guilt that followed always made her more dissatisfied.

Ryder had known she'd wrapped a towel around her nakedness. Was he watching her? She faked a yawn and stretched out on the sofa, letting one leg dangle over the side. This would give him a good view.

What was happening to her? She quickly sat up. She'd never been this brazen in her whole life. Being naked made her feel powerful, but that didn't make it right. The feeling fizzled. Not that she really thought it would last.

"What am I supposed to do all day?" She glanced up.

Silence.

What? Was she expecting the ceiling to open and a voice would tell her what to do?

She drummed her fingers on the arm of the sofa and scanned the room. White, bare walls stared back at her. Her home was boring. Nanny told Haley to put her stamp on it and make it her own. She missed her grandmother. Nanny had been the one person she could talk to.

Her brow furrowed. Nanny had been right about Haley needing to make the house her place. She did have that paint she'd bought with the intention of transforming the whole house. It was a great idea at the time. She liked the colors. Bold blue, canary yellow, and bright orange. Her sister hated Haley's choices, so she put the cans and paintbrushes in the closet.

But it was her house, she reasoned. Her sister's small apartment on the other side of town was almost clinical. She nibbled her bottom lip. Her sister was right about so many things. Haley had really liked the colors, though.

Why not paint the walls? It wasn't as though she had anything better to do.

She jumped up and went to the hall closet. The cans were there, stacked neatly in the back. She dragged all the painting supplies to the living room, then stared at the unopened cans. Her determination faltered. What if Rachael was right? What if it looked terrible?

The doorbell rang. She jumped, then froze, staring at the door as though the wood surface had suddenly become a living, breathing monster.

No one ever rang her doorbell. At least, hardly ever. She glanced down at her naked body, and any smidgeon of courage she might have had crumbled.

The doorbell chimed again.

She would just look through the peephole. Maybe by the time she got to the door, they would be gone.

Her steps were heavy as she took her time getting to the door. She looked through the tiny glass portal.

No one. She let out a sigh of relief, then smirked. She'd open the door, then close it really fast. No one was there, but Ryder couldn't say she hadn't obeyed his rules.

She removed the chain and opened the door.

Her heart skipped a beat.

A man had his back to her. He casually leaned against her door jamb. His white coveralls were paint-stained and he had on worn tennis shoes. She carefully began to ease the door closed, trying not to make a sound.

The man abruptly turned and smiled.

She slapped a hand to her chest. *Ryder!* "You scared the crap out of me!" She glanced down the road, then pulled him inside, quickly slamming the door closed. Her hands were still shaking as she put the chain back on. "That was not funny!"

"But didn't you feel just a little daring going around without clothes? As if you were walking on the wild side?"

"I felt guilty." She certainly wasn't going to admit that she had felt a little naughty, but free, at the same time. He didn't seem to want a response as he stared at her nakedness. She started to cover herself, but he shook his head. Her arms fell to her sides as his gaze moved over her again, stopping at her breasts before moving lower. He caressed her with that one look, teased her body without even touching her. An ache began to build inside her. Then he met her eyes.

"Damn, you're sexy."

"I'm not—"

He stepped closer and placed a finger on her lips. She inhaled his scent. For a second, she had a crazy impulse to suck his finger inside her mouth, but he moved it away before she could.

"Say it." He waited patiently.

"Say what?"

"That you're sexy."

"But…"

He sighed, then turned back toward the door.

"I'm sexy," she blurted.

He looked at her and grinned. She melted on the inside.

"What are you doing here?" she asked.

"I thought you might need help painting your walls."

How did he know she was going to paint?

Really?

As if she didn't know the answer to that one. Well, she could use the help. "Okay, sure, but can I at least put something on so I don't get paint splattered on me?"

He smiled, then moved to the cans of paint.

She guessed that answered her question. Whatever. She certainly didn't know what lesson she was supposed to learn by running around her house naked.

He opened all three cans. "Good color choices," he said.

Something fluttered inside her, making her feel warm all over. "You think so?"

"Yes, I do. You should learn to go with your gut feeling. Most times it won't steer you wrong." He stirred the paint, then handed her a brush. "You do the upper wall and I'll get the lower." He opened the step stool for her.

She drew in a deep breath and stared at the white wall. It didn't really look that bad.

"Haley?"

Yes, it did. Determination filled her. It was only paint. If she didn't like it, she could always paint the wall white again. She dipped her brush into the orange, dragged it over the rim, and then climbed up the two steps on the stool. Her hands trembled as she made the first stroke. She stepped down and stood back, staring at the bright orange streak on her wall.

A smile teased her lips. "It *was* a good color choice."

"Yes, it was."

Maybe that was the lesson she was supposed to learn. She grabbed the can of paint and placed it on the shelf of her step stool, then dipped her brush in again. She pulled the brush down the wall once more.

There was a snap, then a whiz.

She looked over her shoulder. Ryder held a digital camera. The blood drained from her face. "What are you doing?"

"Taking your picture."

Humiliation washed over her. All her insecurities came rushing back. "Please don't."

"Why?"

"Because I'm not pretty."

He frowned. "Why would you think that?"

She set the brush down. "Oh, let me see, because no one ever asks me out. Because no matter what clothes I wear, I look like a frump." She sniffed.

He smiled and took another picture. "But you're not wearing any clothes."

"I'm being serious."

"So am I, and you're not a frump."

There was no reasoning with him. Ryder probably saw the beauty in everything. What did it matter? Let him have his fun at her expense. She was beginning to think he might not be an angel after all. Maybe he came from somewhere else and this was just another way for life to torment her. "Okay, fine. Take your stupid pictures, but they'd better not end up on the Internet."

She grabbed her brush and began to paint the wall with renewed fervor.

For the next couple of hours, she lost herself in the smooth strokes of the brush. When Ryder wasn't snapping her picture, he pitched in and helped. She had to admit, he made the job go by a lot faster. After a while, she didn't even notice when he snapped a picture. There was something about being naked that made her feel not quite so frumpy. She had a feeling she was getting used to her nudity.

When they finished the living room, Haley had a streak of paint on one breast and a couple on her arms. One foot rested on the top step and the other on the next one down. Her back and arms ached, but she felt great as she surveyed the wall in front of her. "I love it," she told him. "What do you think?"

"It's fantastic."

She glanced down to where he was squatted below her. Tingles spread over her body. From his angle, and the way her legs were placed on the steps, one foot planted on the top, the other on the bottom, there was little of her lower region left to the imagination. He snapped four pictures in quick succession. She stepped off the stool and cocked an eyebrow. "Now I know why you wanted to do the lower part of the wall. Are angels supposed to act like this?"

"I'm a nephilim. We don't follow the rules. The view was nice. I enjoyed watching the way you moved. The way your legs would part when you stretched high. The way your breasts bounced just a little. I loved the way you stopped being embarrassed because you were naked."

"Do you want to have sex?" The words tumbled out, but she found that she didn't want to call them back, and maybe she *had* noticed the hungry way he looked at her a few times, and it had been empowering.

"No," he said.

Her heart fell to her feet. Had she just asked him to have sex? Please, just let a hole open in her floor and suck her down. He put down his brush and walked nearer. She wanted to die, but he raised her chin and looked into her eyes. "I want you to make love to me. You're in control. Do whatever you want."

Was he serious? He looked serious.

Her diary! This was one of her fantasies. Except for real. She began to tingle in anticipation of what was to come. "Take off your clothes." He might as well be as naked as she was. But he only shook his head.

"You remove them."

Even better.

She stepped closer. His arms were at his sides. She fumbled with the metal buttons on his coveralls, but finally managed to get them undone. She pushed them off his shoulders and down his arms. He wasn't wearing a shirt. Her knees went weak as she stared at so much beautiful naked skin.

She met his gaze. "Anything?"

"Anything."

How did she get this lucky? She ran her hands over his chest, flicking one finger across his nipple. He drew in a sharp breath. She was just getting started. He'd given her carte blanche and she intended to savor every moment.

"I love the way you feel," she said. "All hard muscles." She twined one hand behind his neck and brought his head closer to her face. The warmth of his breath tickled her cheek. He was hers. All hers, and she planned to savor each moment. She ran her tongue over his lips, tasting him. He opened his mouth just a fraction and she thrust her tongue inside, stroking. She pressed her body closer, her breasts rubbing against him.

Ryder groaned and pulled her in closer, her legs straddling his knee, then he applied just a little pressure. Heat shot through her body like a fire out of control. He grabbed her ass, making the fit a little tighter. She gasped, moving back a step; the connection between them was lost.

"Oh, no, you said I have control," she reminded him, slightly out of breath.

He started to protest then opened his arms in supplication. "Do what you will."

She pushed his clothes down. He helped her by toeing off his shoes, and then kicked his clothes away until he stood in front of her wearing only a pair of dark blue briefs. She barely breathed as she watched his cock grow hard beneath the material.

This was the moment she was waiting for. She knelt in front of him. Her fingers tingled as she grasped the waistband and began to tug the cotton material down. She drew in a sharp breath when the tip of his cock was exposed. He was so damned beautiful. She pressed her lips together and brought his briefs down a little more, savoring every second. He was so big, and she wanted him so much.

"Ahh," she breathed as she drew his briefs the rest of the way down. When he stepped out of them, she tossed them on top of the rest of his clothes. For a moment, she sat back on her heels and stared at just how magnificent he was. Every inch of him was tanned golden brown. He was all tight, sinewy muscles, with hard ridges and planes. Even her imagination couldn't compete with what stood in front of her.

Why should it? Ryder had told her he was part angel, part mortal. He would never walk with mere men. He would always stand above them. And for a little while, he was all hers. Haley planned to enjoy every second.

She leaned forward and placed a kiss at the base of his erection. He jerked. She licked up the length, savoring him. She'd never sucked a man's cock. Ryder tasted like honey. She licked across the velvety soft tip before drawing him inside her mouth.

He gasped, his hand tangling in her hair. Her hands moved to his ass. She began to massage. Another one of the fantasies in her diary was having complete control over a man, but she had much more than that. She had control over an immortal. The frumpy girl disappeared and in her place was a dominatrix.

And she wanted more. She moved her mouth away. Heat flowed through her body, settling in the vee between her legs. "Lie down," she commanded.

He moved to the carpet, obeying without hesitation. She straddled him. He stared up at her. She let him look, but only for a moment. She slowly lowered her body until his cock pressed against her pussy. She wiggled against him, breathing a sigh of pure enjoyment.

Ryder grunted. "You're killing me."

She smiled. "I thought you were immortal?"

"I want to fuck you."

"Not yet." She looked down at him. His eyes were glazed with passion. She had done that. He wanted *her!* She had created the lust she saw in his eyes. She leaned forward, licking up his chest.

"I'm not ready yet," she purred. She slid off him and scooted between his legs until she stared at his magnificent body again. She'd seen pictures of naked men before, but not one of them compared to Ryder. Her eyes shifted downward. Damn, he was bigger than she ever imagined a man could be. And he was all hers.

She ran her tongue up one thigh. The muscles in his leg twitched. Pleasure and pain. She'd read enough books to know foreplay was part of the magic of making love. She planned to do a whole lot of teasing. She outlined his length with her tongue, careful not to touch it. His breathing was labored.

"What do you want?" she asked, turning the tables.

"Take me."

She smiled right before she sucked him inside her mouth. He groaned, his hips shooting up. She doubted she would ever get tired of having him in her mouth. She rolled her tongue around the tip, then sucked him back inside.

"Haley," he moaned.

She took pity and moved on top of him again, sliding him inside her. For a moment she closed her eyes and savored him being inside her, filling her. Then she slowly began to rock back and forth. She heard his indrawn breath, felt his body tighten.

"What do you want me to do?" His words grated.

She raised heavy lids enough to look down on him. He was her slave. Hers to command at will. He told her that she was in control.

But apparently even an immortal had his breaking point. "Fuck me," she whispered.

Saying fuck came so easily to her lips and sounded soft and sexy when the word rolled off her tongue.

Ryder braced one arm behind her and in one swift movement, she was lying on her back. It happened so fast she was momentarily stunned.

"As you wish," he said. He lowered his head until his breath brushed her face and his tongue grazed her lips.

"You taste sweet, but you're not sweet, are you?"

She shook her head.

"Good, because I plan to see how bad you can be."

He pulled out, then thrust back inside her. She gripped his arms and countered each of his movements. Flames licked up her body, shooting down to her lower region. She circled her hips. He groaned and thrust harder. She watched his face, saw the naked emotions of a man in the throes of passion. He was beautiful.

She met each thrust. She tightened her hands on his arms as the friction inside her grew hotter, her body tighter, until everything seemed to explode at one time.

"Ahh, yes," she screamed out as she came. Waves of heat washed over her. Her body trembled in release. She couldn't breathe, she couldn't move. Ryder plunged inside her again and again, then his body grew taut as he climaxed. His hands slid down her thighs, then back up.

Haley went limp, crumpling onto his chest, feeling each rise and fall as he inhaled and exhaled. She vaguely knew when he rolled on his side, taking her with him. It was a few moments before she could think clearly. No, she didn't want to think. She felt too good to analyze what just happened. She wanted to bask in the glow he'd created inside her.

He began to circle one of her nipples with his finger.

"Nice," she said.

"You're beautiful and hot and sexy."

She smiled, loving what he said to her, even though she knew everything was a lie. It didn't matter. Nothing mattered except how he made her feel.

"I'm starved," he said after a moment.

She opened her eyes and looked at him. "I thought you were immortal."

"I am, up to a point. It doesn't mean I don't get hungry."

"I have lunch meat in the refrigerator." She tried to remember how old it was. "I think it's still okay." Most of the time she ate fast food that she grabbed on the way home.

"I have a better idea."

She stretched. "What?"

"Let's go out."

"I thought I wasn't supposed to wear clothes today?" She had a feeling his stomach would win over her being naked.

"You're not. I want to keep you exactly the way you are. I love looking at you."

"Then how are we supposed to go out?"

His grin was wicked. "I'll show you. Close your eyes."

"Close my eyes?" Before she could say anything else, lights began to swirl and she felt herself moving. She threw her arms around his neck and held tight. "What's happening," she cried and closed her eyes tight. He didn't say anything as cool air swept over her. Her stomach lurched. Then everything stopped around her.

Haley had a feeling she wasn't in her living room anymore, nor was she lying on her carpet. No, it felt more like a soft carpet of grass, and she could hear the wind whispering through the trees.

Chapter 6

HALEY OPENED HER EYES. Trees dotted the rolling hills, the gnarled branches stretching toward the bright blue sky like elderly men waking from a nap. A gentle breeze ruffled the vibrant green grass. Horses with long flowing manes grazed nearby, quite unconcerned by their arrival. "Where are we?"

"A place that was created a long time ago," Ryder told her.

Where someone might see her? Being brave in her house was one thing; being brave in the middle of the country where anyone might happen by was another! She pressed closer to him. "Take me home." Her words were muffled against his chest but Haley was pretty sure he understood her plea.

"Mmm, nice," he said, nuzzling her ear.

"It's not nice! Get me the hell out of here!"

Instead of magically whisking her back to the house, he moved away before coming to his feet. For a moment she forgot where she was as she gazed at his perfect form. The sun cast its rays lovingly over him, bathing him in soft light. The man was truly gorgeous.

And an ass! She rolled onto her stomach, shielding her front from anyone who might happen by. She wanted to die. "Take me home," she spoke between gritted teeth.

"Why? No one can see you. It's a private retreat. Look around. Do you see any people?"

She cautiously raised her head. He was right. The countryside was deserted except for the horses. So maybe he didn't plan for her to die of mortification. He leaned over. His hand suddenly landed on her bottom with a light slap.

"Ow!" She cried out in surprise more than anything. But then he began to caress her ass. Her eyes widened.

"Wasn't one of your fantasies that a lover spank you?"

She frowned. "My diary is my personal property and you had no business reading it!"

He swatted her ass again. She jumped, but at the same time tingles of pleasure tickled over her body. The soft grass only added to her pleasure.

"You have a great ass. Nicely rounded and smooth." He slapped her again.

She bit back a moan as a familiar ache began to grow inside her.

"Your diary has a lot of fantasies in it, doesn't it?" he asked.

He read the whole thing? She couldn't even remember everything she wrote. Yes, there were a lot of fantasies, but everyone had secret desires. It didn't mean she actually wanted… to… to do everything.

His palm landed on her ass again, slightly harder. "Answer me, Haley."

"Yes, but—"

"But what? You mean to say you want me to stop this?" His palm landed on her ass again.

She pressed against the grass, then moaned with pleasure as the soft blades massaged her body when she moved. Her face grew warm even thinking about telling him the truth. What would that make her? At the very least, a slut.

"I can't," she whispered. "It's wrong."

He forced her to turn over. She immediately covered herself. He reached down and picked her up as though she weighed nothing at all, and for an immortal, she supposed she didn't. He carried her to the woods, not stopping until he came to a grassy, open area. She heard a waterfall, but was too embarrassed to look around. He set her on her feet. Haley couldn't look at him. She was naked, outside, with a man. She felt like Eve must have after she'd taken a bite of the apple. Haley ducked her head, refusing to meet his eyes.

He wouldn't let her hide, raising her chin with one finger so she was forced to meet his gaze. "There is nothing wrong with admitting you're a sensuous woman. You should rejoice in the fact that you can feel with so much depth. You should never be ashamed of your fantasies."

"But they're… naughty."

He chuckled and her face grew warmer. "Of course they are. That's what makes you so sexy."

She frowned. "Now you're making fun of me."

"I would never make fun of you."

"But Rachael and my mother—"

"Rachael hides her true face, and your mother is locked inside a box she created because she thought she had to live by certain rules. Her world has no color, no vibrancy. You're trying to lock yourself away as well. I have the key. You only need to show me the door."

"I'm not sure I can change," she confessed.

"I'm not asking you to. I only want you to release the person who is locked inside of you. The person you want to be, not the person someone else wants to mold you into. I know it won't be easy, but promise me you'll try."

She finally nodded.

"Come, I've prepared a picnic." He stepped away from her.

Behind him was a pile of pillows in an array of bright colors scattered on top of a pink silk sheet. Only he would think to have a silk sheet at a picnic rather than a coarse, scratchy blanket.

In the middle of the sheet sat a gleaming silver platter with fruits, meats, cheeses, and crackers. Her stomach rumbled. She reached down as though she could stop such unladylike behavior. He laughed.

So maybe she was beyond ladylike since she was as naked as the day she was born. "I'm hungry. I can't help it that my stomach growled." She held her head high as she marched toward the picnic. As Ryder caught up to her, he slapped her on the backside. She jumped and whirled around to glare at him.

"Don't think we've ended the lesson. You will obey me," he warned.

On what page did she fantasize about domination?

Ryder sauntered past as if he was her lord and master or something. She opened her mouth to tell him only if she let him, but even she knew her threat was empty. She *wanted* him to dominate her. The idea of being submissive to his every need sent tingles of pleasure down her body.

She was immediately filled with guilt.

Was Ryder telling the truth when he said her fantasies didn't make her a bad person? She wasn't so sure because right now, she felt pretty bad.

He sat on the sheet, then patted the place across from him. Her gaze swept over him. He did naked very well. Suddenly she wasn't all that hungry, at least not for food. He didn't seem to notice as he took a piece of thinly sliced meat and popped it into his mouth, then slowly chewed as he leaned back on one elbow and watched her.

There was no graceful way she could sit across from him. Not that he hadn't seen everything, but darn it, when they weren't making love her doubts came flooding back. It was so blasted light outside, too. Didn't he ever want to have sex in the dark? Well, except she would hate not looking at his naked body. None of her past dates even came close to his physique.

"Sit," he ordered.

She jumped as the sound of his voice broke through her thoughts. He wanted her to sit. If she kept her legs together, she could sort of lean on one arm and keep her dignity. Oh right, and that thought came to her as she stood stark naked in front of him.

He came to his feet before she had time to attempt sitting and walked toward her, his strides slow, unhurried. He stopped only a breath away. Out of thin air, he produced a pair of handcuffs and quickly snapped them in place over her wrists before she could even think to protest. Soft red fur covered the metal so it didn't cut into her skin, but she was effectively trapped.

"You're mine to do with as I will. You have no choice except to obey me." As if to prove his words, he squeezed one of her nipples.

Haley jumped, not expecting the slight pressure that produced a hint of pain but also pleasure that tingled all the way down to settle between her legs.

Ryder tugged on the chain between the cuffs, forcing her to follow. He released the chain when he sat on the silk sheet once more. "Sit," he commanded, but his voice had turned to a lazy drawl as his gaze roamed over her.

Ryder sat cross-legged in front of her, and he was hard. He reached up and tugged on the chain. She had no choice except to obey or topple over onto him.

Haley sank down in front of him, her legs open, nothing hidden from his view.

"That's better," he said with a rakish grin. He moved the tray of food and scooted closer until there was little room between them, moving her legs until they draped across his thighs. Her senses kicked into overdrive. Ryder was only inches from her body; his thick cock was so close.

"Pay attention," he told her. He slapped her on the bottom.

She trembled, but not because he hurt her. No, she was far from feeling pain or fear. Passion, desire, and horniness was closer to what she felt right then. "Easier said than done," she said as her gaze strayed downward.

He laughed and she realized she'd spoken the words out loud. But rather than tease her for being so blunt, he rolled up a thin slice of meat and brought it to her mouth. She took a bite. The flavor burst inside her mouth. It was like nothing she had ever tasted. Her taste buds screamed for more, but he ate the other half, chewing slowly as he watched her reaction.

"What is it?" she asked.

"A delicacy. Do you like it?"

She nodded, looking around. "You said this was a retreat. What did you mean?" she asked, wanting to know more about the place he'd brought her to. "Do you live here?"

"This place was created a very long time ago. We enjoyed it so much that we eventually bought a ranch. It's as close as any of us could get to being normal."

"We?"

He nodded. "Chance doesn't live at the ranch, but he returns now and then. Hunter, Dillon, and I live there." He glanced around. "The four of us created this place."

"Created it? How? What did you do, scoop up a bunch of trees and dirt then dump them here?"

"Something like that."

She frowned. "Exactly how old are you?"

"Why? Do you have a problem dating older men?"

"Not when they look like you," she blurted.

He laughed as he put some kind of spread on a cracker. She bit half when he brought it to her mouth, then once again he ate the other half.

"You can travel to places. I mean, by magic."

He nodded as if she'd just asked if he took the bus to work. She wondered what it would be like to go anywhere she wanted, anytime. Talk about a cheap vacation. "You're lucky." His eyes clouded for a moment, and Haley knew she'd said something wrong. "What?"

He shook his head. "Sometimes knowing you'll live forever can be a burden."

"Oh, yeah, I can see how it would be a real hardship."

"Have you ever played the same game over and over until you were sick of it and wished you never had to play it again?"

She swallowed past the sudden lump in her throat. "Now I'm just a game to you?"

He frowned. "That's not what I meant. It's just that mortals have challenges and experiences that the nephilim can never quite attain."

"And then we die," she spoke softly. She wondered how he could think her life was so perfect when it wasn't even close.

"But first you live."

She shook her head. "I'm twenty-six years old. I've only been existing. That's not living."

"I can show you how, though." When he looked deep into her eyes something stirred inside her.

"The sex is good, but how will it change anything? I'll still be the same frumpy person when you get tired of hanging around. Only then I'll be a horny frump." Her mouth turned down.

"I promise that if you'll do everything I ask, you won't feel the same way by the time I leave."

"Are you going to wave a magic wand and make me beautiful?"

"You already are. You only have to see yourself as I see you." He reached behind one of the pillows and brought out his camera.

She groaned. He only laughed.

"Bite into the orange," he said, bringing the camera up to his face.

"I hate having my picture taken."

"I love taking your picture." He frowned, then removed her glasses, tossing them over his shoulder.

"Hey, those were my glasses."

"Do you need them to see?" His words softened. "Or as a shield?"

He was right. Haley didn't really need glasses at all, but they were like a barrier between her and the world. "No, I don't need them to see."

"Good. Now take a bite of the fruit or I'll spank you."

She thought about telling him no and wondered if that would be considered disobeying. Her pussy clenched as she envisioned him putting her across his knee, his hand slapping her ass.

He snapped some pictures as he came to his feet. She wondered if he would carry through with his threat anyway. Anticipation built inside her when he tugged the chain. She came to her feet, legs trembling.

Ryder reached into the air and brought a golden cord to loop over the middle of the chain, then led her to a tree, tossing the golden cord over a low limb and pulling until her arms were raised above her head.

"I don't think I will spank you," he said. "You want it too much."

Disappointment filled her.

"I have something better."

Better sounded good, except he moved back to their picnic and picked up the camera. More pictures? Snapping her picture while she was naked and tied to a tree didn't really do anything for her. She wanted his hands on her body, touching and caressing.

A branch snapped. Her heart skipped a beat as she frantically tried to look over her shoulder.

"Someone is coming," she hissed. "Hurry! Release me!"

"No, I don't think I will. Remember, you have to obey me."

"Not if I die of mortification." Please don't let this be happening. Please, please, please.

"You have to trust me. Remember, I said I would never hurt you."

Voices were getting closer.

"I do trust you. Now unlock the handcuffs and make us disappear."

"Trust me."

How could she trust him? Her worst nightmare was materializing. And what was Ryder doing? Nothing. No, he looked calm, but what the hell would he care if someone saw him naked?

Two men stepped out of the woods. Two very naked men. They were both about the same height with blond hair. Any other time, she would say they were hot. But right then she just wanted them to go far, far away.

She held her breath and tried not to move. It didn't work.

They stopped and looked at her, then began walking closer.

"Ryder, get me out of here. If you don't make us disappear I'll—" She frowned. There was something strange about the two men. Something off-kilter, not quite normal. Why the hell were they naked, and looking at her as if she was the first naked woman they'd ever seen? Did they escape from an asylum? Were they on drugs?

"Ryder," she whispered. Oh damn, she wanted to die. She tried to turn away from them, but she couldn't quite manage it. What was happening?

"They're not real," he told her.

Her eyes narrowed. One man stopped in front of her, the other stepped behind her. "They look real to me."

"Holograms. This is lesson three. Never be ashamed of your sexual desires."

She studied the man in front of her. His eyes looked odd. As though he were—programmed? "Seriously?"

"Trust me."

"You're beautiful," the man told her.

So maybe he wasn't real. There was something about him that said Ryder was telling the truth. Until he touched her, she would have probably believed Ryder, but the guy's hand on her breast felt too real for comfort.

"Ryder?"

"You wrote about this in your diary."

"Two men, me tied up?" No way would she ever write down a scenario like this. "I don't think so." Why would she ever want to have sex with two hunks at the same time?

"Page two hundred and one." Ryder snapped a couple of pictures.

She jerked when the man behind her moved closer, his body pressed against hers, his hands moving around to the front to cup her breasts. He squeezed, and against her will, her body responded. What had she gotten herself into when she'd agreed to let Ryder fulfill every desire she had written about in her diary? Her secret fantasies sounded a lot tamer on paper!

The man in front of her leaned down and began to kiss her neck as the man behind her lazily ran his tongue over her shoulder blades. She drew in a sharp breath. The man in front of her suddenly produced scented oil and began to dribble the warm liquid over her body.

I won't respond, she told herself. *Just because I wrote about something doesn't mean I really want to experience it.*

The thick warm liquid ran over her breasts and down her stomach. She couldn't stop her moan when the oil trickled between her legs like lava. The air created a reaction with the oil that heated her body. The two men began to massage the warm liquid into her skin. She felt as if hands caressed her from all angles. They touched her breasts, her bottom, her legs.

"They feel real," she barely managed to say as their hands stirred something deep inside her.

Teeth scraped across her nipples as hands traveled over her body. She held her breath, waiting for the moment when they would take her over the edge, but it didn't happen. The pressure inside her mounted as tongues licked and hands stroked her body.

"Please," she begged.

"Please what?" Ryder asked. "Please spank you?"

She moaned.

One of the men produced a whip, slapping the corded black velvet strings dangling from the end against his hand. She watched, fascinated. He moved to stand beside her. Then moved the handle over her breasts, down her legs. The cold, stiff leather did nothing to cool her skin.

The man brought the corded strings against her bare bottom. She flinched, her thighs quivering as pleasure erupted inside her. Again and again he slapped the whip against her bare ass. There was only the slightest pain, but her nerve endings were raw with the need for more.

"Ryder," she whimpered.

The holograms disappeared. He was suddenly standing in front of her, eyes glazed with passion. The cords were no longer binding her, the handcuffs disappeared. He carried her to the silk sheet and laid her down.

"I need you," she said.

"I know," he whispered as he nudged her legs apart, then slid inside. She wrapped her legs around his waist, drawing him closer.

Yes, that was what she wanted—Ryder sliding in and out.

It was all she could do to breathe as he stroked her, his cock hard as he moved in and out. She rose to meet each thrust, her body taut with need. Harder and faster. She couldn't think past the passion building with each thrust. The friction inside her rose until she thought she would explode. Until she could stand no more.

Then she didn't have to. She cried out his name as her hips met his, flesh pressed tight against flesh, straining toward that final release. Haley knew at that very moment that nothing would ever come close to what she would ever experience with a mere mortal, and it scared the hell out of her.

Chapter 7

GOING TO HER PARENTS' home was not something Haley particularly enjoyed. Her father was laid back, letting his wife rule the roost. He stayed in the background most of the time. Haley saw the way he looked at her mother and wondered if she knew how much he adored her. His love was almost palpable.

"Where are your glasses, Haley?" Her mother set a bowl of mashed potatoes on the table, then took her seat.

Haley touched her face. Where were her glasses? Heat flooded her face when she remembered Ryder removing them and tossing them over his shoulder. "They broke," she mumbled, reaching for her iced tea.

"Not before grace," her mother gently reprimanded and Haley's hand went back to her lap. "Rachael, will you say the blessing?"

Haley dutifully closed her eyes and lowered her head, but when Rachael finished, Haley couldn't have told anyone what her sister had said. Her mind was elsewhere, exactly where she wished she could be.

"How did you break your glasses?" her father asked, passing a platter of ham to her.

For the first time, Haley wished her father had continued to stay in the background. She hated to lie. If she were better at it, then lying wouldn't feel so awkward. She certainly couldn't tell them the truth, although the expressions on their faces would be priceless.

Oh, when Ryder and I were sitting naked in the woods he threw them away, then I had two men feeling me up. After that, Ryder and I had mind-blowing sex.

Her mother would probably run to the bathroom and grab the economy-sized bar of soap to wash out her youngest daughter's mouth. Her sister would open and close her mouth like a fish out of water, and her father... She frowned, not exactly sure what her dad would do. It didn't matter. She couldn't say any of that.

"I accidentally stepped on them." Haley took the plate of ham and forked the smallest slice onto her plate.

"Do you have money to buy a new pair?" her mother asked.

Why did they still treat her as though she lived at home and depended on their generosity to get by? "Mom, I have a good job at the bank, the house Nanny left me is paid for, and I have a minimal amount of debt. Yes, I can pay for them."

"Mom was just asking," Rachael chastised as she passed the mashed potatoes to her mother without taking any.

Their mother, in turn, passed the mashed potatoes to Haley's dad. She didn't take a helping, either. Haley often wondered why her mother cooked such elaborate meals if she wasn't going to eat any of the food.

"Rachael tells me you bought a cowboy hat for the Old Settler's Reunion," her mother said. "I'm glad you've decided to go this year." Her pleased smile stretched across her face.

Cowboy hat?

She must be talking about the one Rachael spotted on the sofa. That was the trouble with lying, Haley always got caught in a trap of her own making. She had already decided to stay home and read, which was what she'd done for the last couple of years. There was no way out, she supposed.

"Yes, I thought I would." She didn't meet her mother's gaze. Her mom would probably suspect something was going on. Her gaze moved around the room until it landed on Fifi instead. Oh hell, her mom had moved her taxidermied pet into a corner in the dining room. The stuffed Pekingese glared back at her with its glass eyes as if the stuffed animal knew the truth.

Haley's stomach rumbled. The dog had always hated her. She loved animals! But her mother had spoiled Fifi rotten, and the crazy mutt had nipped at Haley's ankles every chance it got.

"Well, are you?" her mother asked.

She tried to focus on what her mother had just asked. "What?"

"You really need to try to pay attention when someone is talking to you, dear. I asked if you were seeing anyone in particular." Her mother moved the peas around her plate, reminding Haley of a pinball machine. A pea found an opening between the chicken and a leaf of lettuce and made a run for it. The pea's quest for freedom was cut short when her mother forked the small green ball and brought it to her mouth.

"Ben from the bank bailed on her last night," Rachael supplied.

Sadness filled her mother's eyes. "Oh, I'm so sorry."

Haley shifted in her chair. "It's not as though it was a real date. He was taking me to supper to repay me for putting together his spreadsheet. We'll probably go out some other time."

They didn't buy her story. She could see it written all over their faces. Her mother and sister's expressions were filled with pity. You'd think someone had died the way they were acting.

"Don't worry, dear, I'm sure someday a… very… uh… nice man will come along." She turned to her oldest daughter. "So, Rachael, how's the court case coming along?"

Haley relaxed as her mother and sister carried on a conversation, even though Haley was pretty sure their mother had never even been inside a courthouse.

Again, she felt as though she were the odd one out, that she didn't belong in her family. Maybe she was adopted? Except she looked too much like her father. She glanced his way. He looked up and gave her a weak smile. She wondered if he ever felt like the odd one out.

"Excuse me," Haley said. Her mother and sister looked up. "I'm going to the powder room." They gave her a half smile and returned to their conversation.

Haley scooted her chair back and stood. For as long as she could remember, the bathroom was called the powder room. Her mother said excusing yourself to go to the bathroom sounded crude. A bathroom was a bathroom as far as Haley was concerned.

Once inside, she firmly shut and locked the door, leaning back against the cool wood surface and closing her eyes. "I hate family dinners," she mumbled.

"Then why do you go to them?" Ryder asked.

Her eyes flew open, heart banging against her ribs. "You scared me!" She glared at him, but at the same time a jittery feeling rippled over her. Damn, he was so sexy with that lock of dark hair falling onto his forehead.

"Why do you go to the dinners?" he asked again, not a bit concerned he'd almost scared the living daylights out of her.

"They're family. It's required," she told him as her heart slowed to a more normal rate, then shrugged. "Some kind of unwritten law going back to the dark ages." She wondered if he'd felt her emotions earlier. "I'm glad you're here.

He leaned toward her, his lips brushing across hers. He tasted like cinnamon and when she inhaled, she caught the scent of leather and country breezes. She wasn't sure what brand of aftershave he used, but the scent was heavenly. She sighed, leaning her head against his chest when the kiss ended. She could hear the steady beat of his heart through the cotton of the white T-shirt he wore. It soothed her soul.

"I missed you." He brushed his lips across the top of her head.

"Is this going to be another lesson?"

"Why? Do you need one?"

Haley heard the smile in his voice. Her arms wrapped around his neck, causing her breasts to press against his chest. The friction stirred a need deep inside her. "Yeah, I think I do." Her words were husky, betraying her desire, but she didn't care.

Ryder was so close that she could feel him getting hard. How could her family make her self-esteem sink lower than the *Titanic*, yet a few whispered words from Ryder and it began to rise? She squeezed her eyes shut when the answer popped into her head—he was only answering her prayer. God help her, she didn't care. She only knew she needed what he could give her. Especially when she felt more than a little vulnerable.

"Are you okay?" Rachael asked from the other side of the door, then rapped three times.

Her sister really needed to work on her timing. "Yes, I'm just fine. I'll be out in a moment."

"Mom was starting to worry."

Ryder didn't get in any hurry to release her, but right before he did, he kissed her forehead. "I'll see you later." Then he was gone.

A cold draft of air swirled around her. A band squeezed around her heart. Would this be what it felt like when Ryder left for good? She knew he would leave. There would be more prayers that needed to be answered. More women who needed saving. Would he go straight to the arms of another woman?

Her stomach began to churn. She quickly leaned over the sink and splashed cool water on her face. The sick feeling continued to rumble in her belly. She patted her face dry before opening the door. Rachael was still there. Her sister looked behind Haley, scanning the bathroom, then straightened. She wore a puzzled frown.

"I thought I heard a man's voice?"

"Really? The only man here is dad."

"Odd." Rachael turned her attention back to Haley. "Your skin is pale. Are you coming down with something?"

"I'm a little queasy." At least that wasn't a lie.

Rachael nodded. "Probably because you ate all that ice cream this morning." She turned and went back in the direction of the dining room.

I will not scream! I will not scream!

Instead, she gritted her teeth and joined the others. Her mother studied her as though Haley was a bug under a microscope. Finally, she'd had enough. "I'm fine, Mom."

"Rachael said you were queasy."

"I'm better now." Her mother didn't look satisfied. "Just gas."

Her mother nodded as if that answer was an area she didn't want to explore, which was fine with Haley.

The evening dragged on until Haley finally gave her mother a brief hug, smiled at her father, and told her sister good-bye. She didn't breathe easier until she was pulling into her own driveway. She automatically glanced across the street toward the Monroes. Their lights were out. Only a small glow came from the kitchen window on the north side of the house. Albert liked to get up to raid the cookie jar in the middle of the night. Martha didn't mind. She was the one who left the light on over the sink.

Haley turned the car key and the motor shut off, but she didn't open her door. She sat there for a moment, thinking about her neighbors across the street. They'd married young, and celebrated their sixtieth wedding anniversary last year.

How would she ever find what they had if she stayed in Hattersville? Not for the first time, Haley thought about moving. She was born and raised there. She knew all the secrets. The high school principal had an affair with the Baptist preacher's wife, though no one talked about it. Not out loud, anyway. And Mr. Farley never went bowling like he told his wife. He just wanted to go drinking with his buddies. Misty Ware didn't stay with her aunt two summers ago because she missed her. Ms. Ware admitted to her friend that her daughter was hooked on drugs and they'd sent her to rehab. Misty came back home a lot quieter, thinner.

Living in a small town wasn't always about people knowing your business. If you needed to borrow a tool or a fancy purse, you could always ask a neighbor. As her dad always said, why buy when you can borrow?

Neighbors watched your house when you went away. They brought food when someone died. Every small town was pretty much the same. Haley knew there had to be more.

The farthest she'd ever traveled was to Dallas. She and Alexa had decided they would spend a weekend exploring the big city. Most of the time they were lost or stuck in traffic. Bar-hopping had been dismal. Alexa would have done much better without her tagging along. Like troopers, or fools, they smiled and laughed as though they were having the best time, but it had all been a façade.

She returned home and settled for small town life, but had she given the city a chance?

Her cell began to play "Wild Thing." She pulled it from her purse, her heart beating just a little faster, but it wasn't Ryder. It was Alexa. She brought the phone to her ear. "I was just thinking about you."

"Hey, girlfriend," Alexa said. "I knew this was the monthly dinner and thought you could use a friend right about now."

Alexa knew her well. What would Haley have done without her friend all these years? That was the one really good thing about Hattersville, she'd known Alexa all her life. Maybe Ryder had stirred the restlessness inside her.

"Was it bad?" Alexa asked.

"Nothing ever changes. I think I'm getting used to them. How's shopping for wedding dresses going?"

Alexa's oldest sister was getting married in October and her mother was pinging off the walls worrying about the smallest details.

They were staying at her aunt's house in Dallas this weekend while shopping for dresses.

"Everything looks awful on me," Alexa complained. "Nothing new there. I'm too thin."

"Willowy." Haley heard something different in her friend's voice, but couldn't quite put her finger on it. She didn't sound that upset about the shopping trip with her mother. Before she could ask if anything had happened, Alexa continued.

"You're good for my ego." Her sigh came across the phone. "Anything new happening in town?"

Haley opened her mouth to tell Alexa about Ryder, but then closed it without saying a word. Her friend would think she'd finally lost her mind. She couldn't even tell her that she'd met a hot cowboy. Alexa would think she was pulling her leg.

"Not a thing going on here," she lied, then realized she was lying a lot lately. It started around the time a certain nephilim came into her life. That didn't say a whole lot for the angel side of him.

"Well, I have a bit of news." Alexa's words tumbled out. "I met a man. My sister's future cousin-in-law. He's in the wedding party and we met at dinner last night. I swear we talked for hours. Something just clicked between us. His name is Brian and he's tall and dreamy."

For a moment, Haley didn't say anything. A strange feeling of loss filled her. She'd never heard Alexa so excited about a man.

"Are you still there? No matter what, we'll always be friends." A note of worry crept into her voice.

Haley snapped out of her sudden bout of self-pity. "Of course we'll always be friends!" She laughed, and any lingering tension eased. This was Alexa, her very best friend. "I think I was in shock. You went to find a dress for the wedding and found a man."

"You're not upset?"

"Excited, thrilled, but never upset. How could I ever be upset with you? I want to know every little detail. What's he do? Where does he live? Come on, spill."

Alexa's laughter bubbled over the phone. They spoke for another half hour before finally saying good night. Haley still felt the warm glow of her friend's happiness when she went into the house and flipped on the light.

As soon as her eyes adjusted, she automatically glanced around. The bright orange looked better than she expected. The rest of the decor was another matter.

Her gaze slowly moved around what had once been her grandmother's favorite room. The room where her frail little Nanny had sat in her rocking chair crocheting blankets and doilies and told Haley stories of what the world was like when she was growing up.

Haley didn't think her Nanny would approve of the changes Ryder had obviously made while she was at her parents' tonight. No, she was pretty sure Nanny was turning over in her grave.

Chapter 8

"Do you like it?" Ryder said as he ambled out of the kitchen.

She shook her head. "You're joking, right?"

He frowned. "No."

"How could you do this? The pictures...me..."

His gaze moved around the room. "It's art. What's not to like about it?"

She stared at the pictures on the wall, then slammed the front door closed and firmly turned the lock before sliding the chain in place. If anyone saw the pictures hanging on her wall, she would absolutely die. Not that she thought anyone would drop by so late at night. Still, she wasn't about to take any chances.

Ryder didn't seem at all concerned. Again, she wondered if he was really an angel. That half of him certainly wasn't his dominant side. She dropped her car keys on the side table and glared at him. "How could you think I wouldn't be embarrassed?" She waved her arm to encompass the entire room. "There are nude photos of me plastered on the walls!" At least ten naked pictures mocked her.

The churning she'd felt at her parents' only intensified as her gaze lingered on each picture. There she was, in all her naked glory, painting the living room wall. Another was a close-up of her lying on the pink silk sheet at the picnic. He'd hung that one above the sofa. Not a tiny eight by ten, no, the picture was the length of her sofa and three feet tall. Her eyes were half closed, and her teeth pulled at her bottom lip. Her arms were stretched above her head, the red furry handcuffs on her wrists. Her nipples were hard nubs. Nothing was hidden, including the thatch of dark curls at the juncture between her legs. Nope, almost every inch was exposed.

"You really didn't think this would upset me? My living room looks like a… a bordello!" He'd even changed the furniture. White leather replaced her mismatched sofa and love seat. A glass coffee table sat on a white fur rug. The plain light fixture was replaced with a small chandelier. Crystals draped the fixture, reflecting different hues of light. The room was modern and sleek.

"You're a beautiful, sexy woman," he reminded her. "Maybe if I tell you enough times you'll start to believe my words."

"No, I'm not, and you can repeat it until you're blue in the face and I won't believe you." She couldn't look at the pictures on the wall any longer. All her doubts came barreling at her. She hurried from the room, wanting to put distance between her and the awful pictures.

She didn't stop until she was in her bedroom. How could Ryder shame her like that? Damn him! Tears welled in her eyes. She slammed the door closed and flipped on the light. Her bedroom was bright yellow with orange stripes. Ryder had painted her bedroom. Her boring, hand-me-down, dull brown dresser was now soft white. Hysterical laughter rose inside her. There were more pictures hanging on the wall.

Oh, damn. Had she actually let him take her picture with her legs parted, as though she were begging anyone to f-f-fu… She drew in a deep breath, then slowly released it. As if she was begging someone to have sex with her? Her gaze moved from picture to picture.

Heat flooded her face. There she was with the two men. Holograms, Ryder had told her. They had felt real. They looked real. In the picture, their hands were on her naked body. She might have been handcuffed, the golden rope looped over the tree limb, but she wasn't struggling to get loose. How could something that felt so incredibly erotic make her feel so ashamed?

She gulped back a sob. The photos filled every bit of her wall space. Apparently Ryder was pretty proud of his artistic accomplishment.

She wasn't.

"You're not looking at them," he said, popping in to stand beside her.

Startled, she flinched. Then anger began to build like a volcano about to erupt. "Not looking at them? You're joking, right?" How could she *not* look at them when they were hanging all over her walls? She crossed her arms and glared at him. "And when someone slams the door, that pretty much means they don't want company."

He shook his head. "Look closer."

She pressed her lips together.

"Lesson number three."

Ryder was playing dirty. If she didn't obey, he would leave. Let him!

As quickly as the thought crossed her mind, she dismissed it. She would look at his stupid pictures, but it certainly didn't mean she had to like them. "Fine." Her hands tightened on her arms as she quickly looked at each picture. "There, I'm done and I still hate them."

He opened her bedroom door, and for a moment she wondered if he was leaving. A tremble of dread rippled over her. But he took her hand and led her back to the living room. She supposed he wanted her to look at the other pictures as well. Great, not only had he stabbed her in the heart, he was twisting the knife.

He stopped in front of the picture above the sofa. Her shame was complete. She stared at her nakedness until she couldn't look at herself a second longer and turned away.

"You still don't see," he said.

"I've seen too much."

He raised her chin with one finger until she had no choice but to meet his eyes. "Look again, but imagine you're looking at a stranger."

"I don't know what that will accomplish."

"As if she were a stranger," he repeated.

His eyes were mesmerizing. She didn't want to look at a naked picture of herself, but he wasn't giving her a choice. Her gaze moved back to the picture. A stranger, he told her. Haley wasn't sure she could make the separation, but she would try.

She studied the picture. Before he snapped the picture, he'd fanned her hair out to each side. Light played between the branches of the tree above her, capturing the blonde strands and bringing out highlights she'd never noticed before now. Her cheekbones were high and her lips pouty.

Her gaze moved lower. Why had she thought her breasts were too big? They weren't. Her waist was tiny. Her hips didn't look too wide, either. They were in proportion to everything else. Her stomach was flat. The woman in the picture was haunting. The kind of woman that men fantasized about.

The woman wasn't her. It couldn't be. This wasn't the same picture. It was totally different from when she'd first walked into the living room.

"You touched it up."

"I didn't. That's you."

Her eyes narrowed as she stared at the sexy woman hanging on her wall. "That is not me."

"I never lie."

She studied his face. He didn't look as though he was lying, but he could create illusions. He'd already admitted he helped create the country retreat he'd whisked her off to. This could be another illusion, one to build her confidence.

"Lesson three, leave the pictures up."

The blood inside her veins turned ice cold. Leave the pictures hanging on the wall? Was he crazy? Did he not realize they were in Hattersville? If anyone happened to drop by and see the pictures, it would be all over town by Monday morning. She wouldn't be able to look anyone in the eye. Hanging nude pictures around the house wasn't done. If word got out, it would be a lot worse than the high school principal having an affair with the preacher's wife.

"No one will come over," he said.

"How can I be sure?"

"Trust me."

"You're the one who took the pictures and hung them all over the house. How can I trust you?"

"I will never do anything to hurt you."

What choice did she have?

"All right, I'll leave them up, but no one had better come knocking on my door."

"Good." His gaze drifted over her. Her heart skipped a beat. When he looked at her like this, he made her believe she was the beautiful woman he claimed she was. His attention moved to the pictures he'd hung on the wall. He groaned, and in the next instant, he vanished.

"Ryder?" For a moment, she'd thought he might pull her into his arms. Why had he changed his mind?

———

When Ryder opened his eyes, he was standing at the clearing in the woods where he and Haley had their picnic. Where they made love. The moon cast enough light that he could see everything clearly.

Remnants of their picnic remained. The pink silk sheet, the silver platter. The handcuffs. Ah, damn. Why the hell had he returned when he wanted to make love with Haley again? This place only brought erotic images to mind. The ache grew inside him.

He raked his fingers through his hair. She wanted him. One touch would've been all it took to have her begging him to make love to her. And why not? He was a freaking demigod. The angel side of him drew women like a moth to a flame. He never quite knew if they loved him for himself or the power his kind had over women.

Crap, he was starting to lose control of the situation. He couldn't let that happen. He left the clearing, charging through the woods like an angry bull. He didn't stop until he came to the waterfall. It had been Hunter's idea to add one. The water was cold. Hunter always made sure of that. He kept the pool at the ranch freezing, even in the middle of winter.

Ryder stripped, then dove in.

The water was ice cold. He came up shivering. He was in deep enough the water came up almost to his shoulders. He slowed his breathing, letting his body get used to the temperature.

Maybe there was something to be said about taking cold showers. He dove under the water, swimming toward the waterfall. His strokes were long and even. He swam several laps but he couldn't out-swim his desire to return.

He did the right thing by leaving her. The longer he stayed in Haley's presence, the more she would remember. He could wipe her mind clean to a certain degree, but there would be images that lingered.

She would see the world through different eyes. When the nephilim stayed too long with people it changed them. Suddenly they had dreams of the future, or they could heal the sick through touch. Sometimes they communicated with the dead. Problem was, there were bad things in the world, too. If they couldn't process what they saw, it drove some to the brink of madness.

That's why he left, even though he wanted to pull Haley into his arms and make love to her all night. He couldn't take a chance he would cause more harm than good. It didn't stop the ache from burning deep in his gut.

A branch suddenly cracked.

His thoughts jerked back to the present. How the hell could he be so careless? His gaze searched beyond the trees. Nothing moved. He had a visitor. But who? A demon? The nephilim had moved the entire wilderness retreat to a safe location, but a demon had found it once. Damn near killed Chance in the process. Had another one discovered their hideaway?

"Who's there?" he called out as he swam toward the shallow end.

There was a rustle, then Dillon stepped from the woods. "I saw the pink silk sheet, the handcuffs." His gaze swept over Ryder. "Looked like you've been playing Adam and Eve. Better watch it, you know how that ended." He twirled the red fur-covered handcuffs.

"Why are you here?" Ryder chose to ignore his friend's attempt at humor and walked out of the water.

Dillon wore a pained expression. "Could you put on some clothes before we talk?"

Ryder began to relax. "Why? Afraid I'm putting you to shame?"

Dillon shook his head. "Just because you're hung like a mule doesn't mean you know how to use it."

"I haven't heard any complaints."

"Just put your clothes on."

Ryder grabbed his clothes off the ground and began to dress. "So, why are you here?"

"Chance sent me to try to talk some sense into you, except I couldn't find you. This was the last place to look." He strolled over to a boulder that was near the water and leaned against it.

"I don't need someone to talk sense into me. I'm answering a prayer. It's no big deal." He wished Dillon would drop the damn handcuffs. Every time Ryder looked at them, he had a mental picture of Haley at his mercy. His forehead wrinkled. He was beginning to think he was at her mercy.

Dillon shrugged. "Since you have no emotional investment, I can finish the assignment."

"Like hell you will!"

Dillon studied Ryder. "Then the assignment does mean something to you."

He should've seen that one coming a mile away. "They all mean something to me," he finally admitted. "Each and every prayer I answer. Sometimes I think the next one will be the last, but someone's prayer filters in and I have to help them." He sat down on the ground to pull on his boots but grabbed a handful of grass instead, then systematically began to shred each blade.

"Walk away. We only started answering prayers because we were bored and wanted something else to do. It's not like we have a quota. We answer them or we don't." He dropped the handcuffs and straightened.

Walk away? Walking away had never crossed his mind.

"Mortals are fascinating creatures," Ryder finally said, meeting Dillon's eyes. "They endure hardships, but still their spirit stays strong."

"Sometimes, sometimes not." For a moment, pain flickered across Dillon's face.

He should've kept his thoughts to himself, but Dillon made him forget the past. There had been a girl once. Young, pretty. Dillon knew he could save her and poured everything into doing just that, but he'd looked away for a moment and she gave in to the pain that plagued her and took her own life. The assignment sent him spiraling downward into a deep depression. It took all that Ryder, Chance, and Hunter had in them to bring him back. They stuck by each other; they always had, always would. Which was probably why Chance had sent Dillon to check on him.

"I'll be okay. Haley needs me, though." Ryder wouldn't admit to Dillon that mortals were like a potent drug to him. Everything about their lives intrigued him. When they were hurt, they cried. When they were happy, they laughed. When they were desperate, they struggled to survive. They always fought the good fight. He envied what they had. But he wouldn't tell Dillon how he felt. He was a worrier, even though he rarely let anyone see that side of him.

"You know the rules," Dillon warned. "We're not supposed to

interact with mortals. Not this much. If the higher-ups know you've shown your true self to her, they could make life difficult."

"I couldn't convince her any other way. I had to show her I was real." He pulled on his socks. "She has more emotion inside her than I've ever felt in anyone. She's so beautiful."

Dillon looked at him long and hard. "That's not what Chance said. He thought she was kind of homely. It does make me wonder why you chose to answer her prayer."

Chance had no right to talk about Haley. Ryder tempered his reaction to Dillon's words. He wouldn't play into his hands. Instead, he jerked on his boots then came to his feet. "All women are beautiful if they have a good heart. Every woman has something special about her. Her scent, the way she laughs, each nuance is hers and hers alone." He shrugged. "Can I help it if I love them all?"

Dillon laughed, relaxing. "I told Chance there was nothing to worry about. You're the Romeo of our group, and you'll never change." He walked over, slapping Ryder on the back. "Come on, let's go back to the ranch and have a beer."

Ryder only desired one thing, to return to Haley, but he didn't want the others thinking he was obsessed with the assignment. Maybe he wanted to prove to himself that he wasn't, which was why he left her in the first place. "Yeah, sure. I'll explain what techniques I've used on women in the past."

Dillon closed his eyes and shook his head. "Spare me the details."

If Ryder could convince Dillon he hadn't changed his wicked ways, then he shouldn't have a problem with the others, except maybe Chance. He had a way of looking past the lies and seeing the truth.

Ryder was the only one who knew the truth, though. Maybe in the beginning he enjoyed being with a different female any time he wanted, but not for the last hundred years or so. He was just tired of nothing ever changing. He was tired of never having a long-term relationship with a woman, and he was tired of being immortal.

Only problem was, there wasn't a damn thing he could do about it—unless he had a death wish.

When they got to the ranch, Chance and Hunter were downstairs shooting pool. Hunter looked up from the shot he was about to take, studied Ryder for a moment, then nodded. Chance studied him the longest. So long that Ryder grew uncomfortable. Did he guess Ryder was nowhere near finishing his assignment? That he didn't want to end it? Not when every time he was around Haley, he felt as though he was a part of her life and not just living on the edge.

Hunter hit the cue ball. The loud crack splintered the silence. Striped and solid balls scattered across the table. Chance looked down, frowning. "How'd you drop four solid balls in the pockets? Did you cheat?"

Hunter's forehead creased. "No, I didn't cheat." He looked at Ryder and Dillon. "Did I cheat?"

Ryder smiled. Nothing ever changed. Hunter was a damned good pool shooter, but Chance always accused him of cheating. Not that Chance really thought Hunter cheated, but he'd made it a habit of accusing him anyway and some habits were hard to break.

"No, you didn't cheat." Ryder moved behind the bar and grabbed a beer out of the refrigerator for him and one for Dillon. He twisted off the caps and tossed them into the trash before returning. He handed Dillon one of the beers before raising his and downing a good portion. The ice-cold liquid slid down smooth, quenching his dry throat.

"So, what's going on with you and your assignment?" Chance asked in an off-hand manner. He lined up his next shot but Ryder knew he watched his reaction out of the corner of his eye.

Ryder lowered his beer and shrugged. "What always goes on with them. I'm an answer to their prayer." He laughed as he spread his arms.

"You'll never change," Dillon said with a shake of his head.

Hunter leaned on his cue stick, frowning. "Watch your step. Just remember what happened in Rome."

Ryder grimaced. "You keep blaming the Roman orgies on me when I had nothing to do with them."

"You were there, weren't you?" Chance reminded him.

"I was there, but that doesn't mean I was the instigator." Ryder noticed Chance's half smile. His gaze moved to Hunter and Dillon, who quickly found something else to hold their attention. "That's not funny. I'm not so sure the Powers That Be don't hold me responsible too, and they're not joking! I'd just as soon not remind them."

"Eight ball in the corner," Chance said, then hit the cue ball. The white ball slapped the black one with a thud, sending the black eight ball into the corner pocket. The white stopped a few inches away.

Hunter's gaze whipped to the green felt-covered table. "You cheated."

Chance put the cue stick back in the slotted oak holder hanging on the wall, then turned to the others with arms outstretched. "Would I cheat?"

"Yes," they all said in unison.

"Well, I didn't. " He grinned. "At least not this time."

They took their beers to the sitting area where the chairs were big and comfortable. They had to be. They were all over six feet tall. He was the smallest at six feet one inch. Ryder looked at each one of them. They were more than friends. These were the only brothers he would ever have. They had his back, just as he had theirs.

Dillon was dubbed the blond Adonis. He used to take each of his assignments personally. That's why it hit him hard when Lily took her own life. Since then, he hung back, didn't get quite so close to mortals. He still answered the occasional prayer, but he let them make their own choices. He only guided them in the right direction.

Hunter was big and brawny, more muscular than any of them, and he had an affinity for animals. Over the centuries, Hunter had rescued a lot of animals from abusive owners. He made sure they had a safe place where they could live in peace. Most of them were living at the retreat. They had plenty of water, plenty of food, and no one would ever hurt them again.

Then there was Chance. Ryder frowned. Chance's gaze was locked on him as if he could ferret out his deepest secrets. "What?"

"How close are you to this assignment?"

"Her name is Haley." Ryder was getting damned tired of everyone calling her an assignment. He brought the bottle to his lips again and tilted it. This time he drained the bottle.

"So, you're that close," Chance said.

"No, I just don't like to think of mortals as assignments. They have names. They have lives."

"They have problems," Dillon muttered. He leaned back in the brown overstuffed chair, crossing his feet at the ankles as he stared at his empty bottle. "They have too many problems sometimes," he said.

Ryder wondered if Dillon remembered they were in the room. Pity washed over him. Dillon hadn't answered a prayer in a long time. At least, not one entirely on his own. Ryder thought he hung back because he still blamed himself for Lily's death. He shouldn't. Dillon had done his best to save her. That was all anyone could ask of them.

Dillon suddenly looked up and saw everyone was staring at him. "What?"

Hunter cleared his throat. "I'll take over the assignment— Haley," he quickly corrected. "You've stayed too long. She knows you're nephilim." He frowned. "Why the hell did you tell her?"

"Some people talk too much," Ryder said, looking right at Chance.

"Yeah, well, I'm always the last to find out what's going on." Hunter stood, moving behind the bar and getting another beer. "Doesn't change anything, though. The higher-ups will be pissed. Better to let me take over."

"No," Ryder said. Hunter must really be worried if he would offer to finish an assignment. Ryder wasn't about to let anyone take over. "I can handle it; besides, I'm at a critical point. She's starting to gain confidence. A few more days and I'll be out of there."

"One day." Hunter's words were gruff.

What were they doing? Double-teaming him now? Ryder bristled. "I said I would handle it."

Hunter slammed his bottle down on the bar. "One day," he growled.

Ryder came to his feet. "I'll handle it," he grated. "I'm not going to talk about it anymore tonight. I'm going to bed." He got to his feet and left the room. They might be the only family he had, but sometimes they could be a real pain in the ass.

He started toward the stairs, but at the last minute he turned and strode toward the front door. Once outside, he breathed in the fresh country air. The tension inside him began to ease. He started walking and didn't stop until he was at the barn. He went straight to Baby's stall.

Baby was a rare black Andalusian with a long, thick, black mane and tail. A pure Spanish horse and she had the pride and the temper to go with her ancestry. The horse had the best lineage of all the ones they owned, and a name a mile long, but Ryder had always called her Baby.

The horse nudged his shoulder. He chuckled. "How can I refuse when you ask so sweetly?" He grabbed the halter hanging on a hook beside her stall and slipped it on. Baby whinnied. Ryder unlatched the stall and led her out.

Baby didn't just walk out, no, she pranced. It was as though she said, look at me world, and so they should. She was elegant and she knew it. On more than one occasion, she'd let Ryder know that no one owned her.

A few days had passed since he'd ridden her. They both needed some fresh air and wide open spaces where he could clear his mind. He adjusted the blanket on the horse's back, then lifted the saddle. Baby didn't move when he tightened the cinch, but Ryder sensed her excitement. Her emotions were like an electrical current passing through her, flowing into Ryder.

He was more intuitive than the other nephilim. He *felt* people's emotions. With Haley, her emotions ran through him stronger than any other mortal he'd helped in the past. That wasn't good. He couldn't stay as disconnected. She created a hunger in him that was hard to control. Staying away for a while might be the only solution, but letting someone else help her was not even an option as far as he was concerned.

Baby pushed against his shoulder again. "Yeah, I know what you want, sweetheart." She was ready for a run. He led the horse out of the barn and climbed on her back. Before he was even settled, she took off like a bullet. He gripped the reins and let her run. The wind whipped past, the oak trees blurred. The horse's heart pounded as she ran through the night. It was as though they both tried to outrun their personal demons.

Chapter 9

THE NEXT MORNING, IT was all Ryder could do to drag his eyelids open and stumble to the shower. His dreams had been filled with visions of Haley. Haley naked, Haley spreading her legs in invitation, Haley begging him to plunge inside the heat of her body.

The cold shower didn't help. He flipped the lever that turned off the water and grabbed a towel. Their dreams connected last night. It was a new experience for him and he wasn't sure he liked the guilt that went along with it. He grimaced, knowing she felt rejected. She wasn't, though. He wanted her more than she knew. If he wasn't careful, he'd do more harm than good.

After dressing, he made his way down the stairs. He didn't smell anything burning so no one was cooking. Anyone would think that over the centuries they would've learned to cook at least one or two things that were edible, but they hadn't.

The three men were sitting at the table; an assortment of cereal boxes, a couple of jugs of milk, and a couple of cartons of orange juice sat in the center.

"You look like crap," Chance said as he glanced up.

"Thanks a lot," Ryder grumbled. He didn't stop but went straight for the coffee. Someone had made a fresh pot. A good thing because he needed more than one cup to clear his head. He poured a cup then turned, leaning back against the granite countertop. He closed his eyes and inhaled before taking a drink. This was exactly what he needed.

"Did you think about our offer?" Dillon asked. "One of us can finish the assignment."

Cold dread filled Ryder at the thought of never seeing Haley again. He couldn't let her go. Not yet. "There's nothing to think about," he said. "I don't see the problem. It's not as though I've been with her that long."

Hunter shook his head. "We can tell this one is different. Something about it isn't right."

"Yeah," Dillon added his two cents. "And you did show her who you really are, even though the angel's wings were over the top. You have to end this assignment before it's too late."

"I know what I'm doing," Ryder ground out, then downed the rest of his coffee, almost scorching his throat.

"End it today," Hunter told him. "It's not a life or death situation."

"It might seem trivial to you, but it means a lot to Haley."

"You've helped enough. She'll survive," Hunter continued.

"I need more time." He refused to leave Haley hanging.

"No."

Ryder slammed his empty cup on the counter. The cup broke into three pieces. He was left holding the handle. *Calm down!* He took a deep breath, then exhaled as he picked up the pieces of what had been his favorite cup, then tossed everything into the trash. "I won't be told what I will or won't do."

"You're in over your head," Hunter argued.

"Yeah, well, we've all been there before, haven't we? Nothing ever changes. We continue to live another day, another year, so we can answer more prayers." From the expression on Hunter's face, Ryder knew he'd pushed him past the limit of what he would put up with, so he pushed a little harder. "Do you really think you can stop me?"

Hunter came to his feet so fast his chair shot out behind him, wobbled twice, then crashed to the floor. "Is that a challenge?"

Ryder's eyes narrowed. "No, it's a promise."

"Take it outside," Chance warned as he stood.

"Good idea," Hunter said. "He needs someone to knock some sense into him."

"Bring it on!" Ryder was the first out the back door, but Hunter wasted no time following.

Decades before, they'd agreed not to fight in the house so they'd created an arena. It reminded them of the old days, and it was a way to let off steam. No one was ever seriously hurt. Besides, nephilim healed quickly. Maybe, just maybe, a fight was exactly what Ryder needed. He'd been on edge since he'd heard Haley's prayer and felt the deep emotional turmoil stirring inside her.

Hunter's sudden burst of laughter gave Ryder pause and his momentum waned, but he didn't stop walking. What the hell had he been thinking to goad Hunter like that? The man loved fighting and taking care of animals more than anything. He answered more prayers from animals than he did from mortals. He'd once told Ryder he felt more comfortable with animals. Mortals were too complex for his taste. Anyone would think Hunter a gentle man if they ever saw him with an injured animal. They'd be wrong. Piss him off and the guy came unhinged.

I'm so fucking dead.

Ryder strode past ancient stone pillars, stopping in the center of the arena and wondering why the hell he didn't keep walking. Hunter would laugh and Ryder wouldn't hear the end of it. Being immortal could be a pain in the ass.

Might as well get it over with because he wasn't about to listen to their taunting for the next several centuries. He turned in time to see Hunter's fist flying toward him. Ryder ducked just in time. He brought his fist up and connected with Hunter's ribs and was gratified to hear him grunt.

"That was a good one." Hunter laughed, straightening his shirt. "You've improved since the last time we fought."

Ryder didn't feel quite so proud of the fact that he got the first punch in. Not when Hunter treated the incident as though it was no more than an ant sting.

Dillon chuckled.

Hunter's fist flew toward him again. Ryder ducked, but Hunter's other fist caught him on the cheek. Lights danced in front of Ryder's eyes. He staggered back a few steps before regaining his footing.

"You've gotten soft," Hunter grumbled. "Pussy."

"I resent that remark," a woman spoke.

They all looked toward the voice.

Chance grabbed Destiny in a bear hug and twirled her around. "I missed you." He planted a kiss on her lips.

Ryder couldn't help but stare. He glanced at Hunter and Dillon. Apparently, they felt the same way. The fight was forgotten as envy filled Ryder. Chance had found his destiny, literally. He longed for that kind of connection. His friend had beaten the odds and found his soul mate. The odds were still against Ryder.

"I was only gone a week," Destiny said.

"A week too long," Chance told her. "The baby?"

"A little girl." she said on a sigh. "LeAnn and Duncan are going to be great parents." Her expression turned serious as she looked at each of them. "And you're to be her guardian angels."

Chance paled. "You told her about us?"

She frowned. "Of course I didn't tell her. I'm not stupid. I can't believe you would ask such a ridiculous question. Just because LeAnn is the only friend I've ever had doesn't mean I'm going to confide everything to her. Thanks so much that you would think so!" She shoved his chest and marched toward the house.

"Destiny, I didn't mean that I thought you would say anything. Oh, hell." He took off after her.

Dillon, Hunter, and Ryder grinned.

"See what happens when you fall in love?" Hunter said. "That's why I don't get tangled up with females. Too much trouble."

"But they're soft, and they smell so good, and when you make love to them all their emotions are laid bare," Ryder reminded him.

"I didn't say I don't like to make love to them." Hunter frowned.

"Well, you did say you like your animals better," Ryder joked.

Hunter's fist slammed into his face. *Oh, damn, why'd he have to joke like that?* He dodged the next blow even though blood flowed freely from his nose. The next one landed in his gut. He dropped to his knees as his air whooshed out.

"Apologize."

"Okay, okay, I apologize."

"Now, agree to ending this assignment."

"I can't," he wheezed. The guy swung his fist like a damn sledge-hammer. Ryder wiped the back of his sleeve across his nose.

"Don't go back for a month. See how she does on her own. She might not need you as much as you think."

Ryder clamped his lips together to keep from telling Hunter to go to hell. But what if he was right? Haley might not want him hanging around. A sharp pain stabbed him in the heart worse than any of the punches Hunter landed. He met the other man's gaze and saw only sympathy in his eyes. Deep down inside, Ryder knew he might be right. But a whole month?

"A week," Ryder countered.

"Deal." Hunter nodded. "Are we through fighting?"

"You mean Ryder was fighting?" Dillon asked. "I thought he was just your punching bag."

Hunter's laughter filled the air. "Let's get a beer."

"Beer? This early?" Dillon glanced toward the sun. "The sun's barely up."

"And your point is?" Hunter wore a puzzled expression. Apparently he didn't have a problem with drinking that early.

Dillon shrugged. "I guess I don't have one."

"Good." Hunter stuck out his hand toward Ryder.

Since his nose was out of joint, literally, the idea of drinking a beer sounded great if it would kill the pain. Ryder grabbed his hand, grimacing when Hunter hauled him to his feet. "Easy!"

"You've really gotten soft." Hunter shook his head.

"Only because I don't down a barrel of nails every morning for breakfast like you do." He rubbed his shoulder, wincing.

"Wuss."

Dillon snorted with laughter. "You're both full of shit. Remind me to show you two how to fight some day."

Ryder and Hunter glared at him, but they didn't say anything. They would both rather have a beer than continue fighting. If anyone liked to fight more than Hunter, then it would be Dillon. He might look calm and laid back on the outside, but inside he was a stick of dynamite and you didn't want to get caught in the explosion.

Ryder had gotten a little soft, though. That bothered him. What if he crossed paths with a demon? He didn't want to lose his soul. Since he'd made a promise to stay away from Haley for a week, it might be a good time to practice his fighting skills.

A whole week? His dick would shrivel up.

"The time will fly by," Hunter said, guessing some of Ryder's thoughts, then he slapped him on the back. "I was in the north pasture yesterday and noticed we have a fence down. We'll leave in the morning. The fresh air will clear your mind."

Dillon opened the door and they went inside. "I think I'll join you. I haven't gotten my hands dirty in a while. It will do us all good."

In other words, neither one of them would let him out of their sight until the week was up. They probably knew he didn't plan to keep his end of the bargain. What was Haley going to think? Would she care or would she move on with her life?

Chapter 10

THE MORE HALEY HAD studied the nude pictures of herself last night, the more her confidence rose. She actually thought they were kind of hot. So hot that she really wanted to have sex. She waited, but Ryder never showed.

Had he decided she was too much trouble? Her confidence did a nosedive. It was hard not to think Ryder might have moved on. She didn't know what the norm was for nephilim. Halfway through the night, she finally fell asleep on the sofa dreaming about Ryder taking her into his arms and explaining there'd been an emergency angel conference and that was why he wasn't able to return. She snuggled into his arms, turning so she could get even closer to his warmth—and fell off the sofa.

"Well, hell," she muttered as she sat up.

The lamp on the end table was on but she couldn't make out the hour until she blinked several times and stared at the pale blue hands on the glass clock. She wondered if she was still dreaming until she remembered Ryder had redecorated.

The clock came into focus. "Four a.m.," she moaned. "I've got to get up in a few hours. See what you've done to me, Ryder?" She wiggled around until she could plant one arm on the sofa and leverage her body to a semi-standing position, then dragged herself to bed. Why was life so unfair? She crawled beneath the cover and pulled it up to her ears, yawning before her eyes closed again.

Music blared through her bedroom. Haley sat up with a start, automatically slapping her hand down on the alarm button.

"Oh, Lord, it's morning," she groaned, then looked at the clock, hoping the alarm might have been set early. It wasn't.

She could call in sick. That was an idea. Ryder might pop by. The idea sent a thrill of pleasure through her, but the feeling didn't last. She'd used her sick days when she caught a nasty bug the month before. So much for that brilliant idea.

Morning was not her favorite time of the day. Why couldn't work start later in the day? It made perfect sense to her. Everyone she knew slept until at least ten or eleven on their days off. People would be more rested and probably get more work accomplished if they went to the office late. As it was, they were just lining the pockets of the coffee industry. The working population had to consume massive amounts of caffeine just to get through the morning.

Procrastination was another bad habit Haley hadn't kicked. There was no getting around the fact that she still had to get out of bed and get ready for work. Coffee first. She flung the cover back and climbed out of bed. She lumbered disjointedly toward the kitchen. She had more kinks than she cared to count.

The rich aroma of coffee wafted its way around Haley about the same time she stepped into the living room. Thank goodness she'd set the timer on the coffee pot. Her eyes were half closed as she followed the scent.

Her favorite cup was already on the cabinet. She dumped in two low-cal sweeteners before pouring her first cup, then added two heaping teaspoons of hazelnut-flavored creamer. The cup warmed her hands as she brought it closer to her face. She breathed in the rich aroma, then took her first drink, savoring the taste.

She practically inhaled the first cup, then poured another to take back to the bedroom, but paused in the living room. She stared at the nude pictures Ryder had taken of her, studying each one with a critical eye. They were good. But was that really her? He could've touched them up. Had he only given her a fantasy, then left for good? "Ryder?" Nothing. Only silence. "I don't feel like the woman in the pictures." Was this another test? If so, Haley had a feeling she would fail miserably. She still needed him.

More so when she stood in front of her closet and stared at her wardrobe. The same ugly clothes hung on wire hangers as though they were sentenced to death and sent to the gallows. With her wearing them, she supposed that might just be the case. She grabbed a skirt and sweater and put them on. She tried on almost everything on a hanger.

Minus the black glasses, Haley looked the same as she did on Friday. Nothing had changed. Ryder hadn't sprinkled angel dust on her and made her beautiful. If anything, her life was worse because he gave her a glimpse into another world. One where she would be accepted rather than invisible.

Ryder had thrown her back into the real world, though, and he'd done it in a way that was more cruel than if he'd never entered her life. Now she knew what life could be like, and that made her own more miserable. She was starting to dislike the immortal a whole lot.

She grabbed a pink sweater and skirt out of the pile of clothes on the bed. It didn't matter what she wore to work. No one would notice her anyway.

She ran a brush through her hair, pulled it back into a ponytail, then secured it with pins at the base of her neck. The style aged her. She didn't care. At least it was out of her face.

Taking a deep breath, she grabbed her purse and walked out the front door, locking it behind her. As she walked down the sidewalk, Chelsea came waltzing out her front door in her usual short-shorts and halter top. How did Chelsea always get away with going in late? Drat, Haley's day was already going downhill.

Chelsea glanced her way, but didn't bother to say good morning.

That was fine with Haley. She couldn't help but stare at the other woman, though. How did she manage to look great every day? Her clothes were perfect, her makeup was perfect, every hair on her head was perfect.

Haley smoothed her hand over her hair and got into her little blue Civic. It might be nice to have her hair done by someone other than herself. Not that she was a professional, or even that good. Cutting her hair wasn't exactly rocket science, though. She always pulled it back anyway.

She started the car and backed out of the driveway. It took exactly seven minutes and twenty seconds to drive to the bank. She parked in her usual spot and went straight to her desk. Alexa was already behind her teller cage, but looked up and grinned as though she'd been waiting for Haley to get to work.

"I'm glad you're here," Alexa said as she hurried over, then impulsively hugged Haley.

"Where else would I be?" She grinned. Alexa's excitement was contagious. "You look like a woman in love." Alexa glowed. There was something else different, but she couldn't quite figure out what.

"I think I am." Alexa giggled like she had when they were in high school, when their dreams were still dreams, when the excitement of the unknown was still there. "But I tanned, too. Marion said my color was too washed out."

Marion was Alexa's older sister by three years. She never really paid attention to Alexa. They might as well have been born on different planets as far as having the same interests. Marion had been seriously involved with any and all things sports related. She was a high school coach, which was how she'd met her fiancé. He taught world history.

"What do you think?" Alexa asked with a worried frown.

Haley took a step back and pursed her lips as she studied her friend. The tan was subtle and there was no orange afterglow.

She met her friend's gaze. "I think you look absolutely fabulous."

"Really?"

"Really." She knew Alexa waited for her to say something more and Haley would never dream of hurting her one and only friend. "Are you going to see Brian again?"

Alexa nodded, fairly bursting from the seams. "He's coming down for the Old Settler's Reunion." She grabbed Haley's hand. "But you'll come with us, right? I told Brian we've been friends since forever and he can't wait to meet you."

Great, she'd become the third wheel. She swallowed past the lump in her throat and told herself she would not have a pity party. "I'd love to meet him, but I refuse to monopolize your time."

The worried look returned to Alexa's eyes. "I want you there."

Haley squeezed Alexa's hand. "I know, but this is your time. You would do the same for me. Besides, you'll tell me everything that happens, and how exciting will that be?"

"Of course I'll tell you everything." She bit her bottom lip as her gaze swept over Haley. Haley wondered what she was looking for when Alexa's eyes suddenly widened. "You're not wearing your glasses."

Haley touched her face. She'd completely forgotten about them. How could she forget Ryder tossing them over his shoulder, the two of them completely naked?

"You're blushing!" Alexa quickly looked around. "Tell me what happened. Something happened. You've never been able to keep a secret from me."

Abigail Barnhill strode into the lobby of the bank, effectively ending their conversation. Haley breathed a sigh of relief, never so glad to see her boss as she was right then.

She was average sized and in her mid-sixties. Her demeanor was authoritative. She ran the bank like a seasoned warhorse and brooked no arguments when she decided to do something. Even though Abigail had been married for a number of years, she rarely spoke of her husband, and they had no children. If it wasn't for a solemn photo of her and her husband that hung in her office, anyone would think she was a spinster.

"Back to the grindstone," Haley muttered.

After depositing her purse in the bottom drawer, she got to work. For the next hour and a half she crunched numbers. She was so focused on what she was doing that she jumped when Chelsea tapped Haley's desk.

"Meeting," she said, then smiled with false sweetness. She'd traded her halter top and short-shorts for a bright yellow pantsuit.

"I see you decided to come to work today," Haley said with a smile of her own, but Chelsea had already walked away.

Haley smoothed her hands down the front of her pink skirt and hurried to the meeting room. There was a meeting every month. Normally she wouldn't think anything about it, but this morning she had an odd feeling. As if something was about to change, which was a crazy notion. She didn't have premonitions. Alexa hurried in and they took a seat next to each other.

Chelsea was sitting next to Ben. She leaned closer to him and whispered something, letting her fingers trail down the arm of his dark gray suit jacket.

"She gags me," Alexa whispered, voicing Haley's thoughts. "You still haven't told me why you blushed."

Haley had hoped Alexa had forgotten about that. "I've been reading a really good romance. Very naughty."

Alexa studied her for a moment. Haley kept her features bland. "You'll have to loan it to me," she finally said.

Haley breathed a sigh of relief.

Ben laughed, drawing her attention. He quickly covered the noise with a cough when Ms. Barnhill strode inside the meeting room and glanced his way. He pulled slightly away from Chelsea. Ben wouldn't jeopardize his job.

Chelsea frowned, her eyes scanning the room to see if anyone had noticed his brush-off. Her gaze stopped on Haley. Haley didn't waver, staring right back at her. Chelsea straightened, tossing her pale blonde hair over one shoulder. Haley smiled, enjoying that Chelsea was irritated that anyone might have seen Ben's reaction.

"Hazel, have you finished the Stuart proposal?" Ms. Barnhill asked, drawing all eyes to the front of the room. Her gaze landed on Haley.

Haley could feel the heat travel up her face. "It's Haley, Ms. Barnhill." She'd been at the bank four years and her boss still didn't know her name.

Confusion crossed the other woman's face, then awareness. "Yes, of course. Then, Haley, have you finished the proposal?"

"I'll have it on your desk by the end of the day."

Ms. Barnhill did the final approval on all loans over a certain amount and had the last say on any money that left the building. The Hattersville bank had been in her family for generations. She managed the bank with a tight rein.

"Good." Ms. Barnhill looked toward the other side of the room. "Ben, where are you with the Franklins' home loan?"

He sat a little straighter. "I'm finished. I'll bring the file to you after the meeting."

Ms. Barnhill beamed. "Very good." She looked around the table, her gaze stopping on Haley. "That's the way to move forward. Everyone could learn something from Ben's work ethic."

Haley glanced at Ben, hoping he would at least acknowledge her help with the proposal, but he didn't even look her way. She raised her chin, determined not to let his crass behavior get to her.

How could she have been so stupid to think he was something special?

Haley met Alexa's knowing look, but then she did the unexpected. Alexa crossed her eyes. Haley was the only one who saw, but it was enough that Haley had to stifle a laugh. Once, when they were in fifth grade, the teacher made Haley stand in front of the class because she was caught chewing gum. Yes, she was in the wrong. The worse possible punishment was being put on display while everyone stared at her as though she had a huge wart on her face, until Alexa started crossing her eyes. Then it wasn't so bad. It was as if Alexa stood beside her and said, hey, we'll get through this together.

To hell with Ben! She hoped he'd get… What? She thought for a moment, then smiled. She hoped he got blue balls.

As if he sensed her thoughts, Ben looked her way. She cocked an eyebrow. Ben knew the truth, even if the boss didn't. He lowered his eyes and became very interested in his manicure. *Coward.* He certainly hadn't been worth her tears.

I hex you with blue balls, Ben Swanson!

"I have an announcement to make," Ms. Barnhill said, grabbing everyone's attention. "As you know, the bank has been in my family since the day my great-grandfather opened the front door. We've built a good reputation over the years for being honest." She paused, as though she sought the right words.

Her premonition was back. Apparently she wasn't the only one, either, as some of the other employees began to shift in their seats.

"I know this may come as a surprise to many of you, but I've decided to sell the bank."

Shocked silence followed her words. Haley's secure world began to crumble. She hated change. Change made her nervous.

Alexa's mouth dropped open, then closed. She looked at Haley and mouthed, *you're kidding.*

"Don't worry," Ms. Barnhill quickly reassured everyone. "There's a small but well-established corporation interested in continuing my great-grandfather's tradition of being a bank the people of our county can trust. I'm sure nothing will change and the transition will be completed as smoothly as possible."

A corporation? Haley wasn't comfortable with that.

"When?" someone asked.

"The process will take a few weeks." Ms. Barnhill gave one of her rare smiles, except it didn't quite meet her eyes. "The bank wasn't started in a day. Changing ownership won't be immediate, either. I couldn't, in all good conscience, not inform you, my banking family, of what the future held." She cleared her throat and shuffled some papers on her desk. "The newspaper will be making a small announcement this week."

In other words, the newspaper got wind something was up and started snooping until they discovered the truth. They were running with the story. Ms. Barnhill had no choice but to tell her employees.

"For now, it will be business as usual." She stood and the meeting ended. Everyone filed out of the room without saying much.

Ben stopped in front of Ms. Barnhill. The ones behind him had to detour around. "Let me be the first to congratulate you." His words dripped with enough sugar to send a diabetic into a coma.

"Thank you, Ben." Ms. Barnhill smiled.

Haley didn't hear anything else. Ben was probably trying to find out exactly what his role would be with the new owner. Not that she blamed him. She would love to know the same thing.

"Suck-up," Alexa muttered. "I have no idea what you see in the guy."

"I'm wondering the same thing."

"What do you think will happen?"

A sick feeling crawled over Haley. Where would any of them stand with a new corporation? Hattersville was not the corporation type. Why would someone even bother with a small bank? "I don't know, but they can't fire everyone. It wouldn't be good for business."

"You're right."

Haley hoped so. She didn't want to lose her job any more than the next person.

Why not? The thought streaked across her mind, surprising her. Of course she didn't want to lose her job. She loved her job. She was a loan officer. There was a sense of pride knowing she was able to help someone's dreams come true when they were trying to buy a home or a car. Working around Alexa was an added benefit.

Was it enough to make up for the negatives? Like not getting credit for the work she did, her boss not even remembering her name, the fact that she felt stymied? The money she made was just okay. She could get a lot more in Dallas. When she thought about it, she wondered why she was still working there.

But she knew the answer. She'd grown comfortable where she worked and where she lived. That was the reason she stayed.

"There's something different about you," Chelsea interrupted her thoughts.

Here was another reason why she should've left a long time ago. Chelsea was not her friend and would never be her friend. Occasionally, Chelsea would pretend they were best buds, but it was only so she could run one of her scams. There was always something Chelsea wanted. After working with her for the last two years, Haley learned not to trust the woman. She'd stab anyone in the back while smiling and looking them right in the eye if she thought she could advance her career. Then she would wonder why you blamed her, since you were the one bleeding all over the carpet!

"I'm the same as I was Friday." Haley went around her desk and pulled out the chair. Why couldn't she just tell Chelsea to go away? Tell her to jump off the nearest bridge and, hopefully, there wouldn't be any water in the river below. For once in her life, Haley needed to stand up for herself.

Why stop there? Haley should march in Ms. Barnhill's office and tell her that after working for her four years she could at least remember Haley's name. When she left her office, Haley could go right up to Ben and tell him that he was an ass for standing her up.

She could do all that, but she wouldn't. It was the thought that counted. She would never want to draw that much attention to herself. She sat in her chair and scooted closer to the desk. She didn't enjoy making a spectacle. Life was easier if she kept her mouth shut.

"No, you did something." Chelsea tapped a finger on her cheek. With her other hand, she twined strands of pale blonde hair around one finger. The woman had beautiful hair, she'd give her that. And a nice figure. Haley sighed. Who was she kidding? Chelsea had everything and it was all rolled into a nice little package. Haley smiled. Except for her personality. That sucked. She'd make some poor sap a horrible wife some day. An even better thought came to mind: maybe she would marry Ben—and give him blue balls.

Haley opened her desk drawer and brought out the file she was working on, hoping Chelsea would get the hint that Haley had work to do and go away. Chelsea didn't get the message. She propped her pert little ass on the corner of Haley's desk, bumping a paperclip holder and Haley's nameplate. Haley straightened her things with a sigh. Chelsea wasn't going away.

"No, there's something different." She snapped her fingers. "I know!"

Haley jumped.

"You've ditched the ugly glasses." She grinned as though she'd just discovered her latest pregnancy test was negative.

"How very astute of you." She didn't bother to look at Chelsea.

"You don't have to be sarcastic. You're just upset that I left with Ben the other night and messed up your big date plans," she huffed. "You forced him to ask you out so it's not as though it was a big deal."

Except it was a big deal to Haley at the time. She would never let Chelsea know how hurt she was. She wouldn't give the other woman the satisfaction.

"No big deal," Haley shrugged. "Something better came along."

"Better? In Hattersville?" She snorted. "I wouldn't count on anyone believing that story. Even if there was someone better than Ben, why would they go out with you?"

"Haley, don't you have work to do?" Ms. Barnhill asked.

Haley flinched. She hadn't heard her boss's door open. "Yes, ma'am."

Chelsea quickly scooted off the desk, smoothing her hands over the front of her sweater. "I'm sorry, Ms. Barnhill. It's all my fault." She smiled sweetly.

Haley had a painful sensation of a knife being plunged into her back.

Chelsea lowered her head. "I thought it would be nice to organize a party before you left. You were so right when you said that we're family." When she raised her head, fake tears glistened in her eyes. "We'll miss you so much."

Ms. Barnhill softened. "That's so sweet, Chelsea."

"Well, except Haley is such a workaholic that she didn't have time to talk to me about my silly little party. I thought it would be nice to have an open house so that the public could drop by as well." Chelsea waved her arm dramatically. "This bank isn't just a business, it's an institution."

Oh yeah, that was definitely a knife Chelsea was sticking in Haley. She hadn't even mentioned a stupid party. Haley was going to puke. Chelsea was in the wrong line of work. She should've been an actress.

"I think a party is a wonderful idea." Ms. Barnhill beamed.

"You mean so much to us." Chelsea sniffed. "To all of us. Even Haley, I'm sure."

The knife slipped a little deeper. How could Ms. Barnhill buy every syrupy sweet lie Chelsea uttered? The woman was usually sharp. Why couldn't she see past Chelsea's act?"

"Yes, I'm sure my leaving concerns Haley greatly." Ms. Barnhill spoke with a frown in her voice as she looked down at Haley.

Haley picked up a pencil on her desk, gripping it until she was afraid it might snap. There was nothing she could say. Not one damn thing. People believed what they wanted, and Ms. Barnhill wanted to believe she was a well-loved boss who would be missed.

"Haley, since you were too busy to discuss plans for a party, then you might want to start work by actually opening the file in front of you."

"Chelsea, you're very sweet, and I'm sure the person who steps into my shoes will see your wonderful qualities. Why don't you come to my office this afternoon and we'll discuss the open house. Since the public will be invited, we should make sure my great-grandfather's memory is honored as well." After a discerning nod directed at Haley, she returned to her office.

"I suppose I need to plan the dumb party." Chelsea sighed.

Anger began to build inside Haley like a pressure cooker that should've been turned off an hour ago. No, she would remain calm. She refused to stoop to Chelsea's level! "I have work to do." Her words were clipped.

"I guess work is the only thing you have to look forward to. Hard work doesn't always get you what you want." She picked up Haley's nameplate, running her fingers over the engraved letters. "With Ms. Barnhill promising to put in a good word on my behalf, I might finally make loan officer."

Haley half stood, grabbing her nameplate out of Chelsea's hand. "You have to at least be able to add two and two if you're planning to take my job. Does your brain function reach that high?" She sat back down, replacing the nameplate and gripping the pencil with both hands. Chelsea stared at her as though she was in shock. Haley cringed. There would be hell to pay because of what she'd said. Chelsea had a way of making herself look good. The person at the top of her shit list always prayed for mercy until someone else moved to that spot.

A red glow appeared in Chelsea's eyes. Heat radiated off her in waves, scorching Haley with that one evil look. "I can add, don't you worry about that," Chelsea said with deadly calm. "I know there are two loan officers at the bank. I want to be a loan officer but the bank isn't big enough to support three positions. Someone has to go. It won't be Ben. He has too much pull with the old broad. But you?" Her laugh was light. "You, poor Haley, don't stand a chance against me."

Pushing Chelsea until her true self appeared was never a good thing. Chelsea was scary. It was all Haley could do to draw in a breath. Chelsea started back to her desk, but turned at the last moment.

"Oh, and by the way, losing the glasses didn't really help. You probably wish you could look like me, but that won't ever happen." With a sway in her hips that any hooker would be proud of, Chelsea finally walked away.

The pencil Haley held snapped in two. She wanted to throw the pieces at Chelsea's back, but tossed them into the trash instead. When she glanced up, she met Alexa's crossed eyes. Haley couldn't help it; she laughed.

Chelsea's head whipped around. The look she cast in Haley's direction actually burned. She swallowed hard. Chelsea had expected Haley to be near tears, not laughing. This was not good.

Chelsea's eyes narrowed as she quickly looked at Alexa, who was busy counting money. Chelsea clamped her lips together and marched behind her cage. Alexa looked up and winked. Haley grinned, but she knew her smile was a little weak and a whole lot wobbly. The other woman would crucify her.

She opened the file, but the words blurred. Her life wasn't bad. She made a decent living, and with her savings account and owning her own home, her credit score was high. If she wanted to take a trip to a far off land, she could.

So why the hell had she prayed for a miracle?

Ryder made her want more. Made her feel even more dissatisfied.

She would have been perfectly fine to go through life unnoticed. Where the hell was he, anyway, and more important, was he coming back?

The next few days didn't improve. Haley didn't think they would get any better, but there was a glimmer of hope. Ryder was still a no-show. Life was pretty dismal when even an angel bailed.

"You look as though you're a million miles away," Alexa said as she stopped at Haley's desk.

How far was heaven? At least a million miles. She was thoughtful. Ryder said he lived on a ranch where there were others like him. Were they as much of a jerk as he was?

She glanced up from the file that was open on her desk. She'd been staring at the same numbers for the last hour. "Just concentrating on getting the Andersons their loan." A twinge of guilt settled on her shoulders. They really needed the loan so they could buy new farm equipment. The hard-working couple did everything they could to keep the old hay baler going, but it churned out the last bale a couple of weeks ago before belching a cloud of black diesel and dying a bolt-shuddering death.

"I like the Andersons. Are they going to get the loan?"

"I'll do my best."

"Speaking of which, Ben has been doing his best to ignore you. He acts as though you have the plague."

That was the only bright spot that week. "I've been making a point of going past his desk a few times during the day." Watching him squirm was very rewarding.

"It's about time you showed a little backbone. Your life would be even better if I could just get you to tell your mother and sister they should look at their own faults before judging yours."

Alexa warmed up to her subject, except Haley couldn't get past her best friend judging her, too. She meant well, and Alexa was right. She was a wuss. A doormat people cleaned their feet on.

"Earth to Haley."

"What?" She focused on Alexa again.

"I asked if you wanted to go out to eat tonight."

Alexa hadn't really meant what she'd said about her needing a backbone. Not in a mean way. She only wanted something better for her friend. Haley understood where Alexa was coming from. Going out for supper would be a nice change from eating a solitary meal, which would consist of a frozen dinner. Before she could answer, someone motioned to Alexa that she had a call.

"Be right back. Think about where you want to eat tonight."

Anywhere but home. There were only a couple of decent sit-down places in Hattersville, so choosing wasn't that difficult, but from the sour expression on Alexa's face as she returned, Haley had a feeling it would be a frozen dinner after all.

"That was Mom," she said. "My sister is dropping by her house tonight. They want me there to go over table decorations."

"No problem. I thought I'd take a couple of files home to work on."

"You work too much," Alexa chastised.

"I want to help our customers get what they need. Sometimes their survival depends on getting a loan."

"It doesn't mean you have to kill yourself." Alexa studied her friend. "You're starting to look haggard."

"It's not from staying out late," Chelsea quipped, apparently catching the last of their conversation. She suddenly stopped, her eyes growing wide. "Wait, but you did say something better came along the same night Ben stood you up to go out with me." She covered her mouth with her hand. "Is that why you look old and tired? Has this mystery man been keeping you up late at night?" She chuckled.

"Excuse me?" Alexa socked her hands on her hips. "Maybe you'd better take a second look in the mirror. You might want to invest in a good wrinkle cream."

Chelsea stumbled back. "I do *not* have wrinkles!"

Alexa touched the corner of her eye. "Right about here. You're definitely starting to get crow's feet."

"No, I'm not!" She almost trampled Ben in her haste to get to the ladies' room to see if Alexa spoke the truth. Heaven forbid Chelsea have even one tiny wrinkle to mar her flawless skin.

"Bitch," Alexa muttered, before looking at Haley again. "What was she talking about? Have you met someone?"

Haley shrugged. "No, I just told her someone better had come along when she rubbed it in about Ben standing me up."

"You don't have to lie to anyone."

Ouch. Even Alexa couldn't fathom Haley with a man. She felt like a ship with a small hole where her heart would have been and every second that passed, she sank a little deeper. "What if I had met someone?"

Alexa shook her head. "I don't follow you."

"What if I had met a man? One who put other men to shame because he was so good looking. Would that be so hard to comprehend?"

"Are you feeling okay?" Alexa's eyebrows drew together. "Maybe I should tell Mom I can't make it tonight."

Haley was afraid Alexa would never understand. "No, go to your mom's. I'm fine. It's just been a long day and I'm starting to get a headache. I think I'll just take something, then soak in the tub, and go to bed early."

"If you're sure that's all."

"Positive."

"I'll see you in the morning?"

"I still have to secure loans for these people, so I'll be here." She pasted a smile on her face.

"If you need anything, call me."

"I will."

"And next time Chelsea bothers you, tell her to take a flying leap from a tall building." Alexa laughed. "Or lie and tell her she's getting wrinkles."

"I'll do that."

The rest of the afternoon dragged. Haley couldn't seem to stop wondering why she never stood up for herself. A sick feeling began to grow in the pit of her stomach the more she thought about it. Alexa always fought Haley's battles. In the early days of their friendship, Haley attempted fighting back, but someone always got the best of her. She never won. When Alexa began to jump in and stick up for her, Haley backed off. Life was easier if she let Alexa handle all her problems. Haley had been crippled by Alexa's friendship. Not that Haley thought Alexa would ever intentionally hurt her, but she had.

As she drove home after work, she wondered why she questioned her life. But she knew the answer—Ryder. Had the dissatisfaction with her life always been there? He'd opened her eyes. Showed her what her life could be like—except it was an optical illusion.

Why did he give her so much, then take it all away? Unless she was only a joke to him.

Chapter 11

RYDER GRABBED A STAPLE from the pocket of the tool belt around his waist, then held the u-shaped nail in place while he hammered it into the cedar post. When he couldn't drive the nail any further, he pulled on the four-strand barbed wire to make sure it was tight.

Their fence stretched over the next small rise, and the one after that. The barbed wire marked their side. The woman who owned the other side got upset when their cattle crossed over to her place. She'd leave them nasty notes because they never answered the door. She could be a real pain in the ass.

He could remember a time before wire and fence posts when cattle roamed free. There were buffalo back then. The ugly beasts had survived Indians and people who tried to tame the land, then ended up in preserves so everyone could get a glimpse of the past.

The land the four of them had purchased was raw and primitive, much like the retreat, but the place they created had only been a facade of the real thing. A demon once said they were only playing cowboys. Maybe he was right.

He didn't need to fix the fence, either. None of the nephilim had to sweat under a hot sun. Each one had amassed a fortune over the centuries. They could pay someone to fix the gaps. Or use magic. It wouldn't be the same thing, though. There was a sense of pride when he worked the land. For a little while, Ryder felt almost normal.

Just not that day, or the past three days. Haley's emotions were as strong as if she stood in front of him. Every hour that passed, she withdrew inside herself a little more until the confidence she'd gained drained away. She would be a basket case by the time he returned.

He couldn't let that happen. Hell, he *wouldn't* let that happen!

"Enough," he said, throwing down the hammer. "She needs me." He eyed Hunter and Dillon who were in the middle of setting a new post, daring them to even attempt to keep him from her.

Hunter shook his head. "You're too involved. Don't you see what's happening?"

"Yeah, I do." Ryder removed the tool belt from around his waist and let it drop to the ground. It landed with a dull thud, the silver u-shaped nails scattering on the ground. "I left Haley too soon. I can feel her pain. The pressure is starting to get to her. She won't make it four more days."

Dillon pulled off his leather gloves. "Go to her," he said without looking up.

"We agreed Ryder would stay a week," Hunter reminded him.

Dillon raised his gaze. The pain and regret Ryder saw on Dillon's face cut him to the bone.

"This is between Ryder and Haley," Dillon told Hunter.

Hunter expelled a hard breath. "I can't fight the two of you." He waved his arm. "Go, but you better be damned careful. It won't be on my head—"

Ryder didn't wait to hear the rest of what Hunter had to say. He closed his eyes and Hunter's words faded. Lights swirled around him and the wind rushed past. He didn't blame Hunter for trying to keep him at the ranch. Hunter was more than a friend. The four of them were closer than any brothers.

But man, Hunter could talk for hours. He might not say much for weeks on end, but once he got started, none of them could get him to shut up. Ryder was in too much of a hurry to stick around and listen to his dire warnings. And he wouldn't have lasted another day without seeing Haley.

When he opened his eyes, he stood in Haley's living room. As his eyes adjusted to the dim light, disappointment filled him. She'd taken down the pictures. Every last one of them. She'd lost sight of her own beauty. It only took a few minutes to locate them in the hall closet and hang them again.

Much better. He slowly turned in a circle, drinking in the sight of her naked body. How could she not see what was right in front of her?

A key turned in the lock and the door opened. Haley came inside and closed the door, juggling the files she held as she locked it behind her and slid the chain in place. Even tired, shoulders drooping as though she carried a heavy weight, Haley was a welcome sight. He hadn't realized just how much he missed her until that moment. A weary sigh escaped her lips as she flipped the light on and turned.

"Hello, Haley."

She jumped, dropped the files, and threw her purse at him. He dodged all the flying missiles that exploded from the pockets. A tube of lipstick caught his cheek, an opened package of tissues bounced off his arm, and a change purse hit him in the chest.

"What the hell are you doing here?" She glowered at him.

That wasn't quite the overjoyed welcome he'd envisioned. "I missed you." He stepped over the contents of her purse as he walked toward her. "I'm sorry if I startled you."

"Just stay over there." She held up her hand.

"Is something wrong?" It was pretty obvious she wasn't quite as happy to see him as he was to see her.

"No, why would anything be wrong? You came into my life and made me feel... feel pretty, then you trotted right back out. Now you're asking if anything is wrong?" She bent and began to retrieve her papers off the floor. "Everything is wrong," she said as if he wasn't even in the room.

He scooped up the rest of her files, taking the ones she held as they straightened. After he deposited them on the end table, he returned to stand in front of her. He'd hurt her. His actions were unintentional, but would she believe him? "I never meant to cause you pain."

Her bottom lip trembled. "You left without even saying good-bye."

"I'm here now."

"You made me believe in miracles." Her gaze went to the pictures hanging on the wall. "I'm not her. Nothing changed except I feel more alone than ever."

"You're beautiful," he said as he pulled her into his arms. She resisted, but only a moment before resting her head against his chest. The softness of her body pressed against him. Something squeezed his heart. Her pain became his pain. "I won't hurt you again."

"I don't believe you."

He held her a little tighter. "Trust me."

"I'm afraid to. For a little while I almost thought I could change, but then I woke up to the same old me." Her words trembled. "I know you'll leave again. You can't stay."

His lips pressed against the top of her head. "No, I can't stay."

"Then why come back at all?"

"Because we're not finished."

Someone pulled up next door. A car door slammed, followed by more cars, more slamming doors. There was laughter, then music. A party. How many times had Haley listened and wished she was part of the fun?

"Close your eyes," he said. She tightened her hold, sucked in a breath as lights and a cool breeze danced around them. He wanted to take her somewhere that noise wouldn't intrude. He wanted to reconnect and find what they'd lost.

"You brought me back to your retreat." She frowned, her nose wrinkling. "You're sweaty." She stepped away, then stumbled on the uneven ground.

Ryder caught her arm so she wouldn't fall. "I was mending fences. I couldn't stay away a moment more."

She raised an eyebrow. "On your ranch."

"You doubt I have one?"

"You pop in and out of my life. You transport me to this retreat that doesn't really exist. I'm sure you do own a ranch. You can have anything you want." A bit of defiance crept into her words. "It must be nice to have whatever your heart desires."

There was only one thing he wanted. "Can I have you?" he quietly asked.

Her face took on a rosy hue as she visibly swallowed. "You could have at least showered before you came back," she grumbled, but her gaze slid over him in a way that said she wanted him just as much.

"That's why I came here."

She glanced around. "You have a house?"

"No."

Haley's expression turned to one of puzzlement. He couldn't stop the smile that formed. There was so much that he wanted to show her. She'd been trapped for a long time in beliefs that had been shoved down her throat. He wanted to set her free so she could soar. As soon as the thought crossed his mind, reality set in. When he set her free, it would be time for him to leave. But he had this moment, and he wanted to savor every one he spent in her company, seeing everything through her eyes as if he was seeing it for the very first time.

"This is like no shower you've ever experienced," he promised as he brought his thoughts back to the present.

She raised a haughty eyebrow. "Who said I needed to shower? I haven't been mending fences all day."

"This shower is different. I think you'll like it." He stepped closer, trailing his finger down her cheek, lightly grazing her neck, then dropping down the front of her very virginal pink top. He lightly drew circles around one nipple. It immediately tightened. "Do you want to get naked and shower with me?"

She nodded.

"Then come." He grabbed her hand as he led her through the thick woods, pushing overgrown brush and low-hanging limbs out of the way so she didn't trip.

"Why do you always do this?" she complained as she stumbled behind him.

"Do what?"

She didn't say anything. He stopped and looked at her. Her gaze flitted from tree to tree, refusing to meet his. "Nothing," she mumbled.

"What do I always do?" he asked, curious why she fidgeted. When she didn't say anything, he put his hands on either side of her face and lowered his mouth to hers. She tasted minty and fresh. He explored her mouth as his hand snaked to the back of her neck and tangled in the tight bun there. He freed her hair, running his fingers through the soft tresses. A shudder trembled down her body. She pressed closer, and Ryder knew he had to end the kiss now or they would never make it to where he was leading her. He stroked her tongue with his one last time, then tugged on her pouty bottom lip with his teeth before releasing her.

She leaned against him for a moment, not moving until her breathing returned to normal. "That's what," she finally told him.

"What?" She confused him. She did that a lot.

"This." She stepped away from him. "Just now you kissed me."

He didn't understand a word of what she was trying to tell him. "You don't like when I kiss you?"

"Yes, I do. And before you kissed me you…" Her cheeks infused with color. She glared at him. "And before that you were touching me."

Ryder didn't think he would ever understand the way a

woman's mind worked. Especially Haley's. But she was fascinating. Like now, when she struggled to find the right words to explain her problem.

"You get me all hot and bothered, then you grab my hand and drag me through the blasted woods!" she finally blurted.

His grin was slow. "I got you hot and bothered by only tracing the outline of your nipple?"

She caught her moan, choking on it. "You don't have to talk about it."

"Why? Does talking about sex make you horny?"

She pressed her lips together.

"Want me to tell you what I'm going to do once we get where we're going?" He didn't give her time to answer, but continued talking. "I'm going to unbutton your shirt, then slide it off your shoulders. Next I'll unfasten your bra and free those magnificent breasts. I'm going to roll your nipples between my thumb and finger, lightly squeezing and tugging—"

"Ryder," she moaned.

"You're right. If I don't stop, I'll take you where we stand."

"That might not be a bad thing."

"But not as good as what I have planned." He took her hand and continued through the woods. A bobcat suddenly cried out, telling Ryder and Haley they were disturbing her. Haley came to an abrupt stop, forcing him to do the same.

She nervously looked around. "Are there wild animals around here?"

"A few."

She tugged his hand. "What do you mean, 'a few'?" She stepped closer to him.

Her breast brushed his arm and for a moment he forgot everything except the way she made him feel.

"Ryder, you're not paying attention."

He was; wild animals weren't on his mind. She didn't look as though she was thinking about anything except wild animals, and he didn't want to kill the seductive mood.

"They won't hurt us," he told her as he attempted to stay focused. She wasn't making it easy the way she kept pushing her breasts against him. He grew hard just looking at her. He wanted to strip off her clothes and suck on those sexy high-pointed breasts. He would—

She suddenly punched him on the arm.

He jumped, rubbing the spot. She had a pretty good punch for a girl. "What?"

"You're getting aroused and any second a lion could jump out and rip us to shreds? I mean, *really*? All you can think about is sex when we could die at any moment?" Her eyebrows drew together. "Well, probably not you, but I could."

Was that all? He laughed. "All the animals are people friendly. Hunter wouldn't have it any other way."

"Hunter?" She nervously looked around. "Was he here the… the last time? When we were… uh… you know. Is he here now?"

She was such a mix of emotions. Ryder shook his head. "No, but he does visit often. He has an affinity for animals. Most of the ones here are animals he's rescued. Some were neglected, others abused. By bringing them here, he gave them a safe haven. They're fed very well. He communicates with them somehow."

"Good." She breathed a sigh of relief. Her chest rose.

Temptation. He could never resist a sexy woman. He didn't even try. And her breasts called out to be caressed. He rubbed his thumb over one nipple. She moaned. He closed his eyes and took a deep breath before exhaling.

"Ryder!"

"I know exactly what you mean. I want you naked, but we're almost there."

"Don't talk." She pushed him forward. "Just hurry."

Haley might not have discovered herself in a lot of areas, but when it came to sex, she was becoming quite accomplished. It didn't hurt that she had a head start. She'd been quite explicit in her diary. She was about to experience another fantasy.

The water was getting louder. It was a good thing because Ryder didn't know how much longer he could wait.

"What's that sound?" Haley asked.

They came to the clearing. "The waterfall."

He abruptly halted and she plowed into his back. "Next time tell me when you're about to stop in front of me," she began but her words trailed off as she peeked around him. "Oh my."

"Beautiful, isn't it?" The waterfall never failed to amaze him. He doubted he would ever become so callous that he didn't enjoy the breathtaking beauty of the mountain rising up before them, the waterfall spilling crystal clear water into the pond below. The fading sunlight cast the deep blue and red of the sky into the water where it shimmered with an iridescent radiance.

"It reminds me of diamonds falling over the side of the mountain," she whispered as though she might shatter the image.

"It feels even better." He pulled her along with him until they stood at the edge.

"We're going swimming?"

"Skinny-dipping."

She blushed. He grinned. "You wrote about it in your diary."

She grimaced. "How much of that stupid diary did you read?"

"All of it. Every delicious word."

"Oh Lord," she groaned.

From the way her forehead puckered, Ryder knew she desperately tried to remember everything she wrote about. He didn't want her to worry and he knew there was a way he could make her forget all about the diary. He leaned in and nuzzled the side of her neck, sucking on the tender flesh. Haley grabbed his shoulders, a small gasp escaping her lips.

Ryder marveled at the sensitivity of the female body and how quickly a woman could be aroused. One look, one touch in the right place, and a woman would come alive with passion. It was different with Haley. She was so sexually repressed because she'd tried for so long to conform to certain standards that all it took from him was a look, a light touch, a stroke of his hand and she was on fire.

He slipped the last button through her sweater and moved back a half-step. There was something sexy about a woman partially undressed. He enjoyed knowing the best was yet to come.

"You unbuttoned my sweater." Her forehead puckered. "I didn't even notice. Exactly how many garments have you removed?"

"My fair share. But none before ever uncovered anything close to your beauty."

She cocked a disbelieving eyebrow. "And how long did it take you to learn all the bullshit lines?"

He laughed, but stopped when he saw she was totally serious. Would she ever learn to trust others? "Can't it be enough that I can't keep my hands off you? That you steal my breath away every time I look at you?" He slipped her sweater off her shoulders and tossed it toward a rock.

She shook her head, sadness welling in her eyes. "You're only answering a prayer. Creating a fantasy so I'll think I'm attractive. I bet you didn't know that answering my prayer would be so difficult, or you would have run far and fast in the opposite direction."

"You're wrong. I heard you crying that night. Your tears broke my heart. I came because I wanted to help. When I saw you for the first time, I knew my feelings went much deeper." He lightly rubbed her shoulders. Her eyes told him she thought he was still feeding her a line, except she was caught between doubt and the emotions he stirred inside her.

"Don't lie to me," she whispered.

He shook his head. "Never."

"And the…sex?"

A shudder swept through him. "Don't you know how much you tempt me? I want you naked. I can't stand not seeing your beautiful breasts, the thatch of dark curls."

Her pupils immediately dilated.

"I… uh…" She drew in a deep breath. "See what you do to me? You have me stammering like an idiot."

"You have me horny."

Her eyes immediately lowered. "I can see that," she breathed. "Can we make love?"

"I'll get naked if you will." He wanted Haley to remove her own clothes. He wanted her to strip, to become a willing participant. How badly did she want him?

"Another lesson?" she asked.

He nodded.

Her hesitation was brief before she defiantly raised her gaze to meet his. He loved the rebellious streak that occasionally emerged. He wanted to see more of it.

She reached behind and unhooked her bra. There was a brief pause. She had no idea how much that innocent maneuver turned him on. A professional would automatically draw out the moment. Her shyness thrilled him.

Her breasts were free and the bra joined her sweater on the rock. "Beautiful." He stepped closer, running his hands down the sides of her breasts, testing their weight, then brushing his thumbs over the nipples. She gasped.

"How can you not know your breasts are perfect?" he asked.

"Too… too big."

He shook his head, then moved her hands until she held them in hers. "Feel how they fit in your hands. They're just right for a man's mouth." He lowered his head and took one rosy nipple into his mouth. When she would have moved her hands away, he held them in place, his hands covering hers. He moved them so they both massaged.

"This is wrong," she murmured.

He knew she didn't realize that she spoke the words aloud. He raised his head, but for a moment he could only stare at the tight nipple he'd released from his mouth. It beckoned him to suck a little longer. To roll his tongue around it, to tease it with his teeth.

He ached to his very core and almost completely forgot the lesson he was teaching. He drew in a deep breath, waiting for his mind to clear so he could think straight. "Is it wrong to know your body? To have an understanding of what it takes to give and receive pleasure?"

"I was taught it was wrong to touch yourself. You keep…" Her gaze skittered away. "You keep having me touch myself."

With one finger, he tilted her chin and forced her to meet his eyes. "It's never wrong to find pleasure in your body. For centuries society has either embraced or condemned their sexuality. Those who rejected it were weak and afraid. That's not who you are." He brushed his fingers across her nipples. She jerked, automatically leaning a little closer. "You felt good when I touched your nipples."

"Yes."

"Now you touch them."

Her gaze darted around the clearing.

"We're alone, but it wouldn't matter if there were others watching if everyone was a willing participant." He shook his head. "You need to learn that sexual awareness isn't something to be put in a closet or tucked between the mattresses on your bed."

She tilted her head. "My diary was private."

"You never would have shared it."

Her eyes grew round. "Never!"

"Even with a man you cared about?"

"Especially not then. What would he think about me if he read about my fantasies?"

"That he was the luckiest man alive."

Her shoulders slumped. "I can't win against you."

"I don't want there to be a winner or a loser. Making love should be a gift, whether you're giving it to yourself, or to someone else." He raised her hands to her breasts. "Know what pleases you; only then can you show anyone else what makes you feel good."

"I'm not sure I could show someone."

"Would you want to spend the rest of your life with repressed needs?" He shook his head. "That's what's wrong with committed relationships today. Lives are busy. Everyone is working. People start families. They argue over who should take out the trash or pick up the kids. Does it really matter? People forget how to seduce. They forget how it felt to become one. Partnerships break up."

"But what if you've never had someone like that to begin with?"

"You will."

"What if I want you?" She studied his face, waiting for his reaction.

"You only think you do." All nephilim dreaded this moment. The mortals they helped always formed an attachment. It was understandable. They couldn't prevent the bond that grew between them.

Ryder tried to think how he could explain everything, but the words wouldn't come. How did he tell her what would take place when the very thought made his gut twist with dread?

"It won't always be like this, will it?" she asked. "You'll break my heart."

He hesitated. "Someday you'll meet a man who will be exactly what you want. You'll fall in love and have a family."

"You can be that certain?" Her words held a sharp edge, as though she tried desperately to keep her emotions in check. "I'll just meet some guy and he'll fall in love with me." She snapped her fingers. "Just like that. What? You can read the future, too?"

"No, but I promise to watch over you."

"And what will you do after I find Mister Perfect-for-me?"

He knew before he said anything that she wouldn't like what he told her, but she had to know the truth. "I'll go back to answering prayers and trying to make people's lives better."

The color drained from her face. Haley crossed her arms in front of her as tears swam in her eyes.

Ryder couldn't stand seeing her in so much pain. He turned, staring at the waterfall, and for the first time not even noticing the beauty. The only thing he saw was his never-changing life and there wasn't a damn thing he could do about it.

The worst thing about all of it? Haley was right: he would end up hurting her if he wasn't careful. If he stayed much longer, she wouldn't be able to completely erase him from her mind. There would always be something out of kilter in her life.

He wouldn't let that happen. Nor would he let her have regrets about him being in her life. "I'll erase any memory you have of me."

"You can do that?"

But he would have the memory of her, and it might drive him to the brink of madness. "Yes." He'd watched it almost destroy Dillon when Lily chose the wrong path and lost her soul to a demon. But that time was different. Haley wasn't in danger of losing her soul. She wasn't threatened by any monsters, if he didn't count the ones in her own mind.

"Everything we've shared would be gone? I'll remember nothing?"

He faced her again. "Your life will be better. I promise."

"If I don't have my memories of you, how can anything be better?"

A band constricted around his heart. He didn't mean to upset her, only reassure her. The waterfall, the lesson he wanted to show her, all of it was swept to the side as her attention focused on losing him. He moved closer, taking her into his arms. He was glad she didn't reject his touch because he couldn't stand not holding her. "You'll be fine without me."

"No, I won't." She sniffed.

He pressed his lips to the top of her head, inhaling the scent of the apricot shampoo she used.

"How soon before you leave?" she asked.

"A few days. Maybe a week." Angels sometimes stayed a few months, but he knew this assignment wouldn't last much longer. Haley would learn the lessons he wanted to teach her, then she wouldn't need him. "Don't think about the days before I go. Think about all the hours we still have left." He stroked her bare back.

"You'll remember me, won't you?" she suddenly asked.

She asked some hard questions, but he couldn't be anything less than truthful. "I'll always remember you."

She was silent for a moment then sighed deeply. "I was right, you're only answering a prayer." She hurried on before he could speak. "That's okay, I guess. Answering prayers is very noble and I'm sure I will be a better person because you helped me."

"I won't forget you because I don't *want* to forget you," he broke into her rambling. "I've never cared about anyone as much as I care about you."

"Then why are you here when you know it can't last?"

"Because I can't stay away. I want you more than I've ever wanted anything." He'd finally admitted aloud there was something different about Haley. Not that it would change anything. He had no choice except to let her go when the time came.

"I'm nothing. There are women who have a lot more to offer."

He smiled, some of the tension leaving. "You're who I want to be with and we still have lessons," he told her.

"Will it keep you here if I never learn?"

"But you will, and you'll learn well. I'll pleasure you until there are no doubts left. I'll fulfill every fantasy you wrote about until the sexuality you've been hiding is set free." She trembled. As much as she would like to deny her needs, her body betrayed her every time. "Will you let me help you?"

She raised her face. Her bottom lip quivered. "What's the next lesson?"

Chapter 12

IF THEY DIDN'T HAVE much time left together, Haley wanted to make each second count. Ryder said when the time came that he would erase any memory of him, but she didn't think she would ever be able to forget him, no matter what kind of spell he cast.

"What is the next lesson?" she asked again when he didn't answer.

He lightly ran the back of his hand over her cheek. "Take off the rest of your clothes." He turned and walked away.

The guy had a great ass. Tight, firm. She quickly brought her thoughts back when he turned.

"Seduce me," he told her when he faced her again.

It took a moment for his words to sink in. Not that she was a bit surprised. The guy really did have a great ass. Seduce him, though? How was she supposed to do that? It wasn't as though she went around tempting men all the time. She removed his clothes when he wanted her to take control, but she didn't think seducing and practically ripping his clothes off would be the same thing.

"Don't think about it."

"Easy for you to say," she grumbled. All Ryder had to do was look cross-eyed at her and she was his for the taking. With his looks, she doubted he had a problem getting women in his bed. Which brought up a topic she didn't want to think about.

She could do it. Ryder had already removed her top, so that didn't leave much. She drew in a steady breath and reached behind her to unbutton her full skirt.

"I love the way you thrust your chest out. It makes me want to fondle your breasts, take each one in my mouth, and suck on each nipple."

Her thighs clenched. Who seduced whom? Instinctively, she knew the sooner she was naked the sooner he'd make love to her.

She jerked the zipper down. The material ripped, but she didn't care. She didn't like the skirt anyway. She wasn't fond of any of her clothes. If she lost one ugly outfit, it wouldn't make a bit of difference.

When she let go, the skirt puddled at her feet. She was left wearing only her plain white slip, sensible cotton panties, and plain black pumps. Thank goodness the slip hid her ugly underwear.

"Don't stop there," he urged.

Why didn't she have cute underclothes? What she had on wouldn't excite an old man overdosed on Viagra. But she would get through the lesson as she had all the others because if he couldn't help her, he might leave anyway. She didn't know if there were rules he had to follow.

"Haley?"

She'd zoned out again. He leaned back against a boulder and waited patiently for her to seduce him. He was going to be so disappointed. She wasn't a temptress. She might as well get it over with and hoped he wouldn't laugh.

She kicked out of her shoes and pushed her panties and slip down at the same time. She just couldn't let him see her old lady underwear. She would die of embarrassment. She would much rather him see her naked. But when she stood in front of him without a stitch of clothes, Haley found she couldn't look him in the eye.

"That works for me," he mumbled.

Her gaze jerked up as he strode toward her, pulling his T-shirt over his head at the same time. It wasn't humor that glinted in his eyes.

He tossed his T-shirt away and her attention was drawn to his bare chest and all those beautiful muscles on display for her enjoyment.

He reached for the top button on his jeans and pushed it through the hole, then quickly slid the zipper down. He stopped in front of her and took her into his arms, lowering his mouth until their lips met in a searing kiss. His hard chest pressed against her bare breasts. She slid her arms around his waist, slipping her hands inside his jeans as his tongue stroked her.

She didn't wonder where her newfound boldness came from. She wanted Ryder naked, but she would settle for fondling his ass. He groaned when she squeezed his cheeks, ending the kiss as his hands glided over her back.

She pressed closer as he stirred the fire growing inside her, but it wasn't enough. She wanted to see all of him. It was only fair since she was naked. She moved her hands to the waistband of his jeans and shoved them down. The only thing between her body and his was his briefs, but she wasn't about to let a bit of material get in her way.

"Easy, sweetheart, slow down."

"I can't. How can I when I want to see every inch of you? I want to hold you and take you in my mouth." Oh God, that sounded so pathetic. She was supposed to be seducing him, not attacking him!

"You catch on fast." There was a quiver of need in his voice.

She leaned back to make sure he didn't laugh at her lame effort at seduction, but there was only passion in his eyes.

"You think I'm lying." He took her hand and placed it on his cock. "I look at you and all I think about is making love."

She drew in a sharp breath as erotic visions filled her mind. She could almost feel him sliding inside her.

If he did lie, Haley hoped she never learned the truth. With him, she became everything she dreamed of being. She was the woman men turned to stare at. The woman men desired. The seductress.

Her eyes glazed with passion. "I want you," she said. She grew bolder and slipped her fingers into the waistband of his briefs, then tugged them down, releasing him.

"Beautiful," she said breathlessly.

He stepped out of his clothes. Never in her wildest dreams would Haley have ever thought she would stand so close to someone who looked like Ryder. She planned to take advantage of every moment.

She aimed him toward the boulder, not stopping until he leaned against it. She wanted him fairly comfortable since she was going to seduce him. A moment of doubt assailed her, but she quickly dismissed it. She was no longer Haley the frump. The seductress inside had come out to play.

She wrapped her fingers around his thickness. He drew in a sharp breath. He wanted seduction? She would give it to him. "Does that feel good?" She moved her hand down, marveling at the rosy tip.

"You learn fast."

"You're a good teacher." She ran her finger across the end, enjoying the velvety smoothness, massaging the drop of moisture across the tip. Until Ryder came along, touching a man so intimately was only a fantasy in her diary. She wanted to take full advantage of everything he offered. She touched her lips to his nipple, running her tongue over the tight bud. His hips jerked toward her. She was amazed at the power surging through her.

And how brave she'd become. She was discovering passion could break the chains of the puritanical beliefs that had held her captive most of her adult life. Not one of the men she'd had sex with in the past bothered to learn what she desired. The men she slept with only cared about their needs being met, which didn't take that long. Ryder let her experience everything.

She slid her tongue down his chest, circled his navel, then licked across his erection. He gasped. She smiled right before she sucked him inside her mouth.

"Yes, there," he said, drawing in air.

She cupped his balls, lightly massaging while taking him deeper inside her mouth. His breathing was ragged. She sucked harder. His hips rocked.

"Ah," he moaned.

Was he hurt? She released him.

"No, please don't stop." He tangled his fingers in her hair.

He clamped his lips. The muscles in his neck tensed. It wasn't pain she saw on his face, but pleasure. His words only confirmed how much he enjoyed what she was giving him. She licked down the side, then swirled her tongue over the tip before drawing him back in her mouth.

"Yes, right there."

She moved her hand to the base of his penis and rubbed her thumb against him. Her mouth moved over him, up and down, sucking him in deeper, licking and teasing.

"I can't…" he said as he slipped his hand under her arms and pulled her up. He pressed against her, burying his head in her hair. "Don't move or I'll explode," he grated out. He drew in mouthfuls of air.

Instinctively she knew what was happening and pressed closer, wanting to give him the release he craved. He leaned back against the rock.

"You don't know what you're doing," he tried to tell her.

"Yes, I do," she said and wiggled closer. Flames shot down her. For a moment, she didn't move. She didn't realize how aroused she would get from giving him gratification. After a moment, she regained her equilibrium and continued her seductive assault. "Did you enjoy me sucking your cock? I loved every second I had you in my mouth."

"You're killing me," he said. "I need to be inside you."

"Not yet." She squeezed in closer, rubbing her pussy against him.

Excitement rushed through her. "Rubbing myself against you is incredible."

"Yes, that's it." He cupped her ass, rocking against her.

The friction between them rose. Their hips moved in perfect time. She raised her leg until her thigh rested against his hip. Yes, there. She closed her eyes and let the intensity of their movements send spasms of pleasure over her. Their breathing grew labored as the heat built inside her.

He grasped her tighter. Thick, warm liquid washed over her pussy. She grasped his neck, holding tight as the air around her grew so heavy she couldn't draw in a breath. The leaves didn't move on the trees. The sound of the waterfall faded. It was only the two of them.

He increased his movements. She buried her head against his shoulder and continued to rock against him.

"Let the world slip away," he whispered close to her ear. "Focus on my cock rubbing against you, my come making your clit wet. Think about me sliding up and down, massaging your pussy."

She couldn't...she... Pleasure and pain gripped her. Her body clenched as her release came. She drew in a deep breath as though she'd been holding it for a very long time, then exhaled. A tear slipped from the corner of her eye and slid silently down her cheek.

Ryder held her close until her body stopped trembling, the sound of his heartbeat soothing her. The wind rustled through the trees once more. The waterfall tumbled down the side of the mountain and splashed into the pool.

As she returned to Earth, so did the reality of what she'd done. How could she have been so forward? She'd pretty much jerked him off with her body, then used him to masturbate. What the hell was she thinking? No, that was the problem, she hadn't been thinking. Ryder made her feel like a freaking sex goddess, and she wasn't even close. Now she wanted to die of embarrassment. She kept her head buried against his chest, dreading the moment he would look at her and tell her she was slutty. Why oh why had she read so many dirty magazines? She knew they couldn't be good for her. She'd become a pervert.

When he lightly traced his fingers over her back, she jumped. "I'm sorry," she mumbled. "I guess I got a little carried away with the seduction thing." Her face was on fire! How could she ever look at him again?

He laughed. Great, now she felt a lot better.

"You really don't know how incredible you are."

"I'm sick and perverted."

He moved her away until both her feet were planted firmly on the ground. She kept her eyes lowered until she saw the evidence of what she'd done. "I... I..."

"What are you sorry for?" he asked. "That we both experienced one hell of an orgasm? That with your inexperience, you were still creative and fun?"

Doubt filled her, but she wanted to make sure she'd heard right. "I was? You don't think I was too...too aggressive?"

"Sex is all about having fun. As long as no one is hurt in the process and it's between consenting adults, then why not push the envelope?"

He straightened and held out his hand. "Come on."

Her hesitation was brief. He was right and the sex had been incredible. She sighed, knowing he was breaking through her defenses again, but she felt too satisfied to care.

They splashed into the pond. The water was cool, but not ice cold. Haley didn't stop until the water reached her waist.

"Can you swim?" he asked.

She nodded and dove beneath the water, emerging when they were at the side of the waterfall. "This is fantastic," she said over the roar of the waterfall.

"It gets even better." He pulled himself up on the side of the rocks, then stood on the narrow ledge. "I'll help you," he told her and reached his hand toward her.

She didn't pause as she grasped his hand. She marveled at how much she had come to trust him in such a short amount of time. She wished they could stay like this forever, the two of them living at the fantasy retreat.

She stumbled. His grip tightened until she found her footing and joined him on the ledge. "This is magical," she said with awe as he took her behind the waterfall into a cave. The sun captured the water. It sparkled and shone like tiny diamonds falling in front of her. He'd closed them off from the world beyond as if he'd read her thoughts. "I don't think I've ever seen anything quite like it. But then, I've never left Hattersville." Home seemed like a lifetime ago. She absently leaned closer to him, resting her head on his shoulder. He wrapped his arms around her.

"I used to come here and pretend I was behind a protective shield and no one could touch me," he admitted.

"You're immortal. What could ever harm you?"

"I have something else to show you," he said instead.

Haley wondered if he evaded her question intentionally. She decided her imagination was getting the better of her. He probably didn't mean his words literally, and as she glanced around she doubted he could show her anything that would compare to the cave and waterfall. "What could possibly be better than this?"

"Not better, but I think you'll enjoy it."

"Can't we stay here and let the world move on without us?"

"Not when there are still lessons for you to learn."

Despite the fact they just had incredible sex, she felt the passion start to build. "What kinds of lessons?" She attempted to tamp down her rising desire, but when he chuckled, Haley knew she hadn't succeeded.

"New lessons. You've forgotten everything you learned."

She frowned. "What do you mean?"

"You reverted back to your old way of thinking as soon as you left the house."

"It isn't my fault. Monday morning my alarm blasted me back to reality. Only one thing had changed: I no longer wore my glasses. My vision isn't bad enough that I can't see, and the mirror doesn't lie. I'm still a frump."

"You dress frumpy," he clarified.

Her spirits plummeted as he admitted what she'd known all along. "See, you're finally telling me the truth. I can't be helped."

"I didn't say *you're* a frump. Only your clothes."

"I look terrible in everything." She sighed. "My sister tried to help and she couldn't. Alexa tried. My mother attempted a few times. I don't think it's the clothes."

"Your mother and sister are petite. Alexa is willowy. Their styles would never suit you."

She leaned away from him. "Are you saying I'm tall and fat? That really won't help my confidence."

"Sometimes I want to hug you."

A warm glow swept over her.

"And other times I want to strangle you."

Strangle her? It certainly wasn't her fault clothes didn't hang well or look good on her. She was born with her figure. If he wanted to blame someone, he should look at her father's gene pool. She didn't have to put up with his insults! She sniffed and tried to move away but he grabbed her and pulled her close.

"Your family and Alexa honestly try to help, but they've been the worst obstacles in your path."

"Are you going to strangle *them*?"

"That might still be open for discussion if they don't change their ways." He grabbed her hand and started out of the cave.

"The next lesson?" she asked.

"Exactly, but we need to dress."

That was a disappointment, but he didn't seem to notice she wasn't thrilled. When they were dressed and standing on the other side of the pool, he took her in his arms. She snuggled close. That was better.

"Close your eyes."

She smiled and closed her eyes, but the next thing she knew, air whooshed past. She tightened her arms around him. Her stomach lurched. "A little more warning next time would be nice."

"I'll remember that."

"Where are we going?"

"You'll see."

She peeked from beneath lowered lids, but the dancing lights only made her nauseated so she closed them tight once again until everything felt calm and her feet were on solid ground once again.

A car horn honked; someone yelled at a driver asking where he got his license, from a cereal box?

Haley opened her eyes the rest of the way. They stood in a dark alley. "Where are we?" she asked in a low voice.

"Dallas," he proudly proclaimed.

"My next question is why are we in a smelly alley in the middle of Dallas?"

"I can't just pop in wherever I want. Not if I want to keep my identity a secret. Alleys work well. This is what I wanted to show you." He stepped away from her and started walking toward the light.

Good, because the alley was dark and dreary, but there was also something about walking toward the light with an angel that bothered her too—even if he was only half angel. As soon as that thought occurred, a sweet little gray-haired lady stopped on the sidewalk in front of the alley. "Taxi," she called out in a tiny voice and waved with one hand while her other gripped her walker. A small plastic bag had been tied to the handle, celery poking through the opening.

"Taxi," she called again as another yellow cab zoomed past, but it didn't stop either.

Haley's heart went out to her. Why wasn't anyone stopping?

The elderly woman suddenly raised her middle finger and shook it at the next cab that zoomed past. "Motherfucker! Can't you stop and pick up an old woman?" she bellowed.

Haley stumbled back in shock. Did she really just hear the little old lady say *motherfucker*?

Ryder jogged to the sidewalk, put two fingers in his mouth and whistled loud enough that cars slammed on their brakes, almost rear-ending each other. One happened to be a taxi. He ran over and opened the door, then went back to help the old lady with her walker.

"Thank you. You're such an angel." She smiled and patted his hand in a grandmotherly gesture. "I didn't know there were any left."

Ryder grinned. "You'd be surprised."

The old lady would be more than surprised. She'd probably have a heart attack.

When Ryder joined Haley, he said, "You'll like this place."

"I can already see how lovely it is." She nodded to where the old woman had been yelling for a cab.

"She was nice."

"Nice? Really?"

"She was having a bad day."

"You're right. I'm sure she doesn't go around calling people motherfucker every day." Had she just said motherfucker again? Her own grandmother was turning over in her grave.

"You'll like the place we're going."

"What if I don't?"

"This is the next lesson."

"In other words, I don't have a choice." He nodded. She might as well tell him this wasn't her first trip. "I've been to Dallas. Alexa and I drove up for a weekend. I wasn't impressed."

He laughed and pulled her along with him. She gave up trying to explain how Dallas was too big and getting around in the city could be confusing. Instead, she walked beside him until he stopped in front of a shop with dark windows, and past the windows were heavy, dark curtains. The storefront wasn't the most inviting she'd ever seen. It was kind of spooky. What could the owner possibly sell? Something illegal? A shiver of foreboding raced down her spine.

Her gaze stopped on the dark red door and the silver painted sign. Madame Truffle was written across it in elaborately scrolled lettering. Probably not an illegal drug operation. Not that she really thought Ryder would be involved in something unlawful.

The store wasn't that spooky when she stepped closer. It only appeared closed for the evening. But truffles? Why was he bringing her to a closed candy store?

Except when Ryder touched the knob, it turned. They went inside, the door chiming as it closed behind them. Haley glanced around. This wasn't a sweet shop. Her eyes grew round as she stared at the chandelier dripping with crystals. Plush pale blue carpet covered the floor. It was so deep and so soft that she automatically wiggled her toes. She surveyed the rest of the room. Dark blue sofas and white floral print chairs were grouped in two different areas. The furniture was so delicate the pieces looked as though they would break if anyone sat on them.

There were bold hats on shelves, scarves draped artistically on antique tables. A glass case showcased enough bling to be in direct competition with the crystal chandelier. Her gaze skipped around the room, taking everything in. Clothes were displayed on gold-plated racks. They weren't jammed on them like some of the places where she shopped. There couldn't have been more than eight padded hangers on each rack.

Cold shivers raced up and down her spine. She'd never been inside a high-end store like this one, and she didn't want to be in one now. "I don't belong here," she frantically whispered, scooting behind him. "I'm small-town Hattersville. This isn't even close to small town."

"Too late," he said.

Two women in their mid-sixties with silvery gray hair came around the corner. They each carried an extra thirty pounds of weight, but they did so with grace and plenty of style. There was also no mistaking that they were twins. The similarity between them was too much like seeing double, and at the moment they were arguing.

"I told you to lock the door," one said.

"Today is an even number." The other shook her head. "You were supposed to lock up."

She sighed. "You're right. It was my turn."

Haley scooted behind Ryder. What could he be thinking bringing her to this place? The women coming toward them were dressed exactly alike and very elegantly in beige slacks and beige jackets. The gold tops they wore under their jackets were shot through with gold thread so that every time the light caught them, they shimmered with an iridescent glow. The two women were stylish and chic.

"This isn't a candy store," she nervously told him, tugging on the back of his shirt. She wanted to die! She'd been swimming in a pond. Her hair was still damp and clumped together. Her clothes were rumpled and she'd forgotten to put on her shoes.

"They're two of the best clothing designers in the country."

"I'm going to puke," she groaned.

"Trust me."

No, she didn't want to trust him.

"I told Aggie I heard the door, but I could've sworn I'd locked up. Now I'm glad I didn't. It's been way too long since you've been to our shop, Ryder."

"My apologies," he said. "Maria, it *has* been too many years."

Her eyes narrowed. "And yet, you look as though you haven't aged a bit."

"And who is that hiding behind you?" Aggie asked.

"A friend," he told them, then nudged Haley until she was forced to step forward.

"Oh." Aggie took a step back, her eyes round. She grabbed her sister's arm for support.

"Can we leave?" Haley pleaded.

Maria bumped her sister with her elbow. "You've frightened the poor girl."

"I think I scared *her*," Haley admitted, then lowered her head.

Aggie cleared her throat. "Nonsense. I haven't been frightened in years. You startled me."

Maybe a hole would open up and she could crawl inside. She'd never felt so humiliated in all her life. The one called Aggie, with her honest first impression, had voiced what Haley had always thought—she was a hopeless case. Why had Ryder bothered answering her prayer?

"Haley would like for you to help with her wardrobe dilemma," Ryder explained to break the awkward silence.

"Can we leave?" Haley whispered. "This is a waste of time." But rather than whisk them away, Ryder merely squeezed her hand.

Aggie visibly relaxed. "Is that all? Of course we can help."

"I agree," Maria reinforced her sister's words.

Haley raised her chin, determined to see this through. "You're both very kind, but you don't need to lie. I know you mean well, but no one can help me." Not even an angel, although Ryder tried and she really did appreciate his efforts.

Maria stepped forward and took Haley's hand before she could protest. "You can leave her with us," she pointedly told Ryder, then skimmed her gaze over Haley. "You can come back in three hours. No, better make it five."

Haley turned to Ryder, eyes pleading with him not to leave her, but either he didn't interpret her silent message or chose to ignore her.

Ryder let go of Haley's hand and cast a reassuring smile in her direction.

"Trust me. You'll love the sisters." He left before she had a chance to think of anything to say that would keep him there.

"Come along, we don't have much time." Aggie whirled around.

Maria pulled Haley along with them. What was it with people dragging her places? Did they think she'd run the other way? When she thought about it, that might not be such a bad idea. The two sisters should think about doing the same.

They continued through an area with several doors and a large mirror. The dressing room, she guessed. There were no fewer than three sofas. On an ornately carved coffee table sat a clear crystal bowl filled with silver-wrapped candies. So there *were* sweets connected to the store name. She supposed they were truffles. How appropriate. She never felt more like a loser.

A door at the back of the room blended in so well that Haley wouldn't have known it was there if Aggie hadn't pushed on the panel. Maria continued to drag Haley along with her. There was no escaping. The two women acted as though they were on a mission. They didn't know the war was over before they ever started.

The back room was the complete opposite of the front areas. Every imaginable shade and style of clothing hung from several iron racks that were pushed against both sides of the room. Bolts of fabric were stacked on tables and strewn haphazardly over cushioned chairs. Carpet covered the floor, but in a neutral beige shade. Another table was littered with papers and color swatches. Haley couldn't help being startled by the difference.

The sisters stopped, both looked at her, then smiled at each other. "It's quite a change from the front rooms," Aggie said.

"We didn't want our ideas in competition with what we've

created up front," Maria continued. "It starts up here." She tapped her head. "We have to see it in our mind before we can sketch it on paper."

"Oh." Haley supposed it made sense. What she couldn't understand was why they would even bother with her.

"We like a challenge," Maria said as if she read Haley's mind.

"And Ryder pays very well."

"He'll have to," Haley said with wry sarcasm.

Maria and Aggie chuckled. She was glad they saw humor in the situation. They would need it before they were through trying to find a style that would suit her. She should explain that some lost causes aren't meant to be found.

"First things first," Aggie said, clapping her hands. "Tape measure, paper, pen." She went to one of the tables and hunted for the tools of her trade.

"And second," Maria chimed in, "please remove your clothes. The saleslady who sold you those horrible rags should be shot." She went behind a partition then returned looking quite satisfied.

"You want me to strip?" Haley asked, hoping she'd misunderstood. Her mortification would be complete if she hadn't.

Aggie rejoined them, apparently having located everything she needed. "Behind the partition," she began.

"Is a blue silk robe," Maria finished. "Everything off so we can get measurements."

She breathed a sigh of relief. Not completely naked then. She stepped behind the partition. As she removed her clothes, she thought about how wonderful her life would be if they could at least make her presentable. Haley had no misguided notions that she would ever be pretty, but she would settle for presentable.

She slipped her arms into the silk robe. The softness against her skin was like nothing she'd ever felt. She could learn to like silk. On the other side of the screen, the sisters were talking and starting to sound a little impatient so she belted the robe tight around her waist and came around the screen.

They stared at her long enough she began to fidget. Didn't they know she couldn't help the way she looked?

"This is what you were hiding beneath those tacky clothes?" Aggie said when she finally raised her eyes. Her eyes were wide and the expression on her face was one of disbelief.

For a moment Haley wondered if the robe might be transparent. It wasn't, but the silk material did mold to her body.

"Stunning," Maria said.

The sisters weren't that bad. They seemed rather nice and they were trying to help. Haley hated to tell them age might have caught up to them because they needed to have their eyes checked. She was not and would never be stunning.

"She doesn't see it," Aggie said with surprise.

"I believe you're right," Maria said with just as much surprise.

Poor Ryder. Haley knew he counted on the sisters to help, but she had a feeling he would be very disappointed.

Chapter 13

HALEY WAS MEASURED IN places she had no idea needed to be measured. The sisters turned her every which way but upside down and Haley was afraid they were thinking long and hard about doing that, too. She was poked and prodded until she wanted to cry uncle! Nothing they did would help, so why go through all this torture?

Maria raised a strand of Haley's hair as if it might have something crawling in it. "What in the world have you been doing?"

"We went swimming," Haley muttered.

"Of course, dear," Aggie said and patted her hand, then looked at her sister. "We need help."

"Einstein?"

Haley had finally managed to push one of the sisters over the edge. "He's dead," she told Maria, then looked at Aggie with pity. "Maybe you better take your sister to the doctor." Or a psychiatrist might be better, but she didn't want to scare either one of them.

Maria and Aggie's foreheads puckered, then their eyes rounded and they began to laugh. A light, musical sound, much like the chimes on the front door of their shop.

"Einstein is a beautician. One of the best. He'll do wonders with your... hair," Aggie told her, looking quite sane.

Haley wondered who in their right mind would name their child Einstein, and did she want him doing anything to her hair? She picked up a clump of hair that was drying and decided it didn't really matter if he shaved her head.

Maria whipped out a cell phone from her jacket pocket and speed-dialed Einstein. "Einstein, Maria here." A worried expression settled on her face when she focused on Haley. "I have a job for you. No, no, nothing that will take that long." She nibbled her bottom lip.

Haley raised her eyebrows, her gaze meeting Maria's. Maria only shrugged one shoulder. The woman was lying through her teeth.

Maria continued. "At the shop. Yes, now. It's not really that late. I can order from Alberto's. Yes, I know he only does reservations, but he'll put something together for me. He's a very good friend. Yes, all your favorites."

Maria looked at Haley and Aggie, then rolled her eyes and mouthed *diva*. Aggie delicately covered her mouth to stifle her laughter. Haley wondered what she was letting herself in for with this Einstein guy.

Maria suddenly stilled. "The blue silk cape. Yes, just in from France." She lost a little of her rosy glow. "But you know what it took to get it here. That cape came from the countess's own collection." She shook her head at something Einstein must have said. "It's not the cost, darling."

Aggie raised a clump of Haley's hair and cast a silent imploring plea toward Maria.

"Okay, if you insist, but I expect something absolutely stunning in return. Yes, hurry. Yes, I'll order from Alberto's." She looked upward and shook her head. "See you soon, love." She slipped her phone back into her jacket pocket.

Aggie was already speaking on the phone with Alberto when Maria smiled at Haley. "You'll love Einstein. That isn't his real name, by the way. He's such a prima donna, but he's also a fabulous hairdresser. You'll never meet anyone better."

"But it cost you the cape." She didn't want anyone forced to part with something they so obviously cared about.

"Pfft, that old rag? The countess was in dire financial straits. At one time, she was a very good customer. The color is much too bright. Einstein has been salivating since he discovered we bought her collection."

"Remember the pink chiffon?" Aggie said as she joined the conversation.

Maria smiled wistfully. "The ball gown we created."

Aggie sighed. "She was the darling of the party."

"But then her husband ran off with her maid, took all her money, and the countess discovered he'd spent almost every penny of her vast fortune." Maria pursed her lips.

"We took the blue silk cape off her hands, along with a few more items we want to redesign. We paid four times what everything was worth," Aggie told her.

"But she was a very good customer."

"I hear she met a prince last week," Aggie told Maria. "He has money."

A calculating gleam sparkled in Maria's eyes. "See, Aggie, I told you it's best never to forget a customer. Especially one as pretty as the countess. I knew she would land on her feet. We'll start designing her wedding dress next week."

"Very good idea, sister."

Haley wondered if she might have hit her head or fallen down a rabbit hole. None of this seemed real. She had never met anyone who might remotely know royalty. But then, she'd never met a nephilim until a few days ago.

The sisters moved to one of the tables. Aggie picked up a sketch pad, then studied Haley. After only a few seconds passed, Aggie began to draw something on the paper. "What about this?"

Maria nodded. "But lose the ruffle."

"Good idea. She's not the frilly type." She erased something on the paper. "Color?"

"Green. But not pale. Something bold." She squinted her eyes. "Or red. Deep red. Almost maroon."

"Yes, you're right," Aggie agreed. "Nothing washed out like that horrid pink."

Haley had known the pink didn't look good on her, but once again she'd caved under pressure.

Maria turned and picked up a large ring with squares of colorful material. She chose a deep emerald green, then both women marched over to Haley. She knew exactly how animals in a zoo must feel.

Maria held the material against Haley's cheek. "See how it brings out the green in her eyes."

"Breathtaking," Aggie said. She flipped the squares until she came to a swatch of red, then shook her head. "Not strong enough." She flipped past more shades of red, then stopped and brought another color to Haley's cheek.

"Yes, this is wonderful against her skin. She would be magnificent in red."

Haley had a feeling both sisters needed their eyes examined. Before she could gently explain they didn't need to lie, the door was flung open. All three women jumped.

"Einstein is here!" the man announced in a theatrical voice.

A man of small stature stood in the doorway. At least Haley thought he was a man. It was hard to tell. He was dressed in wild pinks. His boots were pink, his sequined pants were pink, his blousy shirt was pale pink and he wore a large hat with a long fluffy pink feather. He'd finished his costume off with a pink rhinestone-studded cape which he dramatically swept off and folded across one arm. Einstein was a cross between Liberace, Elton John, and Lady GaGa.

"And by the way, darlings, you left your door unlocked again. Did you forget we live in the city?"

That was who would be working on her hair? She took an

involuntary step back. Maria and Aggie grabbed her arms to hold her in case she decided to make a run for it, which wasn't a bad idea.

"Where is she?" His gaze scanned the room.

"This is Haley," Maria and Aggie pronounced at the same time. Maria continued. "The girl I told you about."

"Eghh!" Einstein's hand flew up to cover his mouth. He began to hyperventilate, his face turning bright red. "Oh... I... no... it's impossible." He shook his head. "I need air."

Haley wrapped her arms around her middle and frowned. "No, tell me what you really think," she muttered.

"Shh, dear," Aggie whispered. "He must have his dramatics, but he's worth it."

Haley didn't think so, but she kept her lips clamped together. She was going to kill Ryder. How could he subject her to this kind of humiliation? He was supposed to build her confidence, not destroy it.

Two men came up behind Einstein. Haley wondered if he brought reinforcements until she noticed the black bags with bold yellow letters that read Alberto's.

"The front door was open," the taller of the two said.

Einstein jumped, slapping a hand to his chest. "See, anyone can waltz in and kill us all!"

"It's only the food I ordered," Maria proclaimed.

Einstein sniffed, then shook his head. "I can't eat. My appetite is ruined."

Give me a break!

Aggie rushed over and slipped the two delivery men some money, then motioned for them to set the bags on one end of a table. As soon as they began to unload the bags, Maria lifted one of the lids from a glass-covered dish. "Ricotta and fig canapés."

Einstein raised his chin. "I can't be bought with...food," he exclaimed, but his nose twitched when he inhaled.

Maria quickly set the lid on the table and removed another one. She closed her eyes and inhaled. "Spaghetti and those tiny Italian meatballs you adore. See, I ordered all your favorites."

Einstein examined his nails. "Garlic breadsticks? The soft kind?"

"Of course. How could you think I would forget? And I had Alberto add tiramisu for dessert."

"Tiramisu?" He sashayed across the room to the table, nose stuck in the air.

The waiter removed a china place setting from another satchel, then carefully arranged gleaming silverware next to it while the other waiter removed the cork from a bottle of wine and poured some into a glass. Alberto's gave new meaning to the phrase take-out. It sure beat burgers and fries.

"Maybe I'll just have a peek." Einstein stopped at the end of the table, practically drooling over the feast laid before him. He looked at Haley, back at the food, then Haley. His lip curled while he debated attempting the impossible by doing something with Haley's hair and the delicious food. "I guess I can try."

"Wonderful!" Maria and Aggie said in unison.

"I'll need help, though," he added.

Aggie and Maria hesitated, then Maria spoke up. "We can help."

Einstein carefully laid his cape over a chair, then waited for one of the waiters to pull his chair out so he could sit. "I don't think so, ladies." He picked up a canapé and popped it into his mouth, moaning in delight as he chewed. After swallowing, he daintily patted his lips with the red linen napkin. "I need someone who knows what they're doing. No offense, of course." He reached in his front pocket and brought out a jewel encrusted phone. His fingers moved with lightning speed across the face before he brought it to his ear. "You're needed at Madame Truffle's shop. An emergency. Bring the works." He hung up without apparently waiting for a reply and returned to his food.

"This is going to take longer than five hours," Aggie murmured.

"A lifetime wouldn't be long enough." Haley sighed.

"You haven't seen Einstein at work." Maria fairly glowed with excitement.

The sisters didn't wait for him to finish eating but rather continued draping Haley in expensive fabrics. "Will you be going anywhere special?" Aggie asked.

Haley thought for a moment. "The Old Settler's Reunion is this weekend."

The sisters looked at each other with puzzled expressions. "What is an Old Settler's Reunion?" Maria asked.

She shrugged. "A rodeo, crafts on the courthouse lawn, parades, a country dance. That sort of stuff."

"They have a rodeo in Fort Worth, sister," Aggie said.

"It smelled bad so we left before it started. We're originally from New York."

"Oh, that would explain the accent. I'm from a small town in Texas—Hattersville."

"Hattersville?" Einstein asked, dragging his attention away from his meal. "You're from Hattersville?"

"Yes."

"I went through there once. I grew up in Coyote. It's even smaller than Hattersville." His expression turned sad and his thoughts seemed to drift away from them. "The outcast," he murmured. "The one people talk about when they think you don't hear, but you do. The one without a date for the prom. You feel as though you're skirting the edge of living." He waved his hand in front of his face, blinking rapidly. "Oh, I know the pain you've suffered!" He brought his napkin to his eyes and dabbed at the moisture. "I can't eat anymore," he declared as he came to his feet. The waiters began to gather the dishes. "A to-go box, if you please." He rolled his eyes as though they should have known that already.

Einstein strutted over to Haley, pulled out a pair of jeweled reading glasses, and examined her hair. "It won't be easy, but I can do something with this… this rat's nest. What did you do? Go swimming and come straight here?"

"She's with Ryder," Aggie explained.

"Ryder? Our Ryder?" He fanned his hand in front of his face again. "Why didn't you say that in the first place?"

Two women chose that moment to walk into the room. Each carried a large bag. "The door was unlocked." They gave a bored shrug at the same time.

More doubts rose inside Haley. The two young women couldn't have been more than seventeen and they were stick thin. Black eyeliner and purple lipstick made them look more like they were ready for Halloween than work. When they saw Haley, their eyebrows shot up.

"There's a problem, ladies?" Einstein asked.

"Not at all. Where would you like us to set up?"

For the next few hours, Haley felt as though she was being run through a wringer washer. The two women, who she learned were called Leslie and Julia, washed her hair then combed out the tangles. They tugged and pulled until Haley thought she would scream.

Einstein took over before she freaked totally out, using a paintbrush to apply goop he'd concocted in the bathroom. The stuff smelled horrible. It was all she could do to breathe. He wrapped strands of her hair in foil, then after all that he put a plastic bag over her hair.

Then it was the sisters' turn. They brought out the swatches again, Maria taking notes. She finally nodded and met Aggie's gaze. "This should do it. I'll be right back." She hurried out of the room.

Ryder, where are you!

"Anyone here?" Ryder's voice boomed from the front room as though he'd heard her silent prayer.

"Don't come to the back!" everyone yelled at once.

Haley glanced longingly at the door. She was tired of having her hair pulled, painted, and foiled. She was tired of the sisters measuring and draping. She wanted to go back to the retreat and not worry that she would never measure up to society's standard.

"I'll entertain him," Einstein jumped out of the chair he lounged in and hurried toward the door. "Besides, someone has to lock the front door before we're all murdered by an intruder." He shuddered.

"Do not forget about her hair," Aggie warned.

"I'm a professional, darling, I would never forget anything having to do with hair. Besides, I have a good fifteen minutes." He hurried out the door. "Ryder, hellooooo," he sang out.

"Do I need to be worried?" Haley asked.

Einstein's assistants snickered before quickly turning their attention back to sorting out the next round of products he would need.

"He's harmless," Aggie patted her hand. Her forehead wrinkled. "I think."

Now she felt better. Yeah, right!

Maria emerged from a closet with clothes draped across one arm and an array of scarves across another. Looped over three fingers on each hand were bags, each stuffed which what Haley assumed was more clothes.

"I think we have enough to start with," Maria said with a smile twinkling in her eyes.

Aggie took all but one bag which Maria handed to Haley. "Try this on."

Whatever was in the bag would not transform her, but if it would make the sisters happy, Haley would try it on. They had really tried to help her. She slipped behind the screen, her curiosity aroused. The bag was ultra light. What could possibly be inside? She dumped the contents onto the small table and had her answer.

"You've got to be kidding me." She lifted the blazing-red thong and the matching padded bra that was not going to keep her girls in. Padded? Really? She didn't need extra padding.

"Do they fit?" Aggie called out.

"I doubt it," she answered.

"You have to at least try them on," Maria told her.

The thong looked painful. What was she going to do? The sisters worked so hard and had their hopes so high that Haley had to at least try everything on. So what if she looked like a fool? It wouldn't be the first time.

She slipped out of the robe, tossing it on the table. She grimaced when she had the thong in place. There was something to be said about sensible cotton panties. The bra was next. She was right—too small. She pushed on her breasts and tugged on the material but her boobs refused to go all the way into the cups.

"How does everything fit?" Aggie asked with a note of impatience.

"Too small," she called out.

"Nonsense. I measured everything perfectly." She stepped around the screen, followed by Maria.

Now Haley was sure she would die of embarrassment. She could feel the heat exploding over her body.

"Oh dear, we've made her blush." Aggie's hands fluttered.

"Just think of us as your grandmothers," Maria said. "We don't really have all the time in the world and modesty needs to be tossed out the window." Her gaze studied Haley. "They fit fine."

"You're joking."

"I don't joke about clothes. It's my business." She looked at her sister. "Where's the dress, Aggie?"

"I forgot." She hurried away, but returned before Haley could take another breath, which might not be a bad thing since she was afraid if she took too deep a breath she would pop out everywhere.

Maria took the red dress and both sisters held it open so Haley could step into it. "No slip?"

"Not with this dress," Maria explained. "Less is better."

"Since you're with Ryder, we decided a bold red suited better," Aggie said.

Haley wondered about her comment but didn't have much time to dwell on it as they pulled the dress over her hips then helped her to slip her arms inside. The dress was beautiful, but where would she wear something so fancy? Aggie zipped the back. Haley glanced down. The bra pushed her breasts up so they practically spilled out.

"Where's the rest of the dress?" They looked offended she would ask such a question. "I mean, isn't there a jacket?" They didn't say a word. "A scarf?" She sighed. "This is it?"

"I'm back," Einstein called out.

She breathed a sigh of relief. Maybe her ordeal would soon be over. She really needed to see Ryder.

"What do you think of our design?" Aggie asked.

"The dress is gorgeous." At least that wasn't a lie. It was just a mistake to put it on her.

The sisters smiled. Haley was glad they were pleased.

"The shoes," Maggie exclaimed. "We forgot the shoes." She hurried away, returning a few moments later with a pair of red stilettos.

Haley eyed them warily. "They look dangerous."

"You'll do fine," Aggie told her and helped her slide them on.

She took a tentative step, then another. The heels were more comfortable than they appeared. They probably cost more than she made in a year. She frowned, wondering how much money angels made.

"Hurry, ladies, Ryder won't wait much longer and I still have to finish working my magic," Einstein said from the other side of the partition.

At the mention of Ryder, her pulse skipped a beat. She missed him, and they had only been apart a few hours. What would a lifetime feel like? Her throat clogged. Ryder promised to erase her memories of him. Would it be that easy? She didn't think so. She didn't want to ever forget this time in her life. She'd started living the moment he rang her doorbell.

She walked around the partition behind the sisters, but when she heard a collective sigh from Einstein and his assistants, she looked up and saw shocked surprise on their faces.

"I applaud Ryder for being able to see what was so well hidden. If you were the right gender, I'd jump your bones," Einstein said with the thickest drawl Haley had ever heard. Her surprise must have shown because he continued. "It took a long time and a number of tutors to get rid of the accent. Sometimes old habits die hard."

Haley grinned. Einstein was starting to grow on her. "The dress is wonderful."

He returned her smile. "Oh honey, you don't know the half of it. Now sit." He patted a chair. "Leslie, Julia, moisturizers, sponges, brushes. Hurry, hurry."

"I never wear anything except lipstick," she told him.

"Hush your mouth, child. I'm going to give you a line of my products and you *will* use them. Wearing no moisture in Texas is a sin and you will never ever go out without it again." He paused. "Agreed?"

"Agreed." All this niceness was starting to make her insides mushy.

He nodded and went to work. After helping her slip on a jacket to protect the dress, he rinsed her hair and wrapped it in a towel. Makeup followed. When he finished with the creams, foundation, a light dusting of powder, and eye makeup, Einstein had her pout and he applied a deep red lipstick.

But then he grabbed his scissors. She held her breath as he raised strands of her hair and snipped it with his scissors. He must have noticed her look of fear because he said, "Don't worry, you're in the hands of an expert stylist. Ryder will be trailing after you like a lovesick puppy."

Haley still couldn't calm her nerves and reached toward her hair, but Einstein casually brushed it away. "We still have work to do.

Leslie, blow dryer." His demeanor instantly changed as he held out his hand, palm up. Leslie slapped the blow dryer in his hand. "Julia, round styling brush." He held out his other hand and the brush magically appeared when Julia anticipated what he would be using.

For the next forty minutes, Einstein worked in silence. Haley grew to respect his two assistants. They had everything ready before he asked. She also realized they were probably around her age.

"My best masterpiece," Einstein finally pronounced, stepping back. "Well, am I a genius or what?"

Maria and Aggie clapped their hands. Leslie and Julia bowed to the master hairstylist. Haley was sure her hair looked better. She only wished she could do everything justice.

"She has doubts," Einstein said and tossed his scissors to the table where they landed with a clatter. "She does not believe I could transform her."

"You did," his assistants cried.

"A true work of art," Aggie said.

"None of it matters." He dropped into the nearest chair and slumped forward.

She'd insulted him. After he'd worked so hard. "I'm sorry," she told him, wondering how she could make it up to him.

"A mirror," Maria quickly interjected. "How can she believe if she can't see the results of the magic you created?"

"I have one," Leslie volunteered and grabbed a compact out of one of the bags. She opened it and waved it in front of Haley's face.

An eye flew across the mirror, there were her red lips, wisps of hair—good Lord, she felt like a Picasso.

"Too small," Aggie grumbled. "You're making the poor child dizzy." She hurried to a walk-in closet and opened the door. A moment later, she lugged out a full-length mirror on rollers. Maria rushed to help. When they had it positioned exactly where they wanted, they motioned for Haley to join them.

She loved that they were all so enthusiastic, and she would try hard not to disappoint them when she faked her reaction. She stepped in front of the mirror.

Nothing could have prepared her for the image of the woman who stared back.

Chapter 14

HALEY GLANCED OVER HER shoulder, but no one else stood behind her. "It's a trick mirror," she said. What a cruel game. The woman staring back at her was ravishing. Her hair was streaked with different shades of blonde, the smoky eye shadow gave her an air of mystery, and the dress was beyond anything Haley could have imagined. The neck was rounded and exposed more cleavage than she would ever be comfortable showing. When she moved slightly, the slit on the side of the dress revealed a sexy thigh. The stilettos only added to the allure.

Ryder stepped behind her, resting his hands on her waist. He was handsome in a dark suit. The cowboy was gone, and in his place was a very polished man. Their image could have come from the cover of a magazine for the rich and famous.

But who was the woman standing beside him? Haley felt the warmth of his fingers and knew it was her waist he touched, but the connection didn't quite reach her brain.

"You're exquisite," Ryder told her. "Just like I've been telling you all along. You were pretty before the hair and makeup, before the new clothes, but you couldn't see it."

"It's really me?"

He nodded.

"It doesn't feel like me."

"The image has to catch up to your brain."

She shook her head. The woman in the mirror copied the movement, her hair shimmering. "I'm not sure my brain will ever connect with this. What will people think? How do I act?" She drew in a breath. "I'm scared," she whispered.

"I'm still here. I'll help you."

Maria and Aggie rushed over, Aggie's words pouring out. "We've boxed up some new clothes that will fit, and Ryder has ordered a lot more. We even have clothes for your weekend festivities. That wasn't easy, but we managed to locate something. We'll discard the dreadful clothes you were wearing."

For once, Maria had nothing to say. She gave Haley a quick hug and stepped back, dabbing at her eyes with a tissue she pulled from her jacket pocket.

Einstein beamed. "You give 'em hell in Hattersville. For me." He handed her a bag. "Some cosmetics to take with you. My card is in there if you have any questions, but for you, I had Leslie jot down step by step instructions on how to apply everything."

Haley felt like Dorothy from the *Wizard of Oz* when she's about to return to Kansas. "Thank you so much for everything. Words cannot tell you what I feel. It's very overwhelming." She glanced at the woman in the mirror. It *was* only an illusion. Right?

"Are you ready?" Ryder asked.

Dazed, she nodded.

"Someone will come for the packages," he told the sisters. "Only the best would do, that's why I brought Haley here. I wasn't wrong." He slipped his hand under Haley's elbow and they left.

When they were out the front door, there was a black limo parked next to the curb. A chauffeur standing next to the car straightened, but when his gaze landed on Haley, he froze. His gaze slowly moved over her before he visibly swallowed.

"Leonard," Ryder said.

"Oh, sorry, sir." He rushed to open the door.

"For us?"

"For you," Ryder corrected. "I thought since we're here and all dressed up, we might go out to eat. I don't believe I've ever taken you on a real date. It's about time I did."

Warmth flowed through her, sending a rush of exhilaration with it. Cinderella could not have felt any more special than Haley did right now. She moved into the limo, but as she slid across the seat the slit in her dress parted, showing a long expanse of leg. She quickly pulled the sides together, glancing up as she did. Both men's gazes were riveted on her.

"Ryder?"

He cleared his throat. "Thank you, Leonard," Ryder told the chauffeur as he climbed in.

"No, thank you, sir. I mean, ma'am." He coughed. "Yes, sir." He closed the door and hurried to the driver's side.

"Is he okay?" Haley asked.

"He'll survive."

Haley couldn't understand what had gotten into them, but the same thing happened when the valet opened their door and she scooted out. It was as though his brain stopped working. It happened again when they went inside the restaurant.

Their odd behavior didn't detract from Haley's awe at the elegance of the restaurant. The lighting was low, creating a warm, cozy ambience. They were led to a table overlooking the Trinity. The lights from the city sparkled on the water.

"None of this feels real."

"Give it time."

"People are acting funny."

He smiled. "How?"

"Leonard, for one. I thought he might have swallowed his tongue."

"Physically impossible."

"Huh?" She shook her head. He was changing the subject. "And the valet, then the maître d', and the waiter. It's as though they've lost their abilities to function normally."

"You really don't know, do you?"

"Know what?" She felt as though everyone around her knew the punch line to a joke except her.

"Just how attractive you are. There is no competition. The men are acting funny because they're infatuated with your beauty."

"That was really me in the mirror?"

He nodded.

"I thought you might have put a spell on it. You know, like you touched up the pictures?"

"I didn't change the pictures I took. Those were you, but I couldn't make you see how exquisite you really are."

Cold chills popped up on her arms. She rubbed her palms over them. All her life she'd dreamed of being beautiful and having everyone looking at her in awe. She wasn't so sure she liked all the attention she was getting. When she glanced around the room, people quickly averted their eyes, as though they didn't want to be caught staring. She felt like a fish in a glass tank. An exotic fish that people wanted to admire, even though they had no idea what kind of person she really was. As far as they knew, she could be a monster on the inside. It didn't seem to matter to them.

"Isn't this what you prayed for?"

Her gaze met his. "I thought it was what I wanted."

"Do you want to go back to the way you were?"

She thought about the old Haley. The one who sat at home every weekend. Einstein had said something about giving people hell. She wasn't sure she wanted to do that, either. "I'm all mixed up. I don't know who I am." She folded her hands and rested them on the table.

He reached across and took them in his. "You've kept the real Haley hidden all these years. She's just starting to emerge, and the woman you were is frightened."

"Do I have multiple personalities?"

"You need to learn who the real Haley is."

"What if no one likes her?"

"What matters most is if you like her."

"The sensuous woman. The one who has the naughty thoughts and writes about her fantasies in a diary." She sighed. "I have a feeling that one will get me into a lot of trouble in Hattersville."

"Which is better, being the woman you are or pretending to be someone you're not?"

"I've kept her a secret for a long time."

"It's time you set her free."

"And you'll help me."

"I will."

Their conversation stopped when the waiter brought over a bottle of wine. "The wine you ordered, sir." He poured some in Ryder's glass. Ryder swirled the liquid around, then tasted it. When he nodded, the waiter poured Haley's wine, then added to Ryder's glass.

The meal that followed was like nothing she'd ever experienced. From the creamy soup, to the main course, to the dessert that melted in her mouth. She sighed with satisfaction when they returned to the limousine.

"Now for the next lesson," he said.

She snuggled close to him, resting her head against his shoulder. "What would that be?" she asked, stifling a yawn. Three glasses of wine had made her a little tipsy, and sleepy.

"I want you to see how sensuous you are."

That sounded as if it had possibilities.

"By stripping," he continued. "I know a club that only caters to the wealthy. It's very upscale."

He might as well have thrown a bucket of ice water over her. "You're kidding!" She scooted away from him. The passing lights of a store caught his expression. He didn't look as if he joked. "In front of people?"

"Trust me."

She shook her head. "I don't think so."

"Have you forgotten our deal? The one about obeying."

No, she hadn't. But stripping?

The limousine pulled up next to the curb. A doorman hurried to open their door. Haley began to tremble as she read the discreet sign above the door: MEN'S NIGHT OUT. He really wanted her to remove all her clothes in front of strangers. Ryder wasn't teasing.

He climbed out of the car, then held his hand out for her. "Haley? What will it be?"

She knew exactly what he meant. The decision was hers and hers alone. Would she obey or tell him this was the end of the road for her? But was his threat real?

"Did you lie when you told me you couldn't stay away?" she asked, testing the boundaries.

His expression turned sad. "Sooner or later, I will leave. It's not a choice I get to make. You have to decide if the time has come to say good-bye."

She opened her mouth, but the words wouldn't come. Even if it meant only a few more hours, then she would take what she could get. She kept silent, taking his hand. "If I die of embarrassment, it'll be on your head," she muttered as she slid out of the car and stood. When the doorman hurried to open the door to the club, she held her head high and marched inside because she wasn't ready to give any of it up. She wasn't ready to let go of Ryder.

The inside didn't look like what she imagined a strip club to look like. An elegant, winding staircase led to the next story. The floor was marble. The lighting subdued. A man wearing a dark suit stood behind a podium, much like the man at the restaurant.

He looked up, his gaze quickly assessing. Apparently, they met with his approval because he nodded. "Right this way."

"Backstage," Ryder said.

He didn't blink an eye but Haley could feel the heat creeping up her face. She was pretty sure she knew what "backstage" entailed.

"Very good choice," he said as if Ryder had chosen a bottle of expensive wine.

He motioned for them to follow, then walked down a long hall. Haley's heels clicked on the surface, echoing loudly. Her mind screamed at her to end it all, but her feet kept moving.

They turned a corner, and the man stopped in front of a door and pushed a button. They could have been going to a party or visiting a friend. It all looked so normal. Except she knew better.

A young woman wearing a black uniform opened the door, casting a cursory look in Haley's direction before turning her attention to the man in the dark suit.

"A guest," he said.

"I'll see she's made welcome." She opened the door wider. There was a dark curtain behind her so Haley had no idea what awaited her. The woman took her hand, smiled softly, then lightly pulled her forward.

"I'll see you soon," Ryder said.

"You're leaving?" A tremble of fear swept over her.

The woman squeezed Haley's hand. "My name is Wendy and I'll make sure you have everything you need."

Before she could protest, the door closed and she was in the dark. Panic clogged her throat. There was a click and the whirring of a motor. The curtain parted.

"This way, please," Wendy said softly as though she might shatter the silence. She walked down the hall, expecting Haley to follow.

And why not? She probably thought this was a fantasy of Haley's. She stumbled as she realized the truth of her thoughts. *Oh hell, I wrote about being a stripper in my diary.* She should explain to Ryder that just because she wrote down an erotic fantasy didn't mean she actually wanted to act it out for real.

Wendy stopped, and Haley had to catch herself to keep from running into her. The young woman stepped back, motioning for Haley to go inside. "Someone will be with you in a moment," she said as Haley cautiously stepped inside the room. The door closed quietly behind her.

Her gaze swept the room. A cream-colored screen with flowers and hummingbirds painted on it stood in the corner. A full-length mirror leaned against one wall. There was a pale blue vanity trimmed in gold, with a matching stool, and a heart-shaped love seat in blue velvet. A door was open on the other side of the room.

Haley tentatively stepped nearer and flipped on the light just inside the room. Costumes galore greeted her eyes. Dazzling rhinestone-studded dresses from black to white and every color in between. There was an Elvira witch outfit that left little to the imagination. Hats with huge feathers and hats with wide brims sat on the top shelves. There were boas and silk scarves. She walked farther inside, running her hand over the clothes, smothering a high-pitched laugh. She could be anything she wanted. A school girl, a cheerleader—even a nun.

She could make a run for it, too. She didn't have to strip. Unless Wendy had locked her in. She snapped off the light and rushed back to the door. She tried the knob. Unlocked. She watched too much television. Her situation hadn't changed, though.

How could she strip in front of a roomful of people when she didn't even wear a swimsuit in the summer? Her closet was packed with clothes intended to hide her figure. Ryder didn't know what he'd asked her to do.

The room became incredibly hot. Her stomach churned. She was going to be sick. She was going to barf all over the plush beige carpet.

The door opened. The woman took one look at her and rushed over. "Here, sweetie, sit down before you pass out."

Haley nodded. She couldn't speak. Even that slight motion made her ill. She held the woman's arm until she was safely sitting on the loveseat. One more second and she would have been face down on the floor.

"Serese, pour her something to drink."

Haley looked up. She hadn't noticed the other woman. She carried a tray with a bottle and three fluted glasses. The woman had deep brown hair and wore a long white dress that sparkled when she moved.

The other one patted Haley's hand. She was plump but pretty, and her eyes were kind. "The first time is always the most difficult."

"The first time?"

The woman smiled. "Stripping, dear." She said it as if she were talking about making a pie crust. Haley groaned.

Serese hurried over with the drink and curled Haley's fingers around the fragile stem. "Sip this and you'll feel better."

Maybe the alcohol would at least dull her senses. She chose to err on the side of caution. Rather than gulping the drink, she sipped. They were right, her stomach began to calm down after a few moments.

"Better?" the woman beside her asked.

"A little."

"Good. I'm Zana and this is Serese. We're here to help."

"No one can help," she mumbled and took another sip.

Zana's laugh was light and musical.

"You don't understand."

"But I do. I've been a stripper for seven years. Since I was thirty." She shook her head. "I wish I hadn't waited so long."

"You're a stripper?"

Zana smiled. "Are you surprised?"

The woman was being nice and Haley had insulted her. She felt terrible and quickly tried to make amends. "No, not at all."

"I'm not thin like Serese." She nodded toward Serese. "But some men prefer my more generous figure."

"Sexy comes in all sizes," Serese said.

Haley gripped the stem, then realized what she was doing. The last thing she wanted was to break the obviously expensive crystal.

She gulped the last of the drink and handed the glass to Serese. The girl took it, refilled the glass and brought it back.

"I don't think I want more," she said.

"Drink it," Zana urged. "The wine will relax you."

If she thought it would help, Haley would try anything. She took another sip. The wine tickled all the way to her toes.

"I don't know how to strip," she admitted.

Serese gracefully glided over to a box on the vanity. Haley thought it might hold jewelry, but Serese removed a remote. When she pushed one of the buttons, soft music filled the room.

"Do you like that?" Zana asked.

"It's soothing."

Zana nudged Haley's glass. She'd forgotten about the wine. She took a drink.

Serese pushed another button and the lights dimmed until Serese was bathed in a soft glow.

"When you strip, you have all the control," Zana told her. "You'll have the audience in the palm of your hand if you do it correctly."

Serese set the remote down and began to sway, her body undulating to the soft beat.

"I can't do what she's doing." Haley shook her head. There was a sensuality in Serese that Haley knew she would never master.

Zana stood, taking Haley's empty glass. Odd, she didn't remember drinking the rest of her wine.

"Come," Zana said.

Haley wobbled a little when she stood. She wasn't used to drinking. Two glasses with her dinner, now two more, and she was a little woozy. "I don't think I should've drunk the last glass."

"Wine not only relaxes but the drink helps you get rid of stuffy inhibitions," Zana told her. "Tell me what you see."

Somehow, she stood in front of the mirror, but she didn't remember moving. She stared at the woman. It was the same one from Madame Truffle's. The same low-cut red dress, the same slit up the side, the heels. "Who are you?" she whispered, reaching up to touch her face. Did the woman mock her by copying her movement?

"She is you," Zana said.

"It can't be." But how she wished it was so.

"It is, but you must find her. She's inside you. If you don't set her free, she could be lost forever."

"How do I do that?" When she closed her eyes, Haley still saw the frump. The woman in the mirror was imaginary, a dream that fades with the light of day. She didn't know how to connect with the new image because it didn't seem real.

"Let her lead you in the desires of the heart," Zana said. "Set her free and you will find who you were meant to be."

Serese whispered close to Haley's ear, "Close your eyes and let your emotions take over."

Fear rose inside her, heart fluttering. "What if I lose control?" She kept her fantasies hidden away on the pages of a silly diary. If they stayed there, she was safe and in charge of her life, even if that life wasn't the one she wanted. It was never changing. She was a good girl. Her secrets had been bottled up so long, she was scared of what might happen if she freed them.

"Shh, it's okay," Serese said, her voice soft, hypnotic.

Haley met Serese and Zana's gazes in the mirror before meeting that other woman's, the one she couldn't relate to. Her gaze trailed over her voluptuous figure. There was a hint of shyness in her eyes—Haley's eyes. She stepped closer. They *were* her eyes, not those of a stranger.

Her lips had never been pouty. Full, yes, but they'd never been so kissable. She ran her hand through her hair, the strands shimmering in the muted light. Her gaze lowered. The bra pushed her breasts up, revealing an expanse of bare skin. She trailed a fingernail over the tops of her breasts, sending tingles over her body. *Her* body, not that of a stranger.

She wasn't fat. She had curves in all the right places. Her breasts weren't too big nor her hips too wide. Her legs were long and sexy. Why had she hidden behind heavy black-framed glasses and baggy clothes? She knew the answer and it hurt her to the core. Well-meaning family and friends thought they could improve who she was, mold her into what they thought was best for her. They never once asked what she wanted. She lowered her head.

And she had never once stood up for herself.

"It's not too late," Serese said, guessing her thoughts.

"Close your eyes and let the music become part of you," Zana told her. "Let your inhibitions go and let the woman you are on the outside blend with the woman on the inside. Be strong."

She raised her head, met their gazes, then closed her eyes.

"I'm proud of you," Zana said.

Had anyone ever been proud of her? She didn't think so.

"Feel the music," Serese said. "Let it get inside you."

The tempo changed, the throbbing sound drifting around her like a snake charmer enticing her closer. She didn't think about moving her body, it just happened. She began to sway.

"Unzip your dress," Zana told her. When Haley hesitated, she continued. "Free her. It's all right to have these desires."

Haley reached behind her and slowly began to lower the zipper on her dress. Cool air caressed her skin. She trembled; the zipper slipped from her fingers.

"Remember the music," Serese said close to her ear, her warm cinnamon breath fanning Haley's cheek. She was surprised by the tingle of desire that flashed through her. She opened her eyes and met Serese's knowing look. "Desires are good, no matter where they come from."

"But I've never—" Haley shook her head.

"It's okay." Serese moved Haley's fingers back to the zipper. "Let your desires out. We're not here to judge, only to help."

Haley looked at the woman in the mirror. Her dress had slipped down one shoulder. She looked sensual. A woman who tempted men. She slid the other side off her shoulder and slipped both arms out while still holding the dress in place.

The stranger in the mirror waited, watched to see what Haley would do next. Haley released the dress. It puddled around her feet. Zana stooped, moving it out of the way. The stranger didn't seem embarrassed to stand in front of strangers wearing only her bra and thong. Why should she?

"Take off your bra," Zana said.

Haley met the other woman's gaze in the mirror as her insecurities once again settled heavily on her shoulders. Her eyes searched the mirror, but the sexy stranger was gone and Haley stared at herself. The bra and thong showed too much skin. She quickly brought one hand up, shielding her breasts while the other hand tried to hide her lower half. She was fat and men always stood her up. She was clumsy and she was—

"Slow your breathing," Serese said, moving to stand in front of Haley, blocking her view of the mirror.

"I can't," she gasped.

"You are so beautiful." A tender smile appeared on her face.

Haley was mesmerized by how truly lovely Serese was. She wished she could be half as pretty, but that would never happen. Thay had lied to her. The image of the sensuous stranger was false. She still looked the same, still frumpy.

"Slow, even breaths," Serese told her.

Zana brought the wine glass to her lips. "Drink."

Haley didn't even think about not drinking. All her life she'd tried to please people. Why stop?

She swallowed. The wine was sweeter, warmer, this time. She could feel herself begin to relax. She gulped down what was left. When it was empty, Zana took the glass.

"Better?" Serese asked.

"A little."

"You are not the old Haley," Serese said, then stepped to the side. The stranger was back, and Serese was right. She was a temptress.

"This is who you are now," Serese spoke softly. "This is you, Haley. The erotic thoughts you have are not bad as long as you hurt no one. Everyone has them." She lightly ran a painted nail up and down Haley's arm.

Haley sucked in a breath and watched Serese, but she went no farther. Did Haley want her to? She wasn't sure. She'd never entertained thoughts of being with another woman. They hadn't interested her in the past, but there was something exotic about Serese. Something that made Haley feel things she'd never felt before.

"Take off your bra," Serese said, moving in front of her again.

Haley automatically reached behind her and unhooked the clasp, then let it drop to the floor.

Serese's gaze lowered. "You have beautiful breasts." She ran her fingers over a nipple.

Haley gasped, tremors of delight shooting through her. Serese moved closer, her lips pressing against Haley's, her tongue slipping inside to caress and stroke. Haley closed her eyes, curious to see what would happen next, but it was over too soon.

Serese stepped back. "I couldn't resist."

"I… I liked it."

Serese ran her hand down the side of Haley's face. "But you are attracted to someone else. Just know not many women turn me on enough that I would make a pass." She moved to Haley's side and Haley was looking at the stranger again. Her full breasts were high, the rosy nipples taut. They weren't too big.

"Slide your hands beneath the waistband," Zana explained, then moved Haley's hands so they were inside. "A striptease should always heighten the senses. You want the audience to hold their breath as they wait to see what will be revealed next."

"Move your body to the beat as you remove each article of clothing until there is nothing left," Serese added.

Haley let the music consume her. She rotated her hips to the slow beat as she watched herself in the mirror. No, the stranger. Did it matter? She tugged at the band, lowering it on one side, then letting it snap back into place. She slid both hands inside, then pushed the sides down. When her thong landed on the floor, she kicked it out of the way.

"Don't stop moving," Serese said as Zana hurried away. She quickly returned, handing Serese a long feather. "You're naked but you can still tease your audience."

She moved the feather over Haley's breasts. The caressing movement made her gasp with pleasure.

"You try it." Serese handed her the feather.

Haley stared at it. Touching herself? On stage? In front of strangers?

"Make them want to fuck you," she said, but when she said fuck, it was more like an endearment.

Haley moved the feather over her arm. It was like tiny fingers tickling her skin. She swayed to the music as she moved the feather over her breasts. Warmth began to build inside her. She brought the feather lower, stroking between her legs. She moaned, biting her bottom lip.

"She's almost ready," Zana said.

Haley glanced at one, then the other. Before Haley's fear took hold, Serese placed a finger over her lips and shook her head. "You *are* ready."

Zana handed Serese a makeup brush and they dipped them into a jar. When they brought them out, the bristles were covered in sparkles of silver.

"So you will shimmer on stage." Serese brushed down one arm, leaving a trail of powdery glitter in her wake. With a wicked grin, she brushed across Haley's nipples.

Haley sucked in a breath, jutting her breasts forward. Serese didn't disappoint, scraping across them again.

Zana moved down one leg, over Haley's bottom and up her back. Haley watched the woman in the mirror transform into a beautiful, silvery creature. A silver bra and thong were next, then a black and silver dress. Long black-and-silver silk gloves, black-and-silver heels, and a large black feather fan completed the outfit.

"You're ready," Serese and Zana told her.

She looked at the woman in the mirror, still trying to make the connection. That was who she wanted to be more than anything. It would be nice. Haley smiled. The woman in the mirror smiled back.

Haley's brow wrinkled. So did the woman's in the mirror. Haley stepped closer, tentatively touching the mirror. The woman responded in the same manner.

"Oh." Haley breathed. "It is really me."

The truth hit her and her past flashed before her eyes. She watched the old Haley humiliated by men who stood her up or who fumbled in the dark when they had sex with her so they could pretend she was someone else.

Shopping for clothes. The looks of pity. Her mother and sister trying to help but failing miserably and making Haley's self-esteem sink lower and lower.

Alexa fighting her battles. She couldn't have done worse if she had ripped the backbone out of Haley's body. She couldn't fight back because she forgot how to stand up for herself.

"I'm sorry they hurt you," she told her reflection. "You are beautiful and sexy and always have been, you just didn't know it."

She suddenly straightened, anger burning in her eyes. "I want to do this." She wanted to for the old Haley, for herself. She turned on her heel and marched toward the door. No one would ever tell her what she could or couldn't do. She was more than ready. Hell, she'd been waiting all her life!

Chapter 15

"Don't forget to let the music fill your soul," Serese said as they stood behind a black velvet curtain.

Haley peeked around the curtain, then blinked several times. The effects of the wine she drank earlier still lingered. Eventually, everything came into focus. The lights in the audience were low but she could make out the patrons sitting at the closest tables. She didn't see Ryder. Had he left? There was a flicker of light from a flashlight as a man was led to one of the tables. It wasn't Ryder, but when the light turned on, she thought she caught a glimpse of him. No, he wouldn't leave her to face the new lesson alone.

"There's a dress code," Zana explained. "That's why the men all wear suits."

For everyone except the stripper, Haley thought, but she didn't say anything. Her gaze scanned the room. "There are women, too," she said, keeping her voice low.

"Women have fantasies as well as men. Many women admire the female form."

"Gay?"

"Not necessarily," Serese told her. "They think of it as art with the beauty being in the flow of the body. The men often visit for the same reason."

"Do they know I've never done this before?"

"Once a month, we cater to our clients' fantasies. Tonight, anyone can become a stripper."

"They won't laugh, will they?"

"You will do fine," Zana promised. "No one would be so crude as to ridicule someone on stage. Dance for yourself and nothing else will matter."

The lights dimmed until Haley could barely see across the stage. She noticed her hands were damp. A soothing melody began to play and there was a hush over the audience

"Ready?" Serese asked.

Haley jumped.

Ready?

Yeah, sure, she was more than ready to walk out on the stage and take off her clothes. Who was she kidding? She drew in a deep breath, then exhaled. She fiddled with the loop of silk that was around her wrist so she wouldn't drop the feathered fan. "No. I can't do this. Why did I think I could?"

"Because it's what you desire," Serese told her.

"But when I wrote about stripping in my stupid diary it didn't mean that I wanted to do it for real."

"Didn't you?" Zana asked.

"Come," Serese said.

They took her hands and led her to the center of the stage. She didn't know what else to do, so she followed. They faced her away from the audience.

"Close your eyes and let the music come to you. When it does, you'll be ready." Serese walked away, Zana with her.

Haley trembled. She'd read about stripping in a magazine once. She'd even cut the article out and slipped it between the pages of her diary. Sometimes late at night, she imagined herself on stage with everyone watching her while she removed each article of clothing she wore until there was nothing left. At the time, thinking about it sent a rush of excitement through her.

Serese and Zana told her to dance for herself, to feel the music.

If she pretended she was the only one there, how difficult could it be?

The music grew louder. She began to sway until it became a part of her, filling her senses, flowing with her. She opened her eyes. The lights had changed to muted blue and there were stars above her. The stage no longer felt like a stage, but as though she was outside. She turned, reaching up toward the sky.

The music changed again, throbbing with a primitive beat. A rush of heat blew across the stage. It was so hot. Too many clothes. She reached behind and slowly tugged the zipper down on her dress. It was too hot to move very fast. She slipped one arm out, then the other, holding the dress in front of her.

A shiver ran down her spine. The truth of what she did slowly sank in. She wanted to strip. She wanted everyone to look at her. One man especially. She turned and walked closer to the edge of the stage, her eyes searching the crowd.

She spotted Ryder at a table in the corner, sitting all alone. She met his gaze, then raised her arms. The dress dropped to the floor, but she popped the fan open, holding it sideways so she was partially covered. She heard approval from the audience. When Ryder sat forward, Haley knew she was the one with all the control.

She fluttered the fan, the feathers brushing across her sensitive skin. She leaned her head back, enjoying the erotic sensations. The music changed again and the stage turned a deep red. She looked at the audience and winked before snapping the fan closed. Light reflected off the silvery sheen that Zana and Serese had painted on her. The audience applauded.

She didn't want to dance for herself, she wanted to perform for them, for Ryder. She looked at him and smiled. He didn't look comfortable. She was about to make him a lot more uncomfortable. She reached behind her, unhooking the bra. She held it in place, then turned and with her back to the audience, tossed it over her shoulder. The thong hid nothing. The string across her hips merely teased. She snapped the fan open before she turned, walking back toward the stage. The music was louder. She could feel the vibrations rippling across the stage.

She moved her hips in time to the beat and began to touch her breasts with her free hand. She moaned when she pinched one nipple, rolling it between her thumb and forefinger. Haley knew the audience was aware of what she was doing. When she looked at their faces, she knew they wanted to watch her touch herself. They waited breathlessly for her to move the fan.

It was Ryder's expression she wanted to see the most. He didn't disappoint her when she looked his way. He was mesmerized by her movements. She covered her breasts with her free arm, then moved the fan.

The audience leaned forward. Power surged through her. It was as though someone flipped a switch and her true nature was released. Stopping never crossed her mind. She dragged her hand across her bare breasts, scraping across her nipples. She was naked except for her gloves and thong.

She raised her arms high above her head, then brought them down, caressing her breasts, sliding her hands over her hips, down her thighs as the beat of the music intensified. She strutted across the stage as she rolled down one glove, then tossed it toward Ryder. He caught it, bringing the glove to his lips.

Haley laughed for the pure joy of laughing and walked to the other side of the stage. Her breasts bounced with each step she took. She moved to the rhythm of the music, swinging her hips. She removed the other glove, rubbing it across her nipples before she tossed it into the crowd.

The energy coming from the audience was an adrenaline rush. She faced them, legs slightly apart, and slid her fingers under the little bit of elastic. Lights began to flash around her, bathing her in deep blue, red, purple, green, and gold. She pushed the triangle of material down, sliding it over her legs and kicking it away.

This was what it felt like to be truly alive. She stretched her arms out to each side, moving to the music, letting it fill her soul, then she slowly sank to the floor as the last note died. The room exploded with clapping and people shouting bravo as the curtain closed.

Zana and Serese ran to her. "I knew you were a natural," Serese told her.

"Absolutely breathtaking," Zana said, holding out a white silk robe.

Haley stood, glancing down at her nudity. Where was the shame she should be feeling? It wasn't there. Exhilaration still ran through her veins. She slipped her arms into the sleeves and belted the robe, but she wasn't in any hurry to cover her nakedness.

"What did you think?" Serese asked.

Haley grinned. "I loved every minute of it," she said as they walked back to the dressing room.

"If you ever want a job, I'm pretty sure they'd hire you on the spot."

Loan officer or stripper? A few hours ago and she could have easily answered the question, but now she wasn't quite so sure. The three of them walked down the hall and went into the dressing room. The heady scent of flowers greeted Haley. Serese strolled over to a large bouquet of red roses and looked at the card.

"For you," she said with a saucy wink.

Haley never received roses or flowers of any kind. She felt like a princess. A very naughty princess, but still a princess. She took the envelope Serese handed her. Her name was scrawled across the front. She pulled the card out and read the message.

> *There's a party I want to take you to. The limo will be waiting out front.*

"We're going to a party," she said. "I feel like the belle of the ball."

"Because you are," Zana said, her eyes misting. "But you don't want to be late."

No, she didn't want to keep Ryder waiting. Stripping was a very sexual experience, and she needed the kind of release only he could give her.

"I hung your clothes in the bathroom. There's a shower so you can wash away the silver body glitter," Zana said.

Haley hurried into the bathroom and turned the water on. She took a quick shower, careful not to mess up her makeup, and stepped out. When she grabbed a towel off the warming rack, she caught her reflection in the mirror. For a moment she was startled, then she smiled as though greeting a new friend. The old Haley was still there, but she wasn't as scared or as lonely, and she was a whole lot wiser.

She tossed the towel away and reached for the thong, but stopped at the last minute. There was something to be said about being naked, and she was feeling especially wicked. She grabbed the dress instead and shimmied into it, not bothering with the bra.

It was still almost an hour later before she hugged Zana and Serese good-bye. Ryder leaned against the limo talking to the driver, but he straightened when she stepped out of the club. His gaze slowly drifted over her, stripping her out of the red dress. Her nipples tightened in response.

⁓⁓

Ryder watched as Haley moved toward him. With each step she took, her body told him exactly what she wanted. There was a slight bounce that betrayed the fact that she wasn't wearing a bra. Her nipples were tight nubs poking at the material of her low cut dress, begging him to take them into his mouth and caress them with his tongue.

Her hips had a sassy swing as though she still heard the music in her head. She teased his senses with every step she took. He found he could barely take a breath. He ached to sink deep inside her, absorbing her heat.

She stopped in front of him, running her tongue over her lips nice and slow. "Did you enjoy the show?" Her words were low and husky.

The driver opened the door before Ryder could say anything. Haley slid across the seat. The slit of her dress parted showing a good amount of thigh. She didn't bother to pull the material together.

He climbed into the car and had her in his arms, his lips pressed against hers, his tongue stroking hers before the door closed. He kissed her long and hard and even when he ended the kiss, he still held her tight.

"Did I enjoy the show?" He chuckled. "I've got a killer hard-on and the lady asks if I enjoyed the show."

She leaned back, studying his face. "You did, didn't you?"

He saw a little bit of her confidence slip away. "I loved every moment of your performance. You had the audience, including me, breathlessly waiting for each piece of clothing to fall away. Every man wanted to be the lucky one who made love to you tonight. Every woman envied you."

She laughed and hugged him tight. "Thank you so much for fulfilling my fantasy. I felt so alive on the stage."

"You were a sex goddess."

"And I want to make love with you," she said without hesitation as her confidence soared.

"I have something else planned, but we'll make love tonight because I can't wait much longer either."

She pouted. Ryder almost changed his plans and pulled her back into his arms. Before her transformation, Haley tempted him like no other woman. Her insecurities tugged at his heart, but that wasn't the only reason he wanted to help her. It was the way she raised her hand and tucked her hair behind her ear, the way her forehead creased when she worked long hours trying to find a way for her customers to get the loans they needed, the way she handled each new obstacle that blocked her path to happiness.

She was a survivor, but Ryder knew she could be so much more. She only needed someone to nudge her in the right direction. She needed to stop letting other people tell her who she was supposed to be.

He never expected such a dramatic transformation, though. The new Haley took his breath away. She was saucy and sensuous and—

"You're staring," she said, interrupting his thoughts.

"I know."

She reached up, smoothing her hair. He took her hand and brought it to his lips. "I'm staring because I can't help myself. I thought you were beautiful before; now you're dazzling."

Her cheeks turned a rosy hue and she looked away. He shook his head in wonder that she could have such strong sexual desires and still be shy. Maybe that was what he loved about her. He never knew what to expect. He enjoyed surprises.

The limo parked next to the curb. Haley glanced up. "Where are we?"

"A party."

"You were serious? What kind of party?"

He could see she didn't quite trust him. "You'll enjoy it." The door opened and they got out. The high rise apartment building had forty very exclusive floors. There was also a gym any body builder would envy, a spa, a beauty salon, and daily maid service to name a few of the amenities.

"It looks ritzy," she murmured, looking up.

"It is." He tucked her arm under his.

"Another marble floor," she said, gripping his arm a little tighter as they walked toward a long white counter. A man glanced up and smiled.

Ryder knew exactly what Haley was thinking. Conquering one of her fears while fulfilling one of her fantasies was an adrenaline rush, but she wasn't so sure she wanted to jump another hurdle quite so soon. He patted her hand, but he didn't think his gesture reassured her that much.

"May I help you?" the man asked.

Ryder reached in his pocket and pulled out an envelope, then handed it to the man. He opened it, quickly read the invitation and smiled before handing it back.

"The elevators are around the corner, sir. An attendant will take you to the penthouse."

Ryder nodded. As they walked away, Haley was squeezing his arm so tight he thought she might cut off the circulation. "Relax."

"The *penthouse?*" she asked.

"Yes, the penthouse."

They went around the corner. A young woman wearing a gray jacket with deep blue lapels, white shirt, and a modest A-line gray skirt smiled and motioned for them to go inside. Haley started trembling as the elevator glided up, and hadn't stopped when the elevator came to a smooth stop and the doors opened into the penthouse suite.

Waiters moved about with trays of drinks and hors d'oeuvres. Country music played over the speaker system. The curtains were open and downtown Dallas glittered in the background.

Ryder scanned the crowd of laughing, talking guests. The women casually wore diamonds as if they'd found them lying on the ground. The flash didn't mean much, though. Jewels weren't as important as how many acres a person owned. In Texas, it was all about the land passed down from one generation to the next and how many head of cattle you ran on it. The men weren't as showy. Dressing up to them meant a Western suit that had been recently dry-cleaned and polished boots. It didn't matter how rich you were. There was more money in that room than in the Federal Reserve.

"It is a party," Haley said with surprise.

"What were you expecting?" he asked.

"I have no idea. I'm still trying to remember what I wrote in my stupid diary."

"Do you regret your fantasies, Haley? The sex?"

She opened her mouth, then snapped it closed and tilted her chin at a haughty angle. "No, I don't regret them."

"Good, because I certainly don't." He'd embarrassed her again, but he saw a flicker of pleasure in her eyes, too. He stopped a passing waiter and took two drinks from the tray he carried, handing one to Haley.

"I don't think I've ever drunk this much alcohol in one night." She stared at the tall shot glass with green and chocolate liqueur. "What is it?"

"It's called an After Dinner Mint," the waiter said before he moved through the crowd.

She took a sip. "It takes like a peppermint patty. I like it." She glanced around. "Do you know these people?"

"We're crashing the party."

"Aren't you afraid they'll throw us out?" She finished her drink.

Another waiter took Haley's glass and offered her another one. She didn't hesitate and took it.

"They wouldn't be so crass as to throw us out. Not the way you look," he said as they strolled toward the balcony. "You owned the room as soon as the elevator doors opened, just like you owned the stage tonight."

Her gaze darted around the room. "It felt different when I was on stage." She took a quick sip of her drink, then frowned when she apparently realized it was the last one. "These don't last very long. I wonder why they don't serve them in a bigger glass."

"There are plenty of waiters who have more." To prove his point, a waiter walked by. Ryder stopped him and replaced her drink with a fresh one.

"Thank you." She took a sip. "I think you're stretching the truth, but thank you for that, too. There are a lot of pretty women here."

"Do you know how fucking sexy you look without a bra on? It's all I can do to keep from leaning down and drawing one of those tight nipples into my mouth."

She stumbled. He caught her elbow to steady her. His gaze slowly traveled over her. She raised her glass and gulped the rest of her drink, stopped a waiter and grabbed another one, downing it in two swallows. She took a deep breath and looked down.

"Oh God, why didn't you tell me? I forgot I wasn't wearing one. I know I just... stripped, but this is different. I didn't know we were going to a party. Not a real one. I thought we would probably... uh..."

"Make love?"

"That's pretty much what I thought."

His gaze dropped lower. "I bet you're not wearing any panties. Are you naked under your dress?"

"Shh." She frantically looked around the room.

"How does the dress feel against your naked skin?"

She bit her bottom lip as he continued to maneuver her until they were on the balcony. There was enough of a breeze that it kept the other guests indoors, which suited his purpose beautifully, but not so cold that Haley would catch a chill. She drew in a deep breath then exhaled, not seeming to care that the light wind ruffled her hair. She was more concerned someone would overhear his words. Relief shone on her face since they were outside, but he wasn't about to let up with his assault on her mind or her body.

"Why do you do that to me?" she asked.

"What?"

"You know what." She glared at him before striding to the far corner of the railing, except her gait was a little wobbly. He grinned. The alcohol had started to kick in. Her reactions would be slower, her senses heightened. He should feel bad that he'd set her up, but he didn't. One of her fantasies was to make love in a closet when there was a party going on in the other room. He chose the balcony instead. Much more clandestine.

She grabbed the rail with both hands as she attempted to regain her composure.

The bottom half was clear glass so that nothing obstructed the view of the city. Perfect. He wanted her to feel as though she was naked for the whole world to see and not just an audience. And he would have her naked.

Ryder didn't get in any hurry as he ambled up behind her, slipping his hands around her waist. "Does it bother you when I tell you exactly what I want to do?"

She didn't say anything for a moment. "You make me want you," she finally admitted.

His hands slipped up to her breasts and squeezed. She stiffened. "What are you doing?" she gasped.

"If anyone happens to look out here they'll see two people enjoying the view, nothing more. Besides, it's dark over here." He squeezed her breasts, pinching the nipples. She leaned against him. He closed his eyes for a moment, not sure if he should continue the game he'd started. He wanted her too much and her breasts felt wonderful in the palms of his hands. He hadn't thought he could last long enough to watch the rest of her striptease, but like the audience, she'd put him on the edge of his seat and he had to see what would come off next. They'd painted some kind of silvery glitter all over her so that she sparkled when the light hit her. She reminded him of a naughty little fairy that escaped the confines of her magical land. As she danced, Haley cast a spell over everyone. She worked the crowd like a pro, but with an innocence that captivated them all.

Yeah, it was hard to continue with his plans. It was damned hard. But he would, because he wanted Haley to be comfortable with her new self. When they returned to her home, she would take the town by storm. Then he would leave.

A sharp pain tore through him. Life was so fucking unfair. He took a deep breath and slowly exhaled. He would store the memories. They would have to be enough.

Haley sighed, drawing his attention back to the present. Her body was soft against his, and tempting. He squeezed her nipples. "If I had you naked, I'd be sucking on your breasts. I'd roll my tongue over the nipples, then scrape my teeth across them." He slipped his hand behind her and brought her zipper part of the way down.

She jumped, grabbing the front of her gown. "What are you doing?" she frantically whispered.

"Nothing you don't want me to." He pulled her back against him, moving her hair to the side and running his tongue down her neck and across her shoulder where the strap had slid down and bared her skin. "I want to see your breasts."

"Not here," she said.

"Think how it would feel to expose your breasts to all of downtown Dallas. He rubbed her shoulders, moving down her arms. "I want to see your naked breasts. I want the air to make your nipples hard, then I'll squeeze them until you feel the tingles all the way down to your hot pussy."

She moaned and leaned against him. The fight left her. He tugged her dress down enough so her perfectly formed breasts were bared. Her areolas were dusky red, the nipples tight, begging him to take them into his mouth, but he fought the urge and continued to squeeze and release.

"That's better. Do you like the breeze on your breasts?"

"Feels good." She leaned her head against him.

"How does it feel right here?" He moved one hand down and pulled the slit of her dress back, baring her lower half.

She began to pant in little puffs of air. "Yes."

He ran his fingers through her curls. "I loved sucking on your pussy, running my tongue over your clit." He ran his finger up, then back down, pressing against her. She was already damp with need, but he knew she would be. She had kept her sexual desires dormant way too long. She moved against his finger.

"Ryder, don't," she begged.

"Don't what? Talk dirty? I'm only telling you what I like to do to your body. I want to suck on your tits and your pussy."

"Oh, damn," she choked.

There was a grouping of plants not far from them, a leafy tree in the center next to the side of the building. He guided her behind them, leaning her against the side of the building so that she faced him. The music drifted outside, a slow country song.

"Don't what?" he asked again, nuzzling the side of her neck.

"I need release and we can't, not out here."

"Can't what?" He ran his tongue down the center of her chest, then swirled around the dusky areola before sucking the taut nipple into his mouth. She gripped his shoulders. He reached behind her, bringing the zipper on her dress the rest of the way down. She didn't seem to notice or care. He moved to her other breast, circling the areola with his tongue before drawing her taut nipple into his mouth.

When she arched her back, Ryder knew she was ready for more. His hands were the only thing holding up her dress now that it was completely unzipped. He let go of the soft material and the dress slid to the concrete floor.

"Ryder!" She reached for her dress, but he took her hands and pinned them above her head. Her attempts to break his hold were feeble as her desire to walk on the wild side competed with her upbringing. But her movements were a tease to him. The sway of her breasts, the way she wiggled her hips.

"You're completely naked while there's a party going on inside, and we're going to make love. You can count on that. Another fantasy, remember?"

She groaned. "I don't remember everything I scribbled in my diary. They were random thoughts. They were never meant to be acted on."

"Liar." He chuckled.

"I am not..." She moaned when he tugged on her nipple with his free hand.

Her eyes were glazed with passion. He ignored her words as his gaze moved over her. "No one could want anything more than what I'm looking at," he said. "Your breasts fill my hands and were made for a man's mouth. The temptation would drive a normal man insane with the need to touch and fondle them. Hell, it nearly drives me crazy."

She stopped trying to break free from his hold. He sensed the moment her will to fight her desires crumbled. It didn't help that she was completely naked and there was enough of a warm breeze that her skin probably felt as though it was being massaged by a thousand tiny fingers. But what totally tore away her reservations was the fact that it happened to be one of her very naughty fantasies come to life.

Ryder didn't back off. He wanted her to thoroughly enjoy her fantasy. "Your waist is small." He moved his hands to her waist. He didn't think she realized he'd released his hold. "And your hips flare out. A woman with curves in all the right places." His gaze dropped to the thatch of dark curls. "It's almost a shame your pussy is hidden from my eyes, but if I spread the lips a little, I can see my heart's desire."

"Ryder." His name whispered off her lips. "Please," she begged.

He dragged his gaze back up. Her eyes were heavy with passion. "Please what?" He flicked his thumbs over her nipples. She drew in a sharp breath. "Want me to stop?"

Her teeth tugged on her lower lip.

He made his move. "Because if you want me to stop, I will, but you know you're tempted. You want to live dangerously. You want to fuck out here as much as you wanted to strip. You loved the rush of adrenaline that shot through your veins. Admit it."

She licked her lips and looked toward the light that spilled onto the balcony. "This is different. What if we get caught?" Excitement laced her words.

He ran his fingers between her legs. She arched toward him. He knelt in front of her, his hands grasping her waist. He licked up her slit, then nibbled, before drawing her inside his mouth. She tasted musky. His cock throbbed as the heat running through her flowed through him. She grasped his shoulders, her body quivering with need.

Ryder wasn't ready for her to come yet. There was more he wanted to do, more he wanted her to feel. He stood, moving behind her.

"No," she cried her disappointment when he stopped pleasuring her.

"Did you like when I sucked on you?"

"Yes," she cried. "You stopped." Her words hitched.

"But I'm not through. Open your legs," he whispered close to her ear. "I want to touch your pussy, but you have to spread your legs for me." She slumped against him, but did as he asked.

Ryder could barely focus. The ache inside him was unbearable. The need to slide his cock inside her was becoming more painful by the second. He held her tight for a moment while he got himself under control. Then he slid his hands down. One cupped her breast, his other hand continued moving slowly downward.

The sliding glass door to the balcony didn't make much noise when someone opened it, but enough that Haley froze. "We're not alone," she whispered. She started to reach for her dress, but he grabbed her hands and held them.

"Shh," he whispered near her ear. "They don't know we're here. We're completely hidden by the bushes."

The voices that drifted over to them were those of a man and woman, but they didn't come into view until they were nearly to the balcony edge. The woman stopped at the rail, then whirled around and faced the man. She was petite and blonde. He was tall with dark hair. They both looked to be in their forties.

"Jeff, do you realize I want you more than I've wanted any man?" she said in a throaty voice. Her gaze drifted over him. "Call me loose, call me a slut, I don't care, but the only thing I can think about is having sex with you."

Jeff started to close the distance between them, but stopped, apparently thinking better about his actions and went to the railing instead. "It's killing me too. I want to rip off your clothes, take those luscious tits in my hands and bury my face in them."

She drew in a deep ragged breath. "What else would you do?"

"I'd touch you down there, between your legs."

"My pussy, you mean?" She faced him, raising her chin. "I told you I could be naughty," she said in a flirty voice.

Jeff put a little more distance between them. Ryder felt Haley's growing uncertainty as the man came dangerously close to their hiding spot, but he knew she was also turned on by their conversation by the way she squirmed just a little. When the man faced the woman, Haley exhaled. Ryder began to massage her breast, tugging on the taut nipple. She bit her bottom lip, arching her back.

He moved his other hand down, spreading the lips of her pussy. "Do you like being completely naked and knowing we could get caught any second?" He tugged on the fleshy part of her sex. She wiggled her ass against his cock and he almost came undone.

But he knew the games she played. Her eyes were closed. If she could take his mind off her and transfer his thoughts to what he needed, Ryder wouldn't realize she cheated. The man had been too close for comfort and she'd gotten scared. He knew exactly what she was doing. If she didn't watch, she could pretend there was no danger.

The element of danger *was* there and he wanted her to see how close to the edge she was about to go. He would beat her at her own game. He moved his hands from her pussy and up to her abdomen, running his fingers lightly back and forth. She wiggled her hips in frustration.

"Open your eyes." He kept his words low so she was the only one who heard.

Haley moved against him again in a valiant effort, but he stepped back far enough that she couldn't distract him at the same time he massaged her nipples. She gasped, eyes opening. The man looked their way, but Ryder knew he couldn't see into the dark corner. Haley didn't move. Her body trembled with the thought the man could walk over to them at any moment to check out the noise.

"What?" the woman asked, nervously glancing around.

He shook his head. "Nothing. I thought I heard something but it was probably just the wind."

"Good, because I doubt you'd like anyone hearing me say pussy or that I want you to fuck me."

"I didn't know you talked like that," Jeff said.

She raised her eyebrows. "What are you going to do about it? Nothing, I'd wager. You like my pussy too much, and you like fucking me too much, you won't do a damn thing."

"Then you don't know me very well," he drawled. "I'm going to take you into my office and take off your dress right before I bend you over my desk. All you'll be wearing is your bra and panties. I'll leave your bra on but I'll pull your panties down very slowly." He paused.

"What will you do after that?' she breathlessly asked.

"I'll force you to spread your legs."

"Force me?" She raised an eyebrow.

"Force you," he repeated and continued as though she hadn't interrupted. "Then I'll spank that sexy ass while it's up in the air."

"Will it hurt?" Her chest rose and fell.

"What do you think?"

She nodded. "My ass will sting." She visibly swallowed. "And what will you do after that?"

"After I'm through spanking you, I'm going to get down on my knees, but you will have to stay where you are with your legs spread apart. I'm going to look at every inch of you, from your ass all the way to your pussy. When I tell you to turn around, you'll obey me because you'll be afraid I'm going to spank you again."

"Yes," she breathed.

"You'll take off your bra while I'm watching every move you make. I'll squeeze your tits and pinch your nipples. When I tell you to lie back on my desk, you will because you want what only I can give you. While you're lying there, I'm going to examine every inch of your pussy. I'll touch you whenever and wherever I want."

"Oh, Jeff." She took a step toward him, but stopped when the door slid open. She quickly stepped back and pasted a bland smile on her face.

Ryder could see the effort it took for the woman to quickly compose herself.

Halcy pressed closer to Ryder when she heard someone else brave the breeze on the balcony. Her body trembled.

From fear? Or excitement?

"I love touching you," he whispered close to her ear. "And sucking on your breasts."

Haley brought his hand to her breast. He grinned. Her excitement far outweighed any fear.

A woman stepped into their line of vision. She was older than the couple by a number of years, tall, and wore a diamond necklace that sparkled every time she moved. "Here you two are," she exclaimed.

"Can you see them on the other side of the plants?" Ryder asked, his lips close to Haley's ear.

She nodded, but didn't attempt to cover herself. He slipped a finger inside her, moving in and out, then slid his wet finger up her pussy, then back down again. She moved her body to the rhythm of his movements. There was nothing hurried about it. Slow and easy, letting the passion build inside her.

They can't see us," he whispered. "Our corner is dark. I could slide my cock in you right now and they wouldn't know."

A deep shudder ran through her.

The woman who'd joined the couple began to talk again. "Harry couldn't find you. I told him you two had probably slipped away. I swear anyone would think you were newlyweds the way you carry on." She chuckled. "You must tell me your secret to such a happy marriage. It was all I could do just to have Harry escort me to the party tonight."

Married? Ryder smiled.

"Nothing special," the woman said, "but we'll have lunch soon and talk."

"That sounds lovely. Now come inside out of this dreadful wind. Harry insists on getting home in time to watch the news." She rolled her eyes. "Sometimes I don't know why I married the man."

"We'll be along in a moment," the man said.

"Yes, Harry wants to say good-bye."

As soon as the door slid closed, Jeff turned back to his wife. "Face the rail."

She glanced around. "Why?"

"Do as you're told."

Without another word, she faced the city, the lights on the office buildings twinkling as if it were the holidays.

"What are you going to do?" she asked.

He stepped behind her, reached around her and lifted her dress before pressing his hand between her legs. "You'll have no choice but to bare everything for me. To keep your legs spread open."

She drew in a sharp breath. Ryder could see the man's wife moving against her husband's hand the same way Haley moved against his.

"Then while your legs are still spread open, I'm going to fuck you until you scream my name." He slipped his hand from beneath her dress and the material dropped back in place.

"I can't wait to get home," she said as she turned and walked past him.

He followed, making sure his suit jacket hid his erection. "Me too," he said as they left the balcony. The door closed behind them.

Haley moaned, slumping against him. "They were married. I don't understand."

He nuzzled her neck. "Role playing. It excites them. It's like meeting for the first time, only better. Like I said, everyone has fantasies."

"Then fuck me," she said. "That's my fantasy."

"You and me both."

Ryder couldn't stand not being inside Haley one more second. He turned her until she was holding on to the rail, her ass facing him. The couple's words came back to him and how Haley had squirmed against him when the man spoke about spanking his wife. Ryder couldn't resist. He slapped her ass. She jerked, then moaned. He slapped her ass again. Not hard enough to hurt. She bent over a little more, offering herself to him. Rather than slap her again, he spread her legs open.

"I would never get tired of looking at you." He ran his hand between her legs. "Or caressing your pussy."

"Now, Ryder. Please."

He wouldn't make either one of them wait any longer. He guided his cock inside her, sucking air when her heat surrounded him. She clenched her inner muscles. He jerked.

"Deeper," she said.

He sank farther inside her, then pulled out before plunging

inside again. She ground her ass against him. He grasped her waist. "Ah, damn, lady, you're driving me wild. You're hot and wet. I can't get enough of stroking you with my cock."

"More," she said.

He thrust harder, pulling her against him at the same time. The heat continued to build inside him, growing so hot that he felt like a volcano about to erupt.

"Yes," she cried, her body quivering with release.

His vision blurred. The city lights became a kaleidoscope of swirling colors. He stroked once more, the muscles in his neck stretched taut. He pulled her tighter against him as he came. Making love with Haley was good, so fucking good. So good it scared the hell out of him.

Chapter 16

"ARE YOU READY?" RYDER asked.

She shook her head. "No." She stared at herself in the mirror. What if they thought she was a joke? What if they didn't see the same thing? People often fooled themselves when it came to their appearances. They thought they were prettier or smaller. Their minds had a way of creating an image they could accept. Except Haley, until now. She felt sexy and pretty. She no longer saw the fat frump. A pestering niggle of doubt kept jabbing at her confidence, though. What if—

"Close your eyes," Ryder said, breaking into her thoughts.

Startled, she met his gaze in the mirror. "What?"

He put his hands on her shoulders and squeezed. "Close your eyes."

"Why?" What was he up to? She was positive he wasn't initiating foreplay. Ryder waited patiently. He wouldn't do or say anything until she did. It was a very irritating habit of his. She rolled her eyes. Okay, she would do what he wanted. She closed her eyes.

"Take a deep breath."

She inhaled, smiling as leather and country breezes filled her space. She loved the way he smelled, the way he felt, the way he seduced her. Maybe it was going to be foreplay after all. She imagined him slowly unbuttoning her shirt and letting it drop to the floor. Her bra would follow.

"Pay attention," he lightly scolded.

She frowned as her fantasy ripped into a million pieces and scattered like confetti in the wind. She sighed. It was a nice fantasy.

"Clear your mind," he told her.

Not an easy task when he stood that close to her, but she would try. She inhaled, then exhaled.

"Imagine you're walking down the street. Someone is coming toward you, but you can't see her very well. You only know it's a woman. She's getting closer. You can tell she's dressed much like you."

Haley pictured the woman, but Ryder was right, she was blurry. He didn't give a lot of detail. Who was the mystery woman?

"Open your eyes and look at the woman in the mirror as if you're meeting her for the very first time."

She opened her eyes and was startled to see the alluring woman in the mirror. She knew it was her, even though it still didn't sink in at times. Was the mirror fooling her? With a critical eye, she studied the woman as if a stranger stood in front of her. Her hair was stunning, the light from the window capturing the highlights. She wore just the right amount of makeup. Brown eye shadow gave her eyes a smoky, seductive quality. Her lips were creamy red. An air of mystery surrounded her. Einstein was a good teacher when it came to showing her how to put on makeup, and Haley learned fast. He said less was more. He was right.

Her gaze traveled down. Marie and Aggie delivered on their promise and Haley had a brand-new wardrobe. The scooped neckline of her deep blue shirt was bold. There was nothing frilly about it, but it accentuated her curves, rather than hiding them, and was tucked into a pair of low-rise jeans that showed off her long legs.

Einstein sent along a pair of black boots with yellow roses climbing up the sides. His note said they were so she could "kick some ass." She smiled and was again amazed by the total transformation. Einstein had the right idea, and she was more than ready to show the world, at least Hattersville, the woman she had become.

"I'm ready," she pronounced with confidence.

He smiled. "Good. I knew you could do it."

She walked to the bedroom door, but he didn't follow. "What?"

"This is your day."

Fear trembled over her and suddenly she couldn't swallow. "Are you leaving?"

He shook his head. "I'll see you tonight."

The breath she held whooshed out. "Don't scare me like that."

He closed the distance between them and took her into his arms, holding her close. "I won't leave without saying good-bye, but you have to do this on your own. Do you understand?" He held her at arm's length and gazed into her eyes.

"No, I don't." She didn't want to understand either, but when he kept looking at her, without saying anything, she nodded. She supposed she did understand what he was trying to tell her. "It doesn't mean I have to like it."

He grinned and her heart did a flip-flop. "Own today," he said. "Make it yours. I want you to prove to yourself that you're a different person on the inside as well as the outside."

Haley knew he wanted her to prove it to *him*, even though he didn't say the words. She didn't want to let him down any more than she wanted to let herself down.

Ryder closed his eyes and was gone an instant later. She reached toward where he'd stood. Her pulse sped up. No, Ryder said he would be back tonight. He wouldn't lie to her.

But she was being pushed from the nest and it was either fly or crash, and it was a long way to the ground. She could manage one day by herself. Sure she could. She went back to the mirror, committing her image to memory. "I'm sexy and beautiful." She looked at the woman staring back at her. No, she was more than the outer image. Ryder had given her confidence. Her belief in herself might be shaky at times, but it was there. She only hoped it would last all day.

She marched out of the room and down the hall, grabbing her

keys and slipping the strap of her new black clutch on her wrist. She grinned. There was an embroidered yellow rose in the center. Einstein said it was a reminder from him not to let anyone get the best of her. He was right; she had something to prove and today was her day!

The sun was shining bright as she shut and locked her front door. She looked up and met Chelsea's gaze as the other woman left her house next door.

"Hi," Chelsea said, her smile as false as ever. "Who are you?"

Haley smiled back. She was going to love every minute of this. She didn't answer until she was standing on the sidewalk. She knew the waiting irritated the other woman. "Why, Chelsea, don't you recognize me?"

Chelsea wore a baffled look. "I don't believe we've ever met. Are you a relative of Haley's?" Her gaze swept over her and she chuckled. "Not that there's a family resemblance. She's a dog. You know, bow-wow." She brought her hands up in front of her, mimicking a dog begging for a treat, then laughed at her joke.

A dog. Interesting.

As if Chelsea suddenly realized her blunder, she cleared her throat. She never wanted anyone to know what a real bitch she was. "But sweet," she stuttered. "You know how it is when a woman has her kind of looks. They have to make up for their shortcomings in other areas. She's always ready to lend a helping hand. Do the work no one else wants to do."

"Really? I don't think so. There are some people who enjoy dumping on others, though."

Chelsea frowned. Few people ever disagreed with her.

"So, *are* you related to her?" Chelsea asked with a touch of irritation.

"Maybe you need to have your eyes checked," Haley pondered out loud. "You are getting older."

Chelsea spit and sputtered as she tried to talk but nothing

intelligible came out of her mouth. Come to think about it, nothing ever really did. She was only nice when she wanted something.

"You'll be thirty-two this year, right?" Haley asked.

"I'll be twenty-nine!" Her face turned deep red.

Chelsea had turned twenty-nine for too many birthdays to count. "Really? Do you think *we* were born yesterday?"

Chelsea's eyes narrowed. "Who are you?"

"I bought you a yellow silk scarf last year. I'll never understand why. I guess deep down I wanted you to like me for real. I fell for the mean games you played. I saw the scarf in the trash, by the way. I think you wanted me to see it."

"Who are you?" she asked again, starting to look nervous.

"I'm Haley Tillman."

Chelsea stumbled back. "You're lying! There's no way Haley would look as good as you."

It was Haley's turn to be shocked. Had she looked that bad? Apparently so; add zilch self-confidence, and she became an easy target for people like Chelsea. "I feel sorry for you," Haley told her. "I improved my lot in life, but you'll always be the mean, spiteful woman you are right now." Haley walked to her car, a smile starting. She stood up for herself and it was a heady feeling. She would never again let anyone make her feel like less of a person.

The door across the street opened and Martha and Albert Monroe came out. They looked up and saw her.

"Hello, dear." Martha waved. "Is that a new outfit?"

"Yes, it is."

Martha nodded. "You did something to your hair, too."

"Highlights."

Albert took off his glasses and cleaned them with the tail of his shirt before putting them back on and studying her. "I told Martha you were a pretty gal, but you darn sure didn't know anything about style. Glad you figured out how to get all gussied up." He nodded his head as he looked her over again and chuckled. "We sure didn't realize you were hiding all of that under those fuddy-duddy clothes. I'd burn them if I were you."

"He's exactly right," Martha chimed in again. "We would've mentioned the clothes didn't suit you, but young people don't usually listen to us older folks. They don't realize we didn't get to be old without having a little bit of smarts."

"I think the two of you are very smart." Except she probably wouldn't have listened to them either. It took a prayer and an angel to help her see the light. A shiver of fear rippled over her. Ryder couldn't stay. Was it going to be their last night? She got in the car and started it. He'd said she wouldn't remember him. But how could she forget?

As she backed out of the driveway, Haley knew the thought of Ryder being gone from her life forever left her feeling as if there was a dark cloud hanging over her. She didn't want to lose what they had, but she didn't know how to keep him in her life.

She squared her shoulders and gripped the steering wheel. Another prayer probably wouldn't keep him in her life, but did it have to hurt so much? She glanced next door once more before shifting into drive.

Chelsea sat on the top step looking totally confused, as though she was still trying to figure out how Haley's appearance could change so much. Good, she needed to be taken down a peg or two.

Haley parked the car and pushed the button that locked the doors. She was halfway to the courthouse square when her cell began to blast "Wild Thing." A couple of cowboys looked her way. One tipped his hat and grinned. The other whistled. Haley looked over her shoulder. Other than a married couple with two young children, and obviously pregnant with a third, Haley was the only one the two cowboys looked at.

Do not walk over and thank them!

Deep breath. Inhale.

The cowboys' gazes dropped to her chest.

Do not take deep breaths, either!

She grasped her phone in a death grip and brought it to her ear. "Hello?"

"Haley, where are you? I've been trying to reach you since last night. I was getting worried," Alexa chastised her.

Haley nibbled her bottom lip as she frantically tried to come up with a plausible explanation. "I was reading one of my books." The excuse wasn't that lame. She often got so absorbed while reading she lost all track of time. "My phone was on silent mode."

"Well, at least you're okay. Are you home?"

"No, I've already parked. I'm not to the square yet."

"Brian and I are almost there, too. Oh, I see your car. Wait and we'll catch up so we don't lose each other in the crowd. See you in a sec."

"Wait! There's something I need to tell you," her words trailed off. "I don't look the same," she mumbled. What would Alexa think of her new look? They told each other everything. How could she explain to her best friend that she prayed for a miracle and got an angel? Would Alexa be angry with her for not saying anything? She slipped her phone inside her clutch and nervously glanced around.

There were more people arriving for the parade. They nodded and smiled, but looked at her as though she was a stranger. She didn't know everyone's name but she recognized faces. These were people she'd seen at other parades, in some of the local businesses. Mrs. Reynolds jabbed her husband's ribs when he stared at Haley a little too long. Really? She'd known them all her life.

She breathed a sigh of relief when she heard Alexa say something right before she turned the corner. Being on display, no matter how much better she looked, was not something that made her comfortable.

Haley's gaze slid to the man with Alexa. Not bad looking.

Lanky, light brown hair, strong chin, nice features. His expression was a little on the serious side, his slacks and shirt were starched and pressed. Alexa's usual taste ran toward casual and laid back. This guy didn't seem to fit.

The couple drew nearer and Haley grew more uneasy. They were only a few feet away and her friend was about to pass right by without realizing who Haley was. It was now or never. "Hi," she said, her voice cracking. She cleared her throat and waited to see what Alexa would do.

Alexa stared at her as if she was some crazy woman, then gave a half smile and started to hurry past.

"Alexa?"

Alexa looped her arm through Brian's and increased her pace.

"Lexie?"

Alexa stopped when she heard the nickname Haley had tagged her friend with the day they first met. She turned, her eyes as round as saucers and stared.

Haley tugged on her hair. "I had some highlights put in.

Alexa's gaze moved slowly downward.

"And I went shopping," her words stumbled out. "And the hairdresser showed me some makeup tricks."

Alexa's gaze returned to Haley's face. "Haley? Is that really you?"

"Yes," she hesitantly replied, waiting to see how her friend would react. Her heart fell to her feet when Alexa stepped away.

"I can't believe the difference." She shook her head as tears filled her eyes.

"I'm still the same on the inside where it counts." Oh God, she didn't want to lose her best friend, but she couldn't go back to being frumpy, either.

"You're so beautiful." Her gaze drifted over Haley again. "And… and wow!"

"Don't be mad."

"Mad?" Alexa asked, then hugged Haley so tight that Haley thought she was going to squeeze the breath out of her. "All these years I tried to force you into a style that better suited me. I'm so sorry. I only wanted the best for you. Please don't hate *me*."

Haley hugged back just as tight. "I could never hate you. We'll always be best friends."

Brian cleared his throat.

Alexa stepped back and pulled her boyfriend closer to them. "Brian, I want you to meet my very best friend. This is Haley."

Brian grinned and it transformed his whole face. Haley knew why Alexa was head over heels crazy about the guy. When he smiled, his whole face lit up.

"I feel as though I've already met you," he said. "Alexa talks about you all the time. She's constantly bragging about what a great loan officer you are and how you really try to help people. She has you on a very high pedestal. I have to admit, I've been a little jealous."

"Of me?" She'd always been the one who felt inferior.

Alexa laughed. "The only way I could ever feel worthy of calling Haley my friend was to fight anyone who badmouthed her. Here I was, the skinny kid who wouldn't have graduated high school or got a college degree if Haley hadn't tutored me every step of the way."

"See, what did I tell you? She constantly brags about you." He hugged Alexa close to his side.

"This is a day for surprises." Alexa always showed so much confidence that Haley would never have expected her to feel as though she had to prove her friendship. "We're going to have a long talk later."

"Let's hurry before the parade starts without us." Alexa looped her arm through Haley's and pulled her along. "Oh my gosh, wait until Chelsea gets a look at you."

"She already has. As I was driving off, she was sitting on the porch looking as though she was going to be sick."

"I can't believe you didn't call me so I could be a witness! Serves her right. She's always so mean to people."

The siren blew, signaling the start of the parade at the same time they rounded the corner. They found a good spot and watched as the floats began to slowly move past. The town made a big deal out of the Old Settler's Reunion. The festivities brought needed money to struggling mom and pop stores. Most people went to Canyon Creek twenty-five miles away to shop at the big chain stores.

It was more than the money, though. Children had grown up there, walked across the high school stage to get their diplomas, then went to college. Only a few came back. Most were attracted to the hustle and bustle of city life. The fast pace, the bigger salaries, the fancy cars, and the big expense accounts. There was one thing they left behind—their roots.

As Haley watched the parade, the marching band that was a little off-key but had still won second in the state finals, she felt a sense of pride. Hattersville was her home. She didn't want to move away. Maybe it was familiar, but she liked knowing her neighbors, and she liked living in Nanny's house with all the wonderful memories.

"Look." Alexa pointed to the bank's float. "We should win first place. It's the best one."

They were on the decorating committee, which meant they did a lot of the work but whoever was chosen to ride on the float usually got all the credit. Chelsea always managed to be the main attraction. The theme was the roaring twenties. The float had been decorated to look like a nightclub. Chelsea wore a flapper costume and stiletto heels. The dress was so short it was almost illegal. Ben stood near her wearing a gangster costume, complete with a fake machine gun.

"Except for Chelsea and Ben," Alexa said. "It does look pretty snazzy."

"The office backstabbers?" Brian asked.

"That would be them." Alexa said, then turned to Haley. "I told him how Ben is always kissing someone's butt and Chelsea has been after your job for the last couple of years."

"They deserve each other," Haley said.

"What goes around comes around," Brian said.

She liked the way he thought. "If only that were true, but I've never seen it *come* around. My grandmother was a firm believer in the old saying." The float stopped, unfortunately in front of them, so they were forced to look at Chelsea simpering and blowing kisses to the crowd.

Ben waved as if he was God's gift to women, and pretended to aim his machine gun at spectators. What had she seen in the guy? His smirky smile was so insincere. It would be nice to see them both fall on their faces. Just once.

Ben's gaze swept the crowd, passing over her, then jerking back. Their gazes locked. His expression turned calculating as his eyes began undressing her. When he looked up again, he winked. Ugh! In his dreams.

Wait, he didn't recognize her. She should shoot him her middle finger and see how he liked it when the shoe was on the other foot.

Or play him like he'd played her.

The thought came out of nowhere. But she liked the idea. Flirt with him, then say *too late, jerk. You had your chance and blew it.*

She winked back at him. He raised an eyebrow in question. She slowly ran her tongue over her lips. She had his full attention. The grand finale. She brought her finger to her pouting lips, paused for effect, then sucked it inside her mouth.

His mouth dropped open. He took a step toward her just as the float began to move once again. Except the float was cumbersome and this was the driver's first time to drive in a parade. His foot was too heavy on the gas. The float jerked forward. Ben was just setting his foot down and lost his balance.

As everything happened in what seemed like slow motion,

Haley's first thought was that Nanny was right about what goes around comes around. That, and maybe her *grand finale* moment might have been pushing things.

Chelsea's simpering smile was literally slapped off her face when Ben's machine gun swung around and smacked her on the jaw, knocking her off balance. She swung around, reaching toward the fake marble floor. She landed on her knees, butt in the air. The short dress rode up to her waist. She wasn't wearing panties, proving she was a bottle blonde.

Ben flapped his arms as he tried to keep his balance and might have managed to do so but the driver, who couldn't see what was going on up top, shifted into the next gear. Ben dropped his fake machine gun. It bounced twice and fell to the road. He tried to catch himself but only managed to plant a palm on either side of Chelsea. His face landed in the crack of her ass.

There was a moment of shocked silence. Then pandemonium broke loose. Mothers covered children's eyes; some of the men in the crowd whistled. People applauded and others began to laugh.

Haley marveled at the new age of technological advancement as cell phones snapped pictures of the best float in Hattersville history. She was almost 100 percent certain it would soon be plastered on the Internet. So what if it was X-rated. Within the hour, their little town would be on the map. That should bring in plenty of revenue.

As the float merrily went on its way, Alexa, Brian, and Haley looked at each other. Their expressions all registered different degrees of shock.

"Yeah," Alexa said, nodding her head. "I bet we take first place."

"You did say Ben was an ass-kisser," Brian said.

Haley gripped her hands. Did anyone see her flirting with Ben? They would know she instigated the whole thing. What had Ryder created?

"I could use a drink," Brian said. "Soda?"

"Love one," Haley said, her mouth so dry she could barely talk.

"Me too," Alexa said. As soon as Brian was gone, Alexa leaned close. "I'm pretty sure I was the only one who saw you," she whispered.

"Saw what?" She met Alexa's eyes and had her answer.

"I like the new kickass Haley."

"I didn't know he would lose his balance," she admitted. "I feel so guilty."

"Brian snapped a picture."

Haley stared at Alexa. "That's terrible. No matter how bad they are, we work with them. Ben and Chelsea will never live this down. For the rest of their lives they'll be forever remembered for this one parade."

"Want a copy of the picture?"

"An eight by ten maybe?"

"Perfect. Anything smaller wouldn't do the moment justice," Alexa reasoned.

"And bigger would be tacky."

"Exactly."

Haley sighed. What would she ever do without Alexa?

Chapter 17

"HE'S CUTE. I LIKE him," Haley told Alexa later the same day while Brian and his cousin Conrad, who would soon to be Alexa's brother-in-law, competed in the horseshoe competition.

"I do too," Alexa said.

They wandered through the maze of stalls that were scattered about the courthouse lawn. People had brought their best crafts to sell. Silversmiths displayed a wide variety of belt buckles in different shapes and sizes. In another area the finest leather saddles straddled sawhorses. There were Western hats and jewelry. The ladies' fire department auxiliary was having their bake sale. Yeast breads, cookies, pies, and cakes were set on tables to tempt people. Everything was made from scratch using recipes handed down for generations.

"Sometimes when I look at you, I have to tell myself it's really you," Alexa said, then nodded at a mutual friend. The other woman glanced curiously at Haley, but kept walking.

"Don't feel bad," Haley told her. "I've been doing the same thing."

"I can't stop thinking that I shouldn't have tried to help you so much. I made your life worse."

"Let's just say we both have bad taste when it comes to shopping for my clothes." She didn't want Alexa worrying over the past. She'd tried to help and that was all that mattered.

"I'm still confused." Alexa crinkled her nose, a sure sign something troubled her.

Haley stopped at a booth with scented candles. She picked up one and brought it to her nose, inhaling the rich fragrance. The scent reminded her of a cold winter night snuggled under a down-filled comforter—with Ryder. She read the label: Gingersnap. She held it out to Alexa, who sniffed.

"Nice, but I'm not a candle person."

"I know, but I'll never understand why." She smiled at the woman behind the counter. "I'll take it." After she paid for her candle, they began to walk again. "What are you confused about?"

"Who helped you with your transformation?"

Haley knew Alexa would start to ask questions sooner or later. She had answers ready. "After Ben stood me up, I decided to go to Dallas."

"Dallas?"

Haley nodded. "I passed a beauty shop and something told me to go inside. I was determined to make a drastic change."

"This coming from the woman who dyed her hair orange and swore off hair color?"

"It was time." The lies rolled easily off her tongue. "I met this beautician called Einstein."

"Who would name their kid that?" Alexa sounded doubtful.

"I'm pretty sure that isn't his real name. He performed the miracle." Some of it was the truth. Haley hoped mixing truth with lies would get her past Alexa the inquisitor. Her friend was the only person who could sort fiction from fact. She should've been a lawyer.

"You'll have to introduce me. I'd love a makeover."

Haley breathed a sigh of relief. She was safe.

"So, who's the guy you met?" Alexa asked out of the blue.

Stay calm. "What guy?" She wouldn't even think about Ryder. If she didn't think about him, she would be okay.

Alexa put her hand on Haley's arm so she was forced to stop and face her. "The guy who hurt you?"

"But he didn't!" she quickly protested. "Ryder is perfect. He would never hurt me. It's not his fault..." Too late she realized her blunder.

"I knew there was something different about you. I thought you might be upset because I was dating Brian, but I quickly ruled that out. A guy is the only one who could have put that wistful look in your eyes." Her smile was too smug. "You've never been able to keep a secret from me. I want to know everything. Then you can explain why you didn't tell me."

Haley had a strong feeling she might be in trouble.

Chance strode into the rec room wearing a Grim Reaper expression as Ryder was getting a beer out of the fridge. It was pretty obvious to Ryder that his friend was pissed. He didn't have to overtax his brain to figure why Chance was angry. He'd stayed too long with Haley. Hell, Chance hadn't followed the rules with Destiny either, so he shouldn't be that damn upset.

He twisted off the cap and held the beer out to Chance. When he met Chance's gaze, Ryder wondered if hell had finally frozen over. "You might as well take the beer. If you don't drink it, I will."

Chance grabbed the bottle from him. He downed a big gulp then straddled one of the stools, leaning his elbows on the bar. He didn't say a word, just stared. Ryder always broke first so he'd stopped playing the game and refused to meet his gaze. Confession was good for the soul, but not so much when you confessed to Chance, especially with the mood he was in. Something was up. Ryder might as well get the confrontation over.

"I'm ending it tonight," Ryder said. Nothing could stop the stab of pain that shot through him. Haley would find happiness with someone else when he wasn't around. She wouldn't even know he'd been there. No memories of all they'd shared. He gripped the beer bottle a little tighter.

Chance looked at Ryder, then his beer. He apparently decided the beer was more important. He took a long drink before setting the bottle back on the counter. "Too late."

Ryder's eyes narrowed. Something was going on. A bad feeling began to churn inside him. This was about more than him staying too long with an assignment. "What do you know that I don't?"

"She just told her friend about you."

The ramifications of Haley's confession swarmed around him. Didn't she realize what would happen? He reached inside the refrigerator and grabbed another beer. She wouldn't do that to him. Chance lied. "No, I don't believe you." He twisted off the cap and flung it toward the trash. It pinged off the side, then skittered across the floor. Haley wouldn't tell anyone about him. Cold dread slithered over him. Except he'd never warned her she couldn't tell anyone about him.

"Does the name Alexa ring a bell?"

His head jerked up. "That's her best friend."

Chance shook his head. "You know women better than any of us. They talk, especially to best friends."

"I didn't think—"

"That's pretty obvious."

Ryder took his beer and strode around the bar without saying another word. Chance pushed too hard and he needed to back off. Ryder started toward the sofa but changed his mind and walked to the sliding glass door leading to the pool. He didn't go out, just stared at the glistening blue water.

"You heard her telling Alexa about me?" he asked in a tight voice.

"Haley lied, but her friend isn't buying it. She's demanded to know the truth."

Ryder spun around. "What do you mean?"

"Exactly what I said. She's about to tell her the truth."

"About to tell isn't the same thing as telling. I can stop her."

Chance shook his head. "They're not happy. They don't want

you to see her at all—ever again. You need to clear her mind of all thoughts about you."

They weren't happy? His snort of laughter said it all. "I don't give a fuck if *they're* happy or royally pissed." Chance didn't have to explain who *they* were. Ryder knew. Rarely did they ever call them Father. Chance had met the angel who'd sired him. Michael actually helped Chance out. Ryder had never met his father. The same went for Hunter and Dillon, although they didn't seem to mind that much.

Most of the time, their fathers looked the other way and let them do their own thing, unless the nephilim started screwing up. If they were really pissed, their fathers could block the nephilim's powers.

"You better care," Chance said.

That was the problem, he cared too much. He raised the beer and took another drink, trying to come up with a solution. He knew of only one. "I can keep her from talking."

"I don't think I'm going to like this, but tell me exactly how you plan to make everything better."

Ryder faced him. "I'll go back."

Chance shook his head. "No—"

"It's the only way and you know it."

Chance thought about it, but shook his head. "They won't let you return. It's over."

Ryder's heart began to pound. No, he couldn't let it end this way. "Her friend won't believe her. She'll think she's crazy."

"It's the price you have to pay." Pity shone in Chance's eyes.

"But it's not the price Haley has to pay. When she can't convince her friend, she'll go to her family thinking someone has to believe her. Damn it, Chance, it's happened before and you know it! The insane asylum is filled with people who say they talked to angels. I refuse to let that happen to her."

"You can't interfere in her life anymore."

"The hell I can't." He slammed his beer down on the nearest

table and closed his eyes. In a moment, he would be with her. Everything would be okay when he was with Haley again.

Ryder opened his eyes. He was still in the rec room.

"They've blocked your powers," Chance told him. "They don't want you to see her again."

Chance paused, then took a gulp of his beer, but Ryder knew him too well. There was something his friend wasn't telling him. "What?"

"It doesn't matter." Chance wouldn't meet his eyes.

"It might to me," he quietly told him.

Still, Chance hesitated. Ryder wouldn't back off, and maybe Chance sensed it because he walked around the bar muttering something unintelligible before tossing his bottle in the trash. He leaned his arms against the counter and met Ryder's eyes. That one look made his guts twist and burn as if he breathed in the fires from hell.

"You won't like it," Chance warned.

"I never thought I would."

"They don't want you to see Haley *ever* again. It ends now."

Ryder stumbled to the nearest chair as visions of Haley flashed in front of him. Her laughing face filled his mind, her smile, the way she touched him, her lips against his. He gripped the back of the chair. "No." They couldn't do that! He refused to accept their verdict!

"I'm sorry."

All the anger building inside Ryder exploded. "You're sorry? Is that all you can say?" He shoved the chair away. It slid across the room and slammed into a table. A lamp sitting on the table tilted then crashed to the floor, splintering into a thousand pieces. "I don't give a damn if you're sorry."

Chance didn't say a word. He let him spew all his hate on him until there was nothing left inside. With his anger gone, he looked at Chance. "You have to help me. We're closer than brothers. When we first discovered our powers and people looked at us with fear, when our mothers sent us away from our village, it was just the two of us. Do you remember?"

"I was never so scared in all my life," Chance admitted. "We were kids who didn't know how to survive."

"We made a pact that first night that we would be family. Me and you. We might not be able to count on anyone else, but we could count on each other."

Chance warily eyed him. "Yeah, I remember."

"I'm asking you to send me to her." Desperation laced his plea. "They might have blocked my powers, but they haven't blocked yours."

Chance scraped his fingers through his hair. "You don't know what you're asking. We don't know what they'll do if we defy them."

Everything in Ryder deflated. "I can help her. At least let me do this one last thing for her. Then I'll do whatever they ask of me, even if it means giving up my powers for all eternity."

"You would do that?"

"If I can help her, then yes, I would."

Chance shook his head. "We're probably both doomed anyway."

Ryder came to his feet. "I'll never be able to repay you."

"If we manage to escape the wrath of our fathers then I'll remind you about this for the rest of eternity."

Ryder nodded that he was ready to leave and closed his eyes. He'd pray, but he didn't want any of their angel fathers in heaven hearing him. He would go back, fix everything, and leave as quickly as he could. He would make Haley's life better.

Lights swirled around him as the wind rushed past. He let out a deep breath when his feet were firmly on solid ground again. Ryder opened his eyes. Chance had made sure he was behind a big oak.

When he stepped from behind the tree, he scanned the crowd. He spotted Haley sitting on a blanket spread on the ground. A woman was with her. It had to be Alexa. His gaze quickly swept over her. Pretty, but thin. She had a little better sense of style, but he had a feeling Alexa had tried to dress Haley in the same kind of outfits she wore. He cringed, imagining how Haley felt trying on streamlined clothes meant for a tall, thin woman.

He settled his black Stetson on his head and walked toward them, hoping Haley had not said too much. The closer he got, the more of their conversation he heard.

"Are you going to finally tell me?" Alexa asked with the slightest irritation. "We have our drinks, the blanket you insisted on getting out of the trunk of your car is sitting exactly under the perfect"—she rolled her eyes—"the *most* perfect shade tree, and you still haven't told me your secret."

Haley drew in a breath. "I met an angel when I prayed for a miracle."

Ryder stopped. A minute sooner and he could have prevented her from saying anything.

"An angel after you prayed for a miracle?" Alexa spoke dryly. "If you don't want to tell me just say so."

"Please don't be mad. It's true, I swear."

"Haley, I missed you." Ryder interrupted the conversation. Haley stopped talking and looked up.

"You came back." She took his hand and came to her feet.

Missing her was an understatement. The thought of never seeing her again made him sick, but he knew it would come to that. The Powers would be angry at him and Chance. He hated that his friend would get caught in the middle, but Ryder couldn't survive not being with her one last time. He planned to take advantage of every moment. He kept tugging on her hand even when she was already standing. He didn't stop until she was in his arms, her body pressed intimately against his.

She looked up, her eyes meeting his. All the desire he felt for her was mirrored in her eyes. He lowered his mouth, catching her sigh. Her lips were warm against his. He deepened the kiss, stroking her tongue, tasting her. She wrapped her arms around his neck, pulling him closer. He'd never get enough of her even if they both lived a thousand lifetimes.

Alexa cleared her throat and Ryder ended the kiss with more than a little reluctance. He didn't want anyone intruding on what little time he and Haley had left, but he had to make the transition easy so she wouldn't be more hurt when he left.

"The sun is so bright I can barely see," Alexa complained, shading her eyes as she started to get up.

"Please, I didn't mean to interrupt your visit," he said. "I needed to see Haley."

"That was obvious," she said, sarcasm dripping from her words. "Who exactly are you?"

Haley opened her mouth to explain, but he quickly interrupted her. "Angel Collins." He squeezed her hand.

Alexa cast an exasperated look in Haley's direction, still squinting her eyes. "This is your angel? That was so not funny. I thought you might have lost your mind. I was getting ready to call the men in white coats."

Thunder boomed across the sky, making the ground tremble beneath their feet. Ryder looked up. They were really ticked off now. The first drop of rain slapped him on the nose.

"It's not supposed to rain today," Alexa complained. "Where's Brian?" She looked around as she scrambled to her feet.

"Looks like we're about to get a downpour," Ryder yelled above another boom of thunder, holding on to his hat when a gust of wind threatened to blow it away. "Better make a run for it." He grabbed Haley's hand and dragged her along with him.

"I can't leave her," Haley yelled over the wind that became more than gusts.

"We have to. I can't let her see my face." He stopped. "And you can't tell anyone I was here."

"She's my friend."

"They're angry enough that I returned. We can't make a bad situation worse."

"Who's angry?"

Lightning crashed to the ground near them. Haley screamed. Ryder threw his arms around her, protecting her from the electricity that sizzled around them.

"My father. Where are you parked?" he yelled above the storm.

"Your father's an angel. He's supposed to be—angelic."

"You want to explain it to him?"

"Can't you blink us away?"

"No powers."

Her hesitation was brief before she latched onto his hand. "This way."

They made a run from the courthouse lawn and down the street. They didn't stop until Haley jerked her keys out of her clutch and hit the button to unlock the doors. They were inside the car when the next streak of lightning slashed down near them. She jumped.

"What's going on?" she asked, turning in her seat to look at him.

"I'm being punished."

Her face lost some of its color. "Because of me."

He shook his head. "Because of *me*."

"I think you better explain."

"Let's get out of here first." Not that he thought for one second they could drive fast enough to escape the wrath of an angel. When angels were angry, they could be really mean. He only hoped his father wasn't angry enough to do serious bodily harm.

Haley's foot was heavy on the gas as she sped back to her house. As she slid around a corner, he wasn't sure what scared him the most, her driving or his father's anger.

She cast a quick look in his direction, her frown deepening. "What?"

"I'm amazed you passed a driving test."

"Who said I did?"

Great. If his father didn't incinerate him with a lightning bolt, then Haley would kill him with her driving.

"Yes, I have my license and I'm a very good driver, most days. I thought we were in a hurry."

He'd offended her when Haley had only been trying to help. "You're right, we are in a hurry. You're an excellent driver under the circumstances. I couldn't have done any better."

"Thank you."

She seemed satisfied with his lie. He didn't relax until she pulled into her driveway and turned off the motor. "Can we go inside now? It might be safer."

"I'm not the one wanting proof that I have every right to be on the road."

"Haley?"

"I'm going."

She opened her door. He was already on her side of the car when she shut the door and pointed her key holder toward it before pressing the button. The horn beeped twice. Ryder could only stare. "What are you doing?"

"Locking the car."

"You won't have to worry about it getting stolen if my father shoots another lightning bolt our way." He grabbed her hand before she could protest and they hurried inside, but not before the clouds opened and they were drenched in cold rain.

"I'll get us something to dry off with. Wait here. I don't want puddles everywhere." Haley hurried toward the bathroom. Ryder didn't mention his father could easily flood her home. Why frighten her? When she returned, she tossed him a towel. He caught it and began drying his head. His hat was long gone.

"I want to know exactly what's going on. What did you do to make your father mad?" A shiver trembled over her. "I'm freezing and these wet clothes aren't helping." She began to unbutton her shirt. The material was plastered to her skin.

His father might have wanted to punish him, but as he watched Haley shrug out of her shirt and drop it on the floor, he didn't feel as though he'd been reprimanded. The only thing covering her breasts was a wisp of material that could barely be called a bra

She glanced up as she was about to unfasten her bra. With her hands behind her back, her chest was thrust out.

"Ryder, really? We were almost charbroiled by a bolt of lightning and all you can think about is sex?"

Chapter 18

RYDER DRAGGED HIS GAZE back to her face but Haley could see that it took a lot of effort on his part. She cocked an eyebrow.

He opened his arms in supplication. "I can't help it. I'm half human."

"Only half?"

He grinned. The kind of smile meant to disarm her and make her forget what she was talking about. It worked. The only thing on her mind was getting naked and making love the rest of the day, but when thunder rolled overhead, she remembered how much trouble Ryder was in. Come to think about it, he hadn't explained everything to her either. She released her bra clasp without unfastening it and began to towel dry her hair. "Why are you in trouble?"

He sighed, apparently realizing she was not going to undress until she had answers. Which was a good assumption on his part.

"I stayed with you too long."

"But what about when you left to mend fences? You were gone nearly a week." She'd been a basket case thinking he wouldn't return.

"And I should've stayed gone, but I didn't."

Haley was glad he came back even if he'd pissed off his father. Life without him was not something she wanted to contemplate. "I don't want you to go—ever. We'll leave Hattersville. Find a cave somewhere and become hermits."

He shook his head. "They won't let us be together."

"I'll go with you. Wherever you want."

"You would leave your family?"

The thought of never seeing Rachael or her parents again caused her a moment of panic, but the thought of losing Ryder forever broke her heart. She flung herself at him. "I would leave it all behind if I could be with you." She wrapped her arms around Ryder's neck as the door burst open.

"I can't believe this downpour," Rachael said as she hurried inside with a soggy newspaper spread above her head. "Your house was closer than Mom and Dad's and you know how I hate driving in bad weather. I heard this is a freak storm. One for the records," she said as she carefully folded the dripping paper and propped it beside the door. Then she looked up. Her mouth opened and closed as she stumbled back a step.

Haley had a feeling she might be in trouble. "I can explain."

Rachael's eyes blazed as she glared at her. Haley was stunned to see so much anger directed at her. Rachael was always reasonable and rarely let her emotions show. She was a lawyer, for goodness sake!

"Who the hell are you and where's my baby sister?" she growled like a rabid dog.

Before Haley could explain, her mother and father hurried inside, holding on to each other as they had done for as long as she could remember. If one slipped, the other was there for support. Haley always thought it was more probable they would both fall on their butts, but she thought it wise not to mention that.

"You were supposed to wave at us so we would know the door was open," their mother reprimanded Haley's older sister.

"Stay back, Mom," Rachael warned. "I discovered these burglars when I opened the door. They refuse to tell me what they've done with Haley."

"My baby?" Her mother's expression turned to a look of distress, then with a fierceness Haley had never seen her mother display, she turned on them.

Haley moved out of Ryder's arms and grabbed her wet shirt off the floor, holding it in front of her. "I can explain."

"You're damned right you will," her normally passive father spoke up. "What have you two done with my daughter?"

"I'm your daughter," she finally shouted above another clap of thunder. "And your sister," she said, turning to Rachael.

"She's delusional," Rachael said. "I see it a lot in the courtroom. It's like identity theft, except they steal the subject's life. She actually thinks she's Haley."

Thunder rattled the house. She cringed and turned to Ryder. "You have to do something."

"We can explain—" Ryder began.

Her father raised his fists and took a fighter's stance. "I boxed in the war, fella. I might not be able to whip your ass, but I can cause enough damage until the cops get here."

"You called the cops? Good thinking." Rachael beamed.

He curled his lips to the side and whispered, "Not exactly, but I'm going to."

Everyone looked at him. Haley just shook her head. Her family had lost their minds. "Dad, you were never in the war."

"This is Haley," Ryder said. "Your daughter."

"Pfft." Rachael snorted. "I love my sister, but she doesn't even come close to looking like her."

Haley's mother raised her chin. "My daughter is lovely, but she's not as tall as you and…" Her gaze swept over Haley. "Nor is she so… so curvy."

"Or sexy," Rachael supplied.

"That's right. Haley is a little dumpy, but I love her anyway. You, on the other hand, are not my daughter."

The door opened a little wider and Alexa and Brian squeezed in behind Haley's sister and parents. She looked around the foyer. "Why is everyone standing in here when I know there's hot cocoa in the pantry?" Her gaze moved to Haley. "Ugh, girlfriend, you might want to put on some clothes since your family is here."

"You know this woman?" Haley's dad asked.

"Yeah." Alexa drew the word out. "Did you get hit by lightning, Mr. Tillman?"

"They don't recognize me—even wet they think I look better than the old me," Haley said, shoulders drooping. It was pretty sad when her family didn't think she could improve her appearance.

"Haley?" They turned their attention completely on her.

Haley began to fidget and wished she had her shirt back on, even though it was soaking wet.

"Prove you're our daughter," her mother said.

"Now you want me to prove it?" She pressed her lips together and stubbornly refused. She didn't see any reason why she should.

"Haley," Ryder began. "It's getting a little crowded now."

Oh, right. Their situation was pretty awkward without her making it worse. They wanted proof, she would give them proof. "You loved Fifi more than you did me. So much that you had her stuffed. I mean, really, Mom? She was a terrible dog that bit everyone who came into the house."

"Only once," her mother defended, then lowered her head. "Or twice."

Haley pursed her lips. Her mother still protected the fleabag. "Dad took me to pick Fifi up and bought me that bug-eyed rabbit. I had to hide the damn thing in my closet because it scared the crap out of me."

"Ha!" Rachael raised her arm in the air as though she scored a victory. "My sister doesn't curse."

Haley turned on Rachael. "I do a lot of things you don't know about. I've even stri—"

"Haley," Ryder quickly interjected.

She snapped her mouth closed. It probably wasn't the right time to tell them exactly what she'd been doing since she met Ryder. "When I was six I got sprayed by a skunk and you smeared tomato paste all over me, twelve when I caught a rabbit and had to get a tetanus shot because it scratched me, I died my hair orange accidentally, I broke your favorite carnival glass bowl when I was looking for spare change—"

"*You* broke the dish? There you go, that proves you're not Haley! I broke the dish."

Haley rolled her eyes. "Some lawyer you are. I broke the dish the day before, then glued it back together. Remember that one piece that was never found? I couldn't find it, either. I knew Mom would notice there was something wrong. I told you Mom wanted to set it out when Nanny came over." She hurried on without waiting for a response. "When you grabbed it out of the China hutch, it fell apart. Mom walked in and you were blamed."

"I was grounded a whole month!" Rachael pursed her lips.

Haley shrugged. "I did feel terrible. Sort of."

"That was so mean, Haley Tillman! Mom, ground her!"

"I can't very well ground your sister. She's an adult."

"You're Haley," her father said as he studied her.

"That's what she's been trying to tell everyone," Alexa said, rolling her eyes.

Haley had everyone's complete attention once again and she wasn't sure she wanted it. Maybe now that they knew she was really who she said she was they would leave. She looked at the expressions on their faces. Nope, they still had questions. It was a good thing Ryder was an immortal because she had a feeling he would be here for a very long time explaining a few things.

"You look so… different. Your hair is shorter and there are blonde highlights," Rachael said, her gaze lowering. "I don't think I'm a good shopper, either. You don't need to lose any weight. The clothes I picked out were all wrong." She shook her head as if to clear it and turned her attention to Ryder. "And who are you?"

"He's her angel," Alexa said with a mischievous twinkle in her eyes.

Ryder groaned when they all looked at him. Haley was glad the attention was off her, but she knew Ryder wanted as little attention as possible. Another rumble of thunder shook the house. Ryder glanced up, then looked at Haley.

It was chilly without her shirt, but the look he gave her froze her all the way to the bone. He wasn't happy so many people knew about him. No, his eyes were sad. She drew in a shaky breath and swallowed past the lump in her throat. This was it. Ryder would leave and she would never see him again. She gritted her teeth trying to stop the tears building in her eyes.

"Here, you're freezing," Alexa said as she came from the direction of Haley's bedroom. Funny, she hadn't seen her leave. She shielded Haley so she could slip on a T-shirt.

"This family and your friends are crazy," Ryder proclaimed in a loud voice.

Haley met his gaze. He might have just insulted everyone in the room, but she heard him say something different with his eyes.

I love you and I will always love you. I'm sorry it had to end like this.

"You're the crazy one." *I love you, too.*

"And just what do you mean when you say we're all crazy?" her dad asked.

Ryder looked at each one of them. "And the town is just as crazy. You have X-rated floats. Is that any way to raise kids? Everyone is nosy and no one has any manners. I'm going back to the city."

"I would if I were you," Brian said. "These are good people and none of us appreciate your slurs."

"He's right," her father agreed. "I want you out of my daughter's house."

"And don't come back!" Rachael told him.

"Lady," Ryder said, "I don't ever plan on coming back, but I'm sure your lives will be a lot better off."

No! She knew what he was saying. She would never see him. She swayed. He caught her arm to steady her, then squeezed, his thumb lightly caressing her arm.

Alexa pushed him away. "Don't ever touch my friend again."

"Since I didn't see an extra car," Brian said, "I'll drive you to the bus station."

"I'd rather walk," Ryder growled.

Everyone parted down the middle. Brian opened the door.

"Good riddance." Ryder strode out the door and out of her life. She reached toward him, but Brian slammed the door. Alexa gave her a hug.

"He wasn't worth your time." Alexa shook her head. "That's the trouble with cowboys. They think they're angels."

"Huh?" Her father looked at Alexa as if she'd lost her mind.

"His name was Angel Collins."

"His mother certainly named him wrong," Haley's mother said. "There was nothing angelic about that young man!"

Rain poured from the skies, pelting the house. A streak of lightning snapped and popped like an angry whip. The lights flickered, then went out. Electricity sizzled through everyone in the room, making their hair stand up.

"We're going to die!" her mother screamed.

Haley's father quickly wrapped his wife in his arms. "It's only lightning." But he warily looked around. "That last strike was a little too close for comfort."

Thunder shook the house. Haley cringed, hearing pictures fall to the floor. Furniture slid across the room. Wind moaned outside. Rachael grabbed her and they held each other tight. A window shattered, the white curtain blowing straight out from the rod and giving it the look of a ghostly apparition. A board from the window frame flew off and hit her in the back of the head.

"Mom! Dad!" Rachael tightened her hold. "Haley's been hurt."

The air brought with it a sweet smell. Haley closed her eyes and inhaled. It was nice. It reminded her of Nanny and Christmas morning when they would troop over to her house. She would have apple and pumpkin pies cooling on the counter and a turkey roasting in the oven.

"Get her to the sofa," her father ordered.

How strange that his voice seemed to come from a long way off. They helped her to sit. The air outside calmed.

"You okay?" Alexa asked with a trace of worry in her voice.

Haley rubbed the back of her head. "Yeah, just stunned a little." She smiled. "Not even a bump."

"I think the worst is over," her father proclaimed, patting Haley on the knee and smiling at her. "It stopped raining and the sun is out."

"Really?" Haley came to her feet. "The storm is gone?"

"As well as that awful young man," her mother said. "Why would you ever date a man with red hair? You know they have awful tempers."

"Man?" Had there been a man? She couldn't remember.

"He didn't have red hair," her father said. "It was blond."

"I know what I saw."

"You're both wrong," Rachael joined the argument. "He had brown hair and he was at least a foot shorter than Haley."

"Shorter? You mean taller. The man towered over everyone," Alexa informed them.

"You never can trust a professional basketball player," Brian said. "They say they have a girl in every town."

Haley listened to everyone talk without adding anything. The knock on the head must have dazed her more than she thought. Who were they talking about? She blinked, trying to remember. It felt as though something was missing in her life. Something very important and it made her want to cry.

"How about some of your mother's famous hot chocolate," her dad said. "I got chilled all the way to the bone."

Rachael took Haley's hand. "Sure you're okay?"

"I'm fine," she reassured her sister. "I'll be there in a moment." A shiver ran down her spine as she came to her feet. She was so cold, but before she started toward the kitchen, she walked over and glanced out the window. What did she expect to see? She wasn't sure.

"The storm has passed and everything is all new and fresh," her mother said as she came up behind her youngest daughter and wrapped her arms around her in a hug. "That's what Nanny used to say."

"I remember." Haley smiled and leaned into her mother's warmth. "A time to forget the past and start anew."

"You'll have to tell us all about how you transformed—"

"From an ugly duckling into a swan?" she supplied.

"No, from a woman who had no confidence to someone who does."

"You think so?"

"I've always known you were pretty. Both my girls are. But I never knew how to help you. That's very frustrating for a mother. I wanted only the best, but I'm afraid we hurt you when we only meant to help."

"I love you, Mom."

"And Fifi?"

Haley nibbled her bottom lip. "I don't think so."

Her mother chuckled. "Fifi will go to the attic tomorrow."

She half turned. "Mom, you don't need to do that. You love Fifi, even stuffed, and that's all that matters."

"Like Nanny said, new beginnings. Besides, I've talked your dad into getting another dog. There are so many that need homes. We're going to the shelter Monday morning."

Haley only hoped it wouldn't be another tiny terror.

"Hey, where's the chocolate?" her dad asked as he came out from the direction of the kitchen.

"I'm coming." Her mother laughed and headed toward the

kitchen, but stopped and looked at Haley. "Do you want some hot chocolate?"

"In a minute."

Her mother nodded and continued toward the kitchen.

Haley moved to the middle of the room, then slowly turned in a circle. She could've sworn she'd heard pictures crashing to the floor, but all Nanny's favorite things were still hanging perfectly straight on the pristine white walls she'd loved. Haley's forehead wrinkled. Someday she was going to paint the walls. Nanny had given her permission, but Haley had never gotten around to it.

But hadn't she already painted it? There had been naked pictures of her hanging on the wall. She rubbed the back of her head as a sharp pain shot through. A dream? Probably. Something to write about in her naughty diary.

She walked past the end table on her way to the kitchen, but stopped when her eye caught something on the floor. She hesitated, then walked nearer and picked it up. A feather. Pure white. So white it almost sparkled. She held it close to her face, inhaling the scent of leather and country breezes. How odd. She started to toss it on the coffee table, but stuck it in her pocket instead. She liked the warm feeling it gave her. She smiled. Maybe it was an angel's feather. That was a fanciful thought because she was certainly no angel herself. Nope, her family would need to get to know the new Haley.

The new Haley? Her forehead creased in thought. Where had the old Haley gone? She glanced toward the kitchen, but changed her mind and hurried to her bedroom. She didn't stop until she stood in front of her full-length mirror.

This was the new Haley, after her makeover. "I'm pretty," she whispered. But how? She closed her eyes. A trip to Dallas, a man named Einstein, Madame Truffle's shop. They'd helped with her transformation from frumpy to her new look.

And an angel? No, she'd met a man named Angel. Her head began to pound.

"Are you okay?" Alexa spoke from the doorway.

Haley shook her head. "I think I've forgotten something important. Was there a man named Angel?"

"Wow, that board really banged your head. Angel was a man you met. You didn't have a chance to tell me much. I'm sorry if you liked him, but he was a real jerk."

"What did he look like?"

Alexa shook her head. "It's strange but we all have different descriptions, except for the fact that he was a loser and we're glad he left." She eyed her friend. "You sure you're okay?"

"I can't seem to remember him."

"You better join us. You might have a concussion."

Haley nodded, feeling a wave of fatigue wash over her as she followed Alexa to the kitchen. "And his name was Angel?"

"Something like that. Weird if you ask me."

Haley reached inside her pocket and stroked the feather. Why did she feel like crying?

Chapter 19

"HAVE YOU STARTED LOOKING for a new job?" Chelsea asked sweetly.

Haley sighed. They were back to that again. She wouldn't have guessed in a million years how changing a few things about her appearance would make such a dramatic difference. Chelsea was still out for blood, even though she had finally gotten her dream position of loan officer when Ben quit and moved away. Not that she blamed him. Everyone still talked about the bank's float and what happened. Ben had been called butt-face and ass-kisser one too many times. On his last day at work Alexa had asked him how it felt to be the *butt* of everyone's joke. He didn't laugh. Haley chastised her friend, but Alexa shrugged and said he deserved everything he got.

Chelsea, on the other hand, had risen to fame. She bragged she could have any man kissing her ass, even in public. She didn't realize they were making fun of her as well. Haley was still shocked Ms. Barnhill promoted Chelsea to loan officer. She supposed Ms. Barnhill felt sorry for her. Chelsea wasn't satisfied, though. She wanted Haley's new title of chief loan officer and she would sabotage her any way she could.

"The new owner is arriving today and I'll have him eating out of my hand," Chelsea said with a wicked smile. "I'm throwing a private get-together later this afternoon. If you know what I mean." She smoothed her hands down the sides of her very short skirt.

Haley put her elbows on her desk and leaned forward. "Fuck whoever you want, Chelsea, but as soon as they figure out you don't have any working brain cells you'll be the one out on your ass." She smiled sweetly.

"You know, since you put on makeup and fixed your hair you think you're hot shit."

"Go away, Chelsea, I have work to do."

Chelsea turned on her heel and stomped to her desk, flopping down in her chair. She spun her chair around to face the front, then took a magazine from her drawer and began to scan the pages.

Not that it mattered. Haley looked around to make sure no one watched, then opened her top drawer and reached under her ledger. The feather still looked the same, still felt the same, and still reminded her of country breezes and leather. Odd, but she always felt calm after holding it for a while. Her talisman, she supposed, except it always left her feeling as though she'd let something very important slip through her fingers.

"Have you changed your mind yet?" Alexa spoke low enough that only Haley would hear.

Haley curled her fingers around the feather. "No, I'm still leaving. I've never been out of Hattersville. I have the small inheritance Nanny left me and it's time I used it. I want to travel for a while and see the country."

Alexa shook her head. "You haven't been the same since that freak storm a couple of weeks ago. It's like the whole transformation thing did something to you. Not bad," she quickly added. "It's like you're searching for something."

She smiled. "Maybe I am."

"Well, at least wait until you meet the new owner. I don't want to be stuck here all by myself with Chelsea." She crossed her eyes.

Haley chuckled. "I doubt she'll ever get the best of you."

"Well, she's looking for her next victim since she can no longer get the best of you."

The door to Ms. Barnhill's office opened and she stepped out.

Her gaze swept the room, but Haley didn't think she saw the people who worked for her. It was more like she was memorizing the paneled walls and the pictures of her ancestors that hung proudly on them. She sniffed, then squared her shoulders before clapping her hands to get everyone's attention. When she had it, she said, "Please make your way to the meeting room. The new owner will be arriving soon."

The employees glanced nervously at each other, all but Chelsea, who looked smug in the knowledge that if she could fool Ms. Barnhill, she could fool anyone. Hips swinging, she was the first one to make her way to the other room. She stopped beside Ms. Barnhill. "No one will ever replace you." She sniffed.

"Thank you, Chelsea." She patted her hand. "I've put in a good word with the new owner. You should do fine."

Chelsea lowered her head. "Thank you so much." After she passed Ms. Barnhill, she turned and cast a cold glare at Haley.

"I won't have much of a chance to keep my title after the new owner takes over," Haley told Alexa. "And I refuse to work under Chelsea."

"She's a bitch."

"And she knows it."

Alexa glanced at the clock as they passed by. "I wonder if we'll get overtime?"

Haley looked up and saw that the bank was officially closed for the day. "Doubtful."

They followed the other employees into the meeting room and took a chair beside each other. Haley tried not to look at Chelsea, who was sure to be smirking over her latest victory. The room grew silent when they heard voices in the other room. Everyone sat a little straighter. They were about to meet the new boss.

Ms. Barnhill came into the room alone, then smiled. "I would like to introduce everyone to the new owner of the bank." She waved her arm toward the door as a man joined her.

"Wow," Alexa whispered beside her. "He's the best looking man I've seen wearing a pair of jeans in a long time." She cleared her throat. "Other than Brian, that is."

A breeze swirled into the room from the open door and Haley caught a familiar scent of country breezes and leather.

"I apologize for my informal attire," the new owner drawled. "I feel more comfortable in jeans. That was one of the reasons I wanted to buy the bank. It has that down-home country feel. Ms. Barnhill and her family saw to it that a tradition was carried on, and I plan to do the same." He smiled at everyone in the room.

Haley drew in a deep breath. He had dark, thick hair and the most intense blue eyes. He was tall, maybe six feet one or two inches. And when he smiled he made her toes curl.

There was something vaguely familiar about the man. When his eyes landed on her, she thought she saw a glimmer of interest. She was dreaming, she scolded herself. He was the owner of the bank and it was rumored he had millions. Some even said the bank was a tax write-off. Something in his eyes told her the last rumor wasn't true.

"My name is Ryder Langtry."

"He looks familiar," Alexa whispered. "I don't recognize the name."

"Like a movie star?" Haley thought out loud. Ryder Langtry, she said his name to herself. It sounded vaguely familiar, but she knew she would remember anyone called Ryder. It wasn't a name she heard every day.

"Yeah, maybe that's it. He looks like a movie star."

"I don't want to keep everyone since it's already past quitting time. I wanted to introduce myself and let everyone know I won't be making any major changes. It will be business as usual. I do want to thank everyone for staying over. I'll be meeting with the department heads tomorrow."

The employees came to their feet and began to shuffle out the door. Except Chelsea. Oh God, act one of *How Soon Can I Get the*

New Boss in My Bed was about to begin. She pitied the poor guy. A flash of something unexpected shot through her. Jealousy? That was ridiculous. She had no reason to be jealous. She didn't know Mr. Langtry.

"Could I speak to you, Mr. Langtry?" Chelsea said in her best sugary-sweet voice. "I thought we might discuss a few…"

There was a cold calculating gleam in Chelsea's eyes when Haley looked her way. Dread filled Haley. Leaving of her own accord was one thing; being fired left a sick feeling in the pit of her stomach.

"I might as well go ahead and clean out my desk," she told Alexa.

"I'm sorry." Alexa pursed her lips. "I'll talk to him and tell him the truth!"

"No." Haley sat in her chair, swiveling around until she could reach inside her bottom drawer and get her purse.

"And why not?"

"Because you need this job until you and Brian get married. You'll want to buy a nice place and have money in the bank."

"What if he doesn't ask me?" She twined her fingers together.

"The guy didn't strike me as a fool."

A smile glimmered in Alexa's eyes before traveling down to her lips and curving them upward. "No, he's not."

The door to the meeting room was flung open. Chelsea marched out, grabbed her purse and started out the door, but stopped at Haley's desk. "I wouldn't get too comfortable in that chair if I were you." She stuck her nose in the air and marched out of the bank.

"I hope her heel breaks and she falls flat on her face," Alexa said.

"Careful what you wish for," Haley quickly warned, but a smile was already forming on her lips as a mental image of the parade suddenly flashed in front of her. Chelsea falling, Ben stumbling.

Haley frowned.

The storm. A man. She tightened her hold on the feather as her head began to pound.

"Another headache?"

Haley inhaled, then exhaled. "I'll be okay. It's just that sometimes it's as though I'm trying to remember something and I can't. It makes my head hurt for a little while. No biggie."

"Here comes Mr. Langtry," Alexa whispered. "I'll catch you later."

Haley expected the new owner to walk past her, but he stopped in front of her desk. "Yes, sir? Was there something you needed?" Here it comes. The death blow. She waited for him to tell her she was fired and Chelsea would be taking her place.

"Would you like to have dinner tonight?"

"Sir?"

He cringed. "Ryder, if you don't mind."

"Ryder?"

"Yes, it's much less formal."

"Am I being fired?"

He smiled and warm tingles spread over her. "Is that what Chelsea said?"

"More like implied."

"She won't be returning. I've read everyone's files and Chelsea isn't the kind of employee I want at this bank."

"Then I'll be keeping my job?"

"Not exactly."

She had never been fired and she didn't think she liked the feeling. "When would you like me to leave?" She only hoped he didn't want her to train her replacement. That might be pushing her generosity a little too far.

"I'm actually looking for a vice president. I've read your file and it's very impressive."

"VP? You're serious?" Surely he wasn't giving her a promotion. This had to a joke.

"It'll mean long hours."

"A bonus every year?" She could play games, too.

"Certainly. Lots of traveling. I like investing in new ventures. Will you consider the position?"

She studied his face. "You are serious."

"I wouldn't joke about something this important."

"I'll have to think about it."

"Naturally. Shall we shake on it?" He reached out his hand. She automatically took his.

It was almost as though a current of electricity shot between them.

He jumped, apparently feeling it too. "Sorry, static electricity I suppose."

"I suppose," she mumbled, wondering what was happening.

He released her hand and her feather floated to the desk. He picked it up. Heat spread up her face as he studied the feather. "Interesting." He looked puzzled. "Have we met before?" he asked, handing her the feather.

"I don't think so."

"Dinner tonight? Seven? I'll pick you up at your house and we'll discuss the position."

She swallowed then nodded. He turned and left as she picked up the feather. It suddenly began to sparkle, then it disappeared. Her heart pounded as she watched Ryder leave the building. Haley had the oddest feeling she'd found what was missing from her life since the storm and her world felt right once again.

~~~

Chance watched as Ryder left the bank. There had been one condition when Ryder chose mortality: he wouldn't remember his past or the fact that he'd once been a nephilim.

But Chance hadn't made any promises. He grinned. There was no way he would let his friend wait a lifetime to find the woman he loved. Not if he could help it, and he could, and he did. He had a feeling Ryder and Haley would have a blessed life together, and why not, they had three guardian angels watching over them. Well, half angels, anyway.

About the Author

Karen Kelley is the award-winning author of twenty books. *I'm Your Santa* spent three weeks on the *USA Today* bestseller list. Karen lives in a small Texas town with her very supportive husband and their very spoiled Pekingese, along with many wild birds that can empty two large feeders in the course of a day. She makes jewelry as a hobby because she's a firm believer that you can never have enough bling-bling. You can visit Karen at www.authorkarenkelley.com.

Where There's Smoke

by Karen Kelley

The Devil went down to Texas...

Sexy wannabe demon Destiny Carter has pissed off the people downstairs and has been kicked out of Hell. Now she's in Ft. Worth, Texas, with one week to corrupt a soul. Or else.

Lookin' for just One Soul to steal...

When smokin' hot Destiny strolls into The Stompin' Ground bar in a slinky red dress, she has a feeling her assignment might not be so bad. The cowboy at the bar looks pretty darn delicious and oh-so-corruptible.

But Chance Bellew is no ordinary cowboy, and Destiny gets way more than she bargained for when she rubs up against that sexy dark angel perched on a barstool like sin just waiting to happen...

"Kelley burns up the pages... This book is witty, sexy, and a lot of fun. Readers won't be able to wait to read the next installment!"
—RT Book Reviews, *4 stars*

"Bestseller Kelley (the Princes of Symtaria series) launches a sultry paranormal series with this smoky, sweet, and surprisingly touching tale."
—Publishers Weekly

For more Karen Kelley, visit:

www.sourcebooks.com